PRINGLE PRAWN

MICHAEL SCOTT CLIFTON

BOOKS BY
MICHAEL SCOTT CLIFTON

YA Science Adventure

Edison Jones and the Anti-Grav Elevator

Hank Harper Magical Adventures

The Treasure Hunt Club
The Janus Witch
Pringle Prawn

The Conquest of the Veil Series

The Open Portal
Escape From Wheel
A Witch's Brew
Cavern of the Veil Queen

Book Liftoff
1209 South Main Street
PMB 126
Lindale, Texas 75771

Interior's book design by Champagne Book Design
Cover design by Evelyne Paniez www.secretdartiste.be
www.secretdartiste.be/digital-art
RESOURCES:
Clock: depositphotos 2735704
Frame: depositphotos 339357048
Clock arrow: shutterstock 94417423
Wings and ears: depositphotos 470646606
Costume and body: depositphotos 360422954
Pouch: depositphotos 50966663
Leaves: depositphotos 184429560
Sparkles: depositphotos 157239980
Female face: 100856854 and 102616972
Branches: www.hwwostock.com
Fireflies and effects: www.neo-stock.com
Cloth: www.fantasybackgroundstore.com
Brushes: Jeff Brown and Storywrappers

Library of Congress Control Number Data
Clifton, Michael Scott
Pringle Prawn / Michael Scott Clifton
Magical Realism/Fiction.
Dragons & Mythical Creatures/Fantasy/Fiction.
3.Paranormal/Fantasy/Fiction
BISAC: FIC061000 FICTION / Magical Realism
FIC009120 FICTION / Fantasy/Dragons & Mythical Creatures.
2023916584

ISBN: 978-1-947946-90-3 (Kindle Direct Publishing)

www.michaelscottclifton.com
www.bookliftoff.com

To Caleb Pirtle

A mentor, friend, and an author's author. The world is poorer without you, but heaven is now so much richer.

"Second star to the right and straight on 'til morning."

J.M. Barrie—*Peter Pan*

PRAISE FOR
MICHAEL SCOTT CLIFTON

"Mike Clifton is a truly gifted author."

Teresa Syms—*Reader's Favorite*

"Author Michael Scott Clifton is a master at crafting three-dimensional and interesting characters."

K.C. Finn—*Reader's Favorite*

PRINGLE PRAWN

CHAPTER 1

BEN HASTINGS PLUMMETED INTO THE DARKNESS, falling faster and faster...

Into a scene of madness.

A scream rose from Ben's throat, but before it could leave his lips, he slammed into the ground. The wind knocked out of him, he labored to breathe. Bright sunlight, diluted by swirling clouds of thick dust, greeted him. The air rang with the sharp clash of weapons, inhuman screams, animal snarls, and shouts in an unfamiliar language. Coughing and choking on the dust, Ben struggled to his knees—and froze. His disbelieving eyes revealed a sight that caused him to immediately doubt his sanity.

Men, some mounted, others on foot, fought a furious battle all around him. But when gaps in the dust allowed him to get a closer look at the combatants, he realized the fighters were not men at all but *creatures* whose appearance bore only a tenuous resemblance to humans. Squat and powerfully built, the being nearest him had a triple ridge of bone that ran across its skull. The bony ridges met at the creature's forehead, giving him a perpetual scowl. A beak-like snout protruded from the creature's face, sharp fangs exposed when it opened its muzzle to snarl.

The growl abruptly ended when one of the mounted

combatants rammed a spear through his opponent. Bright yellow blood fountained from the gory wound, and the creature collapsed.

Fear gripped Ben with icy fingers, and he began to hyperventilate. Petrified, he watched the mounted creature struggle to pull his weapon from the carcass. Subtle differences distinguished the mannish beast from its dead opponent. While of the same general size and physique, the being's snout was more abbreviated, and its mouth wider. A purple wattle of flesh—much like the comb on a rooster—protruded from the top of its anvil-shaped head. The warrior rode a mount with a horse-like body. This resemblance terminated at the mount's long scaly neck attached to a blunt head, its wide mouth filled with sharp teeth.

Loud, unintelligible curses came from the rooster-combed fighter while he struggled to yank the spear from his dead adversary. He finally jumped off the bizarre horse-like creature and ripped the pike free. With the battle still raging, Rooster-comb looked for his next opponent.

And straight at Ben.

For a moment, time stopped as Ben and the strange warrior gaped at each other. The pause ended when Rooster-comb raised his spear, released a guttural cry, and charged at Ben. The sight of the warrior bearing down on him with the sharp-tipped lance broke Ben's paralysis.

"Shit!" Ben cried.

He jumped to his feet and blindly fled. The thick, choking dust kicked up by the fierce fighting made it difficult to see. The dim images of tents appeared through the haze, their bulky shapes forcing him to zig-zag around them. As he rounded one pavilion, he tripped over a guy rope. With an *oof*, he sprawled face-first into the parched loam.

Ben rolled into a sitting position and spat out grass and dirt. A lance point suddenly speared the ground between his legs just inches from his crotch, followed by Rooster-comb's leering face. As the surreal being pulled the lance back to make a killing blow,

Ben grabbed a handful of the dry, loose soil, and in desperation, threw it into Rooster-comb's face. The creature howled in pain, dropped the spear, and clapped claw-tipped hands to its eyes.

Driven by terror so sharp his heart felt like it might explode, Ben leaped to his feet and ran. Tents and fighting creatures flew by in a blur as he sprinted headlong away from the battle.

The noise of the struggle abated, and the dust had thinned when Ben rounded another large pavilion and skidded to a stop. Bent over, his chest heaved like a bellows. He turned his head, and saw a different set of strange animals picketed not ten feet from him. Startled by the sight, he almost bolted again. After a hesitant moment, he crept closer for a better look.

Saddles on the creatures' backs identified them as riding mounts. The beasts resembled horse-sized versions of a Tyrannosaurus Rex. Large, leathery wings lay folded behind their backs, held immobile by a mesh net secured with leather thongs. They stood upright on large, muscular hind legs, with vestigial front legs held folded and close to their bodies. Each T-rex had a short, thick tail as a counterweight to help with balance.

Leather muzzles held the rounded, horny snouts of the creatures shut. The purpose of the muzzles became apparent when the T-rex closest to him turned and tried to remove his hand with its rows of needle-sharp teeth. Ben jumped back, and as he cast about for another avenue of escape, Rooster-comb rounded the tent. A cry of triumph left his snout at the sight of Ben.

Trapped between the pavilion and the line of winged mounts, Ben took the only choice left to him. He jumped onto the back of the nearest T-rex. He wriggled into a saddle obviously designed for a different butt than his. His hands scrabbled at the mesh net hobbling the creature's wings. Something flashed by so close to his face he felt the wind of its passage. The spear, thrown by Rooster-comb, quivered with its point buried in the ground twenty feet away.

Gibbering in fear, Ben redoubled his efforts. He tore the net from the creature's wings and tossed it away. He risked a look over his shoulder. Rooster-comb took an object from a broad leather belt at its waist and placed a short arrow in it. Ben blinked—then realized the weapon must be a crossbow.

Frantic, he grabbed the leather reins tethering the creature to the picket line. He ripped them free, and the picket line shook wildly. This caused an immediate reaction among the other winged beasts. They hopped about, calling out in short, high-pitched barks. Ben's back itched in anticipation of the crossbow bolt sure to bury itself there. He sawed at the reins and kicked the creature's sides with his heels.

Nothing happened.

His shouts, shaking of reins, and sharp digs of his heels did nothing but anger the T-rex. It repeatedly nipped at Ben.

Snap!

At the sound, Ben gripped the pommel and threw himself to the opposite side of the winged T Rex. A feathered bolt missed him and plunged into the meaty flank of his riding mount.

The creature reacted instantly.

With an earsplitting honk of pain and outrage, the mount vaulted ten feet into the air. Its wings open to full extension, the T-rex glided a short distance away and landed. The action took Ben completely by surprise, and without his firm grip on the pommel, he would have fallen off .

Ben had just righted himself when the T-rex pitched its head forward, powerful hind legs moving like pistons. They shot away, the wind whistling past his eyes and ears.

Bent over low like a jockey on a racehorse, he risked a look back. Rooster-comb brought the crossbow up and took aim. Ben shouted and kicked his heels savagely into the mount's ribs. This time he got a reaction. The creature once again leaped high into the air and spread its wings, the crossbow bolt passing harmlessly beneath them. Because of their rapid forward motion, they glided a much longer distance. When the beast touched the ground, unlike before, it needed no further urging. The riding mount kept up the pattern of jumping and gliding.

All Ben could do was cling to the pommel.

The ground beneath them flew by as Ben struggled to stay in the saddle. Again, he looked back at the shrinking battle scene he had been in the thick of moments earlier. The veil of dust kicked up by the fierce fighting still obscured much of the detail, but now he could see the murky forms of dozens of the high-peaked tents.

He was about to turn away when something emerged from the dust and turmoil and raced after them. With the great distance already between them and the constant struggle to stay seated in the saddle, Ben found it difficult to make out much detail about who or what pursued him. During one particularly long glide, however, he managed to stay steady in the saddle long enough to get a good look. His heart sank when he spied another of the running/gliding mounts with something riding on its back. A moment later, a moan escaped Ben's lips.

An unmistakable swatch of purple crowned the head of the mounted rider.

Cold fear filled Ben, and he leaned forward to provide as little wind resistance as possible. He shouted encouragement to his strange mount and was rewarded when the beast increased its speed.

The miles passed in a blur, Ben's T-rex continuing the odd cadence of running and gliding. With nothing left to do but hold on, Ben studied the land around him. Prairie-like with scrub grasses and stunted trees, the generally flat topography was relieved here and there with rocky escarpments creased by dry washes and gullies.

In contrast to the cloudless blue sky, a dark smudge appeared low on the horizon. As Ben and his mount drew closer, it began to resolve into the bright green of vegetation. Ben squinted in the rushing air for a better look. When they drew near enough he could make out more detail, he recognized the sight.

A forest!

The forest would make it far easier to escape from Rooster-comb than on the open prairie. Although his T-rex wouldn't be able to fly, the trees would provide camouflage to lose the pursing other-worldly being and to hide in. Hope blossomed in his chest.

Then his riding mount faltered.

So concerned with escape from Rooster-comb and the raging battle, he had given little thought to the odd mount he rode. Now given pause to consider, he realized the expanse they had traveled was considerable. No ordinary horse would have made it even half this far. Yet his steed had gone full bore the entire time, an incredible act of endurance.

An endurance with limits.

The line of green beckoned and became better defined. At the same time, Ben's T-rex continued to struggle. The beast's mouth issued hoarse rasps and dripped mucus, its long neck covered in a lathery, pungent sheen. Their speed continued to drop off, and the long, ground-eating strides and glides became shorter and shorter.

Ben glanced back. Rooster-comb and its mount continued to close the distance between them. *Why hasn't his riding mount tired like mine?* The only thing Ben could think of was Rooster-comb *knew* how to ride these strange creatures, and his mount didn't have an arrow sticking out of its haunch.

Ben tried to gauge the distance between the forest ahead and his diminishing lead over his otherworld adversary. A lump rose in his throat.

It would be a close thing.

His thoughts drifted back to the sequence of events that brought him to the life-or-death situation he now faced.

Why did I take that damn key and use it?

CHAPTER 2

Forty-Eight Hours Earlier

THE TENNIS BALL ROCKETED OVER THE NET. Ben lunged at it, his racket extended in a desperate effort to return the serve. He missed badly, and the ball skipped past him.

"Game, set, and match!" his opponent's triumphant voice called.

Bent over, chest heaving, Ben couldn't summon the energy to reply. When at last he caught his breath and straightened, he looked up to see his girlfriend approach. Sweat dripped from him like rain off a roof, while Cara looked like she'd just enjoyed a spa treatment. Her blond hair, held by a scrunchie in a ponytail, gleamed in the late morning light. Long, tanned legs disappeared under a short, white tennis skirt, while a form-fitting dry-fit blouse clung to her breasts and accentuated her small waist. In fact, the only evidence Cara had just played a tennis match was the rosy hue on her perfect cheeks.

Kicked my ass again, and she's not even breathing hard.

Ben's humiliation might have stung more, except by now, he was used to the beatdowns. "Why don't you play someone who's actually good at tennis instead of me?" he groused.

Cara produced a spotless white towel and dabbed his face and neck. "I do, but none of them are as cute as you." She kissed his cheek and handed him the towel. "Remember, my parents are expecting you for dinner tonight."

Ben groaned. "Every time you invite me over, it's like an inquisition. Your dad quizzes me about my job, my career plans, and if I'm ever going to be a homeowner. Damn it, I have a PhD and teach history at UT-Tyler. Doesn't that pass the test for gainful employment?"

"Daddy is just concerned about your future, *our* future."

Cara held up her left hand. A dainty diamond bracelet that cost more than Ben's car dangled from her slim wrist. "What's missing from this picture?"

Another silent groan echoed in Ben's mind. "I thought you, of all people, would be more enlightened about relationships. People live together all the time, and are just as happy without a ring, ceremony, or a legal piece of paper."

Cara crossed her arms. "My grandmother had a saying she used to tell me. 'Cara, why buy the cow if the milk is free?'" Her expression hardened. "Well, I'm not a cow, and I'm not free. We've been seeing each other for almost a year, and I don't think I'm being unreasonable to expect a commitment."

She spun on her heel and marched away.

Ben ran after her. "Cara, stop!" He grabbed her shoulders and turned her so she faced him. "I've got an appointment with a real estate agent today. I'm going to meet her after my last class this afternoon."

Cara's expression transformed from frustrated anger to excitement. "You do?"

"Yes. Is that commitment enough for you?"

Cara clasped her hands, oblivious to the question. "Daddy will be so pleased. You *must* tell him when you come to dinner tonight!"

She kissed him and ran off, tossing her racket and bag in the back of her convertible BMW sports coupe. For grins, he had googled the model and found the price tag north of a hundred grand—more than his entire year's salary at UT-Tyler.

She started the Beamer and roared off.

Ben shook his head. For the hundredth time, he wondered if he was treading in water far too deep. Cara never acted like the stereotypical *rich kid*, but he'd be fooling himself if he didn't admit she must be used to a certain lifestyle—one he couldn't come close to matching. She did have a degree in fashion and design, but other than working as a part-time receptionist at her father's law office, her work history took up less space than most website addresses.

He swore when he looked at his phone. His *Myths and Folklore* class was in less than an hour. Fortunately, his apartment was nearby. Time enough for a quick shower if he hurried. He ran to his vehicle parked beside the tennis complex. Like Cara's, his car was the product of German engineering. Unlike hers, he bought the vintage red and white '70 Volkswagen van at a much lower price tag. He tossed the sweat-soaked towel in the passenger seat, climbed in, and started the van. It rumbled to life with the throaty sound only an air-cooled VW engine could make.

He turned onto the street beside the tennis courts and headed home.

"Dr. Hastings, are you saying the legend of Coronado's gold is true?"

Ben chuckled. "No, Armando. Although the Conquistadors searched far and wide, they never found the fabled Seven Cities of Cibola. Unfortunately for the Aztecs, they *did* discover the gold in the Aztec's Central American cities."

Ben clicked off the data projector. "The point is, that *all* myths and legends have a grain of truth. Finding this grain is the challenge historians face." He glanced at his phone. "Okay, be sure to check the class website for your upcoming assignments. Have a great spring break, and I'll see you in a week."

A cheer rose from the students as they jumped up and filed out. Ben picked up several file folders, dropped them in his leather briefcase, and snapped it shut. He checked the time on his phone again. If he left now, he'd make it to his appointment with the real estate agent with time to spare. He grabbed his briefcase and headed for the faculty parking lot. A short time later, the VW rolled out of the lot, and he headed for his appointment.

Ben glanced at the GPS on his phone propped on the dashboard. A melodic voice issued from the device. He dutifully followed the directions and fifteen minutes later, turned onto a residential street. One and two-story homes with manicured lawns and flowering shrubs, lined each side of the street in a picture-perfect snapshot of suburbia. The VW's open windows swept in the cool spring air, and carried the smell of a barbeque grill.

Ben shook his head. *These homes must go for a quarter million and up.*

"Looks like my meeting with the real estate agent will be a short one," he muttered. "There's no way I can afford any of these houses."

The rent on his modest apartment was high and growing higher. His lease expired in a month, and he had hoped to exchange the lease payments for a mortgage on a house. Hopes dashed, Ben considered phoning the real estate agent and calling the whole thing off. But, since he'd already made the trip, he grudgingly decided to see it through.

The road ended at a cul-de-sac. "You have reached your destination," his phone announced. Ben peered through the windshield…and his breath caught in his throat.

A gothic mansion occupied the end of the street. Three stories tall, it looked like the Munster's house on 1313 Mockingbird Lane. Rounded spires anchored each side of the structure. Gabled arches stabbed skyward, their gilded edges faded. Mullioned windows, like the black eyes of some colossal beast, stared outward from each level. Two stone lions flanked gray, quarried steps that led up to a large, elevated porch, and a metal railing decorated with gargoyle heads ran the length of the veranda. An ancient four-foot iron fence, peppered with rust, circled the property.

The enormous yard was overgrown. Vines ran up the fence, and knee-high grass and weeds obscured the flagstone path from the gate to the porch. Ivy grew up the brick facing of a colossal chimney leaving only the crown visible. What must have once been flowerbeds and shrubs were now weed-choked plots of wild growth.

The old mansion—like an onion amid a field of poppies— couldn't be more out of place among the new homes in the subdivision.

When Ben got out of the VW, a woman emerged from a small sedan parked at the curb. Middle-aged with tidy, medium-length brown hair, she wore a gray pantsuit that matched the drab color of the mansion. She made a beeline for Ben.

"Dr. Hastings, so good to meet you!" she gushed, pumping his hand. "I'm Gayle Robinson, the realtor you talked to on the phone." She waved at the old structure. "Well, what do you think?"

Before he could answer, she looped her arm around his and guided him toward the gate and up the pathway to the porch. "Wait till you see the inside. It's so much better than the outside."

No doubt, Ben thought. *The outside could be on a postcard from Transylvania.*

They reached the porch and approached a large door with a brass gargoyle fixed in the middle, a knocker in its fanged mouth. Gayle dug around her purse and pulled out a large, old-fashioned key. She unlocked the door and pushed it open. The stale odor of mildew and dust assaulted Ben's nose. The entryway led to a large open room with scattered sheet-covered lumps.

At Ben's questioning look, Gayle quickly said, "The house comes furnished. The furniture's been covered to protect it."

A grand staircase that could have come from the set of *Gone With The Wind*, led from the room to the second story. At the base of the staircase, the largest grandfather clock Ben had ever seen stood against the wall. Amazed, he walked over and studied it.

Easily eight feet tall, carved woodland creatures adorned the crown of the clock. Other carved forest animals decorated the sides. Roman numerals etched the clock face, the hands gilded in gold trim. The moon's phases, also filigreed in gold, formed a semicircle on the clock face. The glass front panel displayed an enormous pendulum and two weighted chains inside the clock.

Ben asked, "Does it work?"

Gayle shrugged. "We don't know." She pointed at the keyhole on the front panel. "We never found a key to open it and reset the weights."

Ben noticed that, unlike all the other furniture, no protective sheet covered the grandfather clock. "Why isn't a sheet over it like everything else?"

"Well, uh, you see, we've tried, but every time we cover the clock, it soon slips off. Nothing has worked."

"You mean a ghost or something takes it off?" Ben teased.

"Hee, hee, you're quite the jokester, Dr. Hastings." Then, quickly changing the subject, Gayle said, "Why don't I show you around?"

The tour took an hour, and by the time it ended, Ben discovered the mansion contained five bedrooms, and four bathrooms. Only one bathroom contained modern plumbing with a sink, toilet, and tub. The other three were water closets. The large kitchen included a sink the size of a bathtub, an old gas stove, and a refrigerator that looked like a refugee from the1960's. An old-fashioned boiler heated the house.

The tour over, they stepped out onto the porch, and Gayle locked the door behind them. "I can give you *very* good terms," she said.

Ben shook his head. "I'm sorry. This is way too much house for me. Besides, I'm sure it's way out of my budget range."

Gayle took a small notepad from her purse and scribbled on it. She ripped off the sheet and gave it to Ben. "This is a very generous price."

Ben looked at the note. "You're kidding!"

"No. We've had this property on our books for a long time. The seller is very motivated."

Ben thought it over before handing the offer back. "I'm sorry. I couldn't possibly—"

Gayle scribbled another number and shoved it in his hand.

It took a few moments for Ben to find his tongue. "You can't be serious. You're practically giving this property away." He glanced at Gayle. "There has to be a catch."

Gayle sighed. She led him to a plaque mounted on the wall several feet from the door. She pointed. "The Grange House has been designated a historical building. An entire set of rules governs what can and cannot be done to renovate the house. For example, it can't be torn down, nor the property sold for new construction."

"You could've told me before we spent an hour touring the place," Ben chided.

"I did my research, Dr. Hastings. I know you teach at the university and I thought a history professor might like to live in an *actual* historic structure."

At the realtor's comment, Ben paused. He walked down the steps, turned, and studied the old mansion. It checked off a lot of boxes. *It's available, furnished, and—best of all—cheap.*

He thought of the upcoming dinner with Cara's parents. A smile creased his lips. He turned to Gayle and held out his hand.

"I'll take it."

CHAPTER 3

ZELKOVA PETROVA FOLLOWED THE BOGUS FEDEX TRUCK AS it turned off the rural East Texas road onto a private drive. The eighteen-wheeler's impeccable paint and labeling made it look just like a delivery vehicle in the shipping giant's fleet.

The lane curved around a copse of trees and disappeared. Five minutes later, Zelkova's large estate appeared. The cubist architectural structure made the manor look like a collection of child's blocks. The *cubes*, stacked three high, towered over the flat open ground leading to the estate. Even painted a soft beige, the structure exuded a sterile, harsh vibe—like a maximum-security prison. Petrova smiled. If anyone ever attacked on her "home," the thick walls of her mansion would stop anything short of an armor-piercing missile. The open ground also provided a clear line of sight and a free-fire zone.

A prostitute by age twelve, Petrova grew up in a brutal Belarus brothel. By twenty-one, with a trail of bodies in her wake, she owned the bordello. Besides honing her survival skills, the experience also developed her keen sense of paranoia. More than once, this had saved her life while her rivals perished.

Then America beckoned.

With its wide-open borders, lax policing, and an astonishing number of the rich and super-rich, Petrova found the perfect atmosphere to profit from the extravagant tastes of the wealthy. It allowed her to expand far beyond simple prostitution to drugs, money laundering, and the most profitable venue of all—human trafficking. Now, with an annual income most Fortune 500 CEO's could only dream of, her criminal organization stretched to every continent.

The pair of vehicles pulled up to a six-car garage adjacent to the estate. The faux FedEx truck pulled into one bay, while Petrova's Hummer rolled into another. The bay doors closed with a *thump*. Petrova exited the Hummer and stood next to the truck. She retrieved her cell and entered a code. A low *thrum* resonated in the air, and the deck beneath the truck began to descend. Lower and lower it went until, with a gentle bump, the section of floor came to a halt. A large open area with loading docks occupied the subterranean space.

Petrova stepped off and signaled the driver. The truck backed up to a loading bay. Two burly men jumped out of the delivery vehicle and opened its locked back doors. Boxes filled the trailer's interior, and Petrova climbed up a set of stairs to supervise the unloading. Workers wheeled the boxes into the warehouse, then stacked them against a wall. Soon the freight area in the truck lay empty. Petrova motioned to the men.

Now the *real* cargo could be unloaded.

"A good catch, boss?"

Petrova glanced over her shoulder. Her chief bodyguard and assistant, Georgi Ivanov, stood beside her observing the transfer of cargo. Brutality dripped from him like an exotic cologne. A large man, his head and shoulders met in a fusion of flesh that left little room for a neck. A square jaw thrust from a bulldog face like the prow on an Artic icebreaker. Beneath dark eyes and thick brows, severe lines etched his cheeks. His nose, broken so many times it resembled a turnpike, perched above thick lips. Ivanov's teeth, a startling white, gave him a predatory look when he smiled. Petrova had never met a more dangerous man. It gave her no small amount of satisfaction to know he worked for her—an even *more* dangerous woman.

Petrova clucked her tongue. "Not as good as I would have liked." She moved to get a better view of the truck's interior. "Get them out."

Ivanov nodded and gestured to the men. They re-entered the trailer armed with electric drills. At the back end of the trac-tor-trailer, they removed screws from the metal panels. The whine of the drills echoed off the walls, followed by the *plink* of bolts hitting the floor. One-by-one, the workers removed the false wall's panels. Inside, packed like fruit in a crate, stood a huddled group of men, women, and children.

The smell of stale sweat, urine, and feces erupted from the enclosed space. Petrova waved a hand in front of her face. "Get them cleaned up, then tested and sorted."

A volcanic rage bubbled inside her. This sorry lot could barely stand. She would be lucky to recover the cost of transporting them.

She whirled on Ivanov. "Find that bastard Farshad and bring him to me!"

Petrova sat at her desk and studied a medical readout on her computer monitor.

None of it contained good news.

Her spartan office in the underground complex contained none of the frills of her office in the above-ground estate. The concrete walls, a dark gray, matched her mood perfectly.

A knock came from the door.

"Come."

Ivanov entered and pushed in a swarthy man. Farshad Hosseini barely came up to the enforcer's shoulder. He bowed.

"Blessings, mistress. I'm at your service."

Petrova remained silent, regarding the Iranian through slit-ted eyes. Although he claimed to be a devout Muslim, she knew Farshad's lifestyle was anything but. His unbuttoned black, silk shirt displayed a forest of bristly hair, and a thick gold chain dan-gled from his neck. Jeweled rings adorned each of his manicured fingers. His thick, black hair, gelled to the point it swept back across his scalp like an oil slick from a leaking tanker, gave him the look of a Vegas high roller. All of it evidence of a lavish lifestyle.

A lifestyle *her* money made possible.

She turned the monitor to Farshad. "Look at these medical reports and tell me what you see."

"Mistress, I don't—"

Ivanov caught the Iranian's neck in one massive hand and shoved his head within inches of the screen. "Don't speak. Look!" he snarled.

"Yes, yes, of course," Hosseini gibbered.

The smuggler's eyes locked on the monitor. His lips moved as he silently read a series of medical reports. He paled as he scanned each summary. Petrova twitched a finger, and Ivanov jerked him back.

Words rushed from Hosseini's mouth. "Mistress, there must be some mistake. My suppliers assured me the commodities were healthy and whole."

Petrova eyed the smuggler and struggled to keep her hands from closing around his throat. She held no illusions about her own character—a cold, calculating, murderous bitch. In her world, the best enemy was a dead one. But she didn't make the rules of survival. She just played by them. Even she, however, never re-ferred to other humans as a *commodity*.

"Your 'commodities' are starved and dehydrated," she spat. "Several are missing teeth, one is pregnant, and two suffer from dysentery. The only good news is that none of them have covid."

She stood, kicked her chair out of the way, and stalked around the desk to Hosseini. "We serve high-end clients. Do you know what 'high-end' means you worthless pile of shit?"

Hosseini cringed. "Yes, mistress."

"They expect healthy, flawless, men and women, boys and girls. *Instead, you brought me a collection of refugees better suited to a concentration camp!*" Petrova shrieked.

"It-it's getting harder to kidnap people," Hosseini babbled. "International authorities are cracking down on smugglers."

Petrova towered over the Iranian. She snatched his shirt with both hands and jerked him toward her.

"The cartels send truckloads of fentanyl across the border while immigrants just walk across, and *you* claim it's more difficult?"

Hosseini swallowed. "No, mistress. I'll take care of it. The next shipment will be of the highest quality, I swear!"

Petrova released the Iranian. "Good!" She smoothed his shirt. "Of course, this delivery is on you. I'll keep this rabble, but I'm not giving you a ruble."

The smuggler opened his mouth, then snapped it shut when Ivanov moved closer. He bobbed his head. "Of course, mistress."

He fled from the office.

CHAPTER 4

"SO, CARA TELLS ME YOU MET WITH A REAL ESTATE AGENT today."

Mitchell "Mickey" Sledge, Cara's father, took a sip from his chilled martini, then leaned back in his chair. They sat outside beside the pool bungalow in the backyard. An expensive privacy fence encircled the yard, the perfect green lawn bordered by flowering shrubs. Located in the exclusive Cascades Country Club, Mickey's house, even at five thousand square feet, seemed ordinary when compared to the other palatial homes in the country club.

A successful trial lawyer, Micky Sledge made a fortune suing businesses and large corporations for workplace accidents and injuries. His highway billboards—an image of Mickey holding a sledgehammer with the caption, *Injured? Let Mickey Sledge put the hammer down for you!*—followed travelers up and down the interstates from Texarkana to Shreveport and Dallas.

Ben took a sip of his beer, imported of course, and considered his answer. "Uh, yes. I'm supposed to close on Monday."

"Great!" Mickey beamed and drained the vodka martini. "Tell me about it."

"Well, uh, it's a bit of a fixer-upper, but it's located in a new subdivision."

"I see. Have you shown it to Cara yet?"

Although Mickey wore comfortable khaki shorts and a Hawaiian shirt rather than a pinstripe suit and tie, the tone of his questioning made Ben squirm—like he was under cross-examination in one of Mickey's trials.

"No. Like I said, the house needs some work, and I want to, ah, you know, fix some things, clean it up before she sees it."

Ben breathed a sigh of relief when Cara skipped out of the house and announced, "Supper's ready!" Spared from further explanation, he jumped up and followed her inside.

A table that could seat an entire football team, held settings for three people. Ben knew Cara couldn't boil water, so the "cook" for the evening was takeout from a nearby upscale bistro. The absence of a setting for Cara's mother—soon to be Mickey's ex-wife number three—was because she lived in a condo on the southside of Tyler.

Cara threaded her arm through Ben's and led him to his seat. Since he told her about his meeting with the real estate agent and plans to buy a house, she had paid him *extra* attention.

Before he could sit down, she whispered in his ear, "You're going to get lucky tonight. *Very* lucky."

They sat down to eat, Cara and Mickey chattering away. Ben nodded at their remarks and dutifully ate, but his mind, fixated on Cara's whispered comment, couldn't be farther away.

Lucky!

Ben yawned and rolled out of bed.

He stood and stretched, then checked his phone. *Nine a.m.* An early riser, he rarely slept past seven. *Last night's gymnastics drained me more than I thought.*

Ben glanced back at the bed. Cara lay on her stomach, her shapely butt partially exposed by the tousled sheets. Even his most fervent imagination could never have prepared him for Cara's definition of *lucky*. Their wild lovemaking lasted most of the night, their heated fog of passion merging one tryst with another. Had he kept score, he guessed it must have ended at an crooked number.

On shaky legs, he went into his tiny kitchen and put a K-cup into the coffeemaker. While it brewed, he studied a framed picture on the wall. In the photo, he and Cara stood arm-in-arm at a faculty mixer, happy smiles on their faces. He wore a blazer and tie, and Cara, a tight black skirt and blouse.

The envious looks on the faces of the male faculty members were his first clue at the effect Cara had on other men. At first, it had thrilled him. *She's with me, fools. Eat your hearts out!* But lately, another thought had inched its way into his mind.

Why me?

He peered closer at himself in the picture. At six feet two inches, a hundred and eighty pounds, he supposed his physique could be considered slim. His face, with its sturdy cheekbones, square chin, and blue eyes, when combined with his longish brown hair, might put him in the category of mildly handsome. Further, his PhD—with the academic title of "Dr."—gave him a bit of gravitas but nothing with serious weight. His old-school VW van spoke more about the state of his finances than any bank statement could.

Why me?

Ben shook his head. He could think of no good reason why Cara would fall in love with someone like him. Maybe that's why he bought the old mansion when every instinct screamed at him to walk away. He needed to do something, anything, to make her happy. A thought chilled him.

Maybe it's not Cara I'm in love with, but instead, the idea of someone like her.

Cara's sleepy voice interrupted his ruminations. "Ben, come back to bed."

"It's past nine o'clock."

She giggled. "I know."

Coffee forgotten, Ben raced back to bed.

Ben rolled to a stop in front of the old mansion.

He stifled a groan at the enormous amount of work ahead. But he didn't dare show Cara the place until he put it in some semblance of order. He got out of the VW and checked his phone. The cleaning service he hired was late.

The decision to dip into his meager savings was an easy one. He couldn't possibly tackle the entire mansion himself. Even then, he could only afford to have the service clean the first floor. The rest was up to him. He planned to do it in stages, starting with the "modern" bathroom and the bedroom he chose for himself. Later, he'd move his stuff in, then work his way from one room to the next.

"Well, what are you going to do about it?" a voice demanded behind him.

Startled, Ben turned. A woman in a beige dress and brown Sketcher sneakers stood next to the van. With arms folded over an enormous bosom, she tapped her foot impatiently.

"Wh-what?" Ben sputtered.

The woman thrust out a hand. "Maude Thorne, president of the neighborhood HOA."

Ben cautiously gripped Maude's hand. "Ben Hastings. Good to meet you, Maude."

Maude's hair, a coiffed mound of dark brown, reminded him of a puff pastry left to bake too long. Squint lines etched the corners of her gray eyes, and her nose ended in a peak like it had been honed by a pencil sharpener. The corners of Maude's mouth curved down as if a bad taste refused to go away. He guessed her age ranged from the mid-fifties to early sixties.

"I've written to the Historical Commission about moving this,

this *monstrosity*, but they refuse every reasonable request. So, what do you plan to do about it?" she demanded again.

Ben, at a momentary loss for words, finally said, "I've hired a cleaning service, and I'll be here all week working on the house."

Maude huffed. "Good luck with that! You can pin wings on a pig, but it's still a pig." She leaned closer. "If it were me, I'd take out insurance and burn the place down."

She stepped back. "In the meantime, you need to clean up your yard. HOA rules require pristine yard maintenance must be kept. The Historical Commission rules do *not* exempt that."

Maude raised two fingers to her eyes, then pointed them at Ben. "I'll be watching you."

She spun on her heel and walked away. To Ben's dismay, she entered the house next to his.

Shit! Maude is my next-door neighbor.

Could things get any worse? On top of the enormous task of getting the old mansion in order, his new neighbor was not only the HOA president, *but she lived right next door!*

Ben studied the yard. It looked straight out of a jungle scene from the *Jumanji* game. How was he ever going to meet Maude's *pristine* yard maintenance requirement?

A sinking feeling followed him as he opened the gate and started for the mansion.

CHAPTER 5

Exhausted, Ben collapsed into the old chair, his feet sprawled in front of him.

The Louis XV chair, a neo-renaissance piece fashionable a century earlier, had a thickly padded seat and back upholstered in a red brocade. With a groan, he pushed himself up and surveyed the mansion's interior.

Due largely to the cleaning service's valiant efforts, the first floor actually looked presentable—in an old school sort of way. Mountains of dust had been swept up and removed, the dust covers on the furniture taken away, and the floor vacuumed and mopped. The mansion still reeked of stale air and mildew no amount of polish or scrubbing could dispel, but all-in-all, Ben was pleased.

His gaze settled on the tall grandfather clock. An idea formed in his mind. *I'll bet it's worth something if I can get it working again.* Excited, he sat up.

Maybe I can sell it for enough money to have the yard landscaped and get Maude off my back.

Thrilled, he retrieved his phone. A quick google search determined the clock's value could range from a couple hundred bucks to twenty-thousand dollars. The amount sent his hopes soaring. A moment later, his initial optimism crashed.

The realtor said the grandfather clock had no key.

Without the key, the clock couldn't be opened, the counterweights re-set, and the pendulum set in motion again. He supposed he could force it open or hire a locksmith, but neither prospect appealed to him. Anything that damaged the clock would lower its value, and a locksmith cost money. Besides, he *still* wouldn't have a key to open and close the panel, something any buyer would want.

With a bitter sigh, Ben stood and walked up to the clock. It towered a good two feet above his head. He leaned closer and studied the keyhole. A brass plate etched in strange designs encircled the keyhole, and by the looks of it, an old-fashioned skeleton key fit the lock. He took a picture of the keyhole with his phone, then stepped back and took several pictures of the clock. Another google search produced a list of antique stores within a sixty-mile radius of Tyler. He emailed each store the pictures, along with an inquiry about old skeleton keys that might fit.

Ben pocketed his cell. With a tired sigh, he trudged up the staircase.

Time to get back to work.

Sweat dripped from Ben's face as he scrubbed the old cast-iron bathtub. Like some mythical creature, it crouched on four clawed feet, patches of rust appearing where the enamel had cracked.

Ben wiped his face with a rag, and reached for the patch kit beside him. Before he could grab it, *The Walker* by Fitz and The Tantrums, blared from his cell. *Harper's Antiques & Oddities* appeared on the screen.

"Hello."

"Is this Dr. Hastings?"

"Yes, it is."

"I think I may have the key you're looking for."

"Really?" Ben could hardly contain himself. "Are you sure?"

A chuckle sounded in his ear. "Pretty sure. An Otto Albrecht clock is both rare and hard to mistake for anything else. They're among the largest grandfather clocks ever made."

"Awesome!" Ben whooped. "Where is your store located?"

"In Mt. Pleasant. I'm the proprietor, Hank Harper."

"Thank you, Mr. Harper. How late are you open?"

"Until six." Another chuckle came from the phone. "And call me Hank. *Mister* is much too formal."

Ben laughed, already liking Hank. "Sure, Hank. I'm Ben." He glanced at the time on his phone. Mt. Pleasant was over an hour away. He had just enough time to clean up and make it there before Hank closed.

"Hank, I'll be there in about an hour and a half."

"I'll have the key waiting for you, Ben. See you then."

After the call ended, Ben danced around the bathroom at his stroke of luck. Hank confirmed the grandfather clock's rarity. It might be worth even more money than his google search had revealed! Once he acquired the key and got the clock working, he'd put it up for sale.

Ben rushed out of the room, dollar signs floating through his mind like party balloons. He'd finally have the money to really fix the old mansion up. Once he showed the renovated mansion to Cara, she'd fall in love with the place. He might even get *lucky* again.

He sprinted down the stairs and ran for his VW parked at the curb. The curtains twitched behind the window at the house next door, and Maude's pinched face appeared. Despite the overwhelming urge to flip her the middle finger, Ben waved instead.

He jumped into the driver's seat. With a grinding of gears, the van roared off.

The GPS led Ben to the downtown area in Mt. Pleasant. Buildings composed of weathered, orange brick flanked a square anchored by a large, multi-storied courthouse. Unlike some of the small towns Ben had visited, Mt. Pleasant's downtown contained no vacant buildings. In fact, it buzzed with activity.

He pulled into a parking space in front of a store with large picture windows. A sign with *Harper's Antiques & Oddities* hung above the brick structure. Ben checked his watch. Five p.m. He'd made it with plenty of time to spare.

Ben got out of the van and stretched. The display window ran the length of Hank's store. He paused to examine the objects on display. A mannequin wearing a prisoner's black and white striped uniform, sat in an old electric chair next to a whaling harpoon jutting from a block of Styrofoam. Further down, a Lionel model railroad track and train set circled the display area. Ben guessed it dated from the early 1900's.

Intrigued, he opened the door and the pleasant tinkle of a bell announced his entry. Warm scents of old leather, incense, and Burberry greeted him. After a few steps he stopped at a slab of stone mounted on a sturdy metal stand. The stone contained the fossilized remains of a birdlike creature. A sign attached to the stand identified the fossil as a pterodactyl, a flying reptile from the Jurassic period.

"A real conversation-starter isn't it?"

Startled, Ben looked around for the source of the voice… and received a second surprise. The speaker, a dwarf, was only four feet tall!

He thrust a hand up to Ben. "Hank Harper. You must be Dr. Hastings."

Ben managed to swallow his astonishment and gripped

Hank's hand. "Good to meet you, Hank. And it's Ben. No one calls me 'Dr.' except at formal university affairs."

A broad smile creased Hank's face. "Got it, *Ben*." He gestured with his hand. "C'mon. I've got your key in back."

Hank led Ben to a long, wooden counter that looked like it would be right at home in an old west saloon. Ben used the time to study Hank. Black hair, tied in a ponytail, curled over the dwarf's neck, and he wore black jeans, T-shirt, and boots. A trio of red, white, and blue feathered earrings dangled from both ears. Hank ducked behind the counter and returned with a large skeleton key.

Hank's blue eyes twinkled as he handed the key to Ben. "I think this is what you want. Try it, and if it doesn't work, return it, and I'll give you your money back."

Ben held the key up to the light. Four inches long and made of brass, the strange etchings on the key's surface struck Ben as vaguely familiar. He fished out his phone and looked at the picture he took earlier of the keyhole. The brass plate had similar runic symbols. Excitement bubbled up within him.

"I think it's a match!"

Ben turned the key. The light caused the engravings to flash in colors of red, green, blue, and yellow. "That's odd. Look how the light reflects off the metal in different colors."

"Metallurgy is not my specialty, but nothing made by Otto Albrecht surprises me," Hank said. "In the words of the poet Robert Frost, Albrecht followed the road less traveled. But, his craftsmanship was unmatched."

Ben shook his head. "I've never heard of him."

Hank laughed. "Well, let me give you a history lesson, professor. Albrecht was born in the early 1800's in the Black Forest region of Germany. He apprenticed under his father, a master clockmaker, and took over the business at his father's death. He soon became known for his, shall we say, *eccentric*, clocks."

Ben raised an eyebrow. "What do you mean?"

"The Black Forest is replete with the tales of fairies, forest sprites, and other mythical creatures," Hank explained. "Albrecht grew up immersed in this culture, and his clocks reflect that."

"You mean he believed them?"

Hank shrugged. "There's a fine line between belief and imagination, Ben. Who can tell when the line is crossed? Maybe Otto Albrecht wanted to enshrine the fairy tales in his clockmaking, while others, like the Brothers Grimm did it with books. I guess we'll never know."

Hank went around the counter to an old-fashioned cash register. "How's twenty bucks sound?"

Ben nodded. He fished the money from his wallet and gave it to Hank.

Hank rang up the purchase, then dropped the key and receipt in a paper sack and handed it to Ben. "Be careful with the key, Ben. You never know what forces are at work."

Ben laughed. "Oh, yeah. Fairies and sprites. Thanks for the advice."

Ben shook Hank's hand and left the store. The shopkeeper's eerie warning followed him all the way back to Tyler.

Hank was joking…right?

CHAPTER 6

Zelkova Petrova walked down a wide concrete corridor.

On either side of the passage, rooms were laid out, motel-style. Each room, built like a bunker, consisted of a single open space with concrete walls, bunk beds, a steel sink, and a toilet and shower. A locked metal door and an observation window with two-way glass fronted each chamber.

Petrova stopped at a room, and studied a trio of teenagers through the window. The three girls, dressed in blue disposable surgeon's scrubs, sat huddled on their bunks. The scrubs, cheap and easily available, were worn by all her captives. She pulled a folder from a plastic file rack mounted beside the door and studied it.

Without taking her eyes from the folder, she raised a hand and crooked her finger. Farshad Hosseini sidled up to her. "Mistress?"

"Congratulations, Farshad."

"Thank you, mistress." The Iranian swallowed. "Uh, for what am I being congratulated?"

Petrova pointed at a thin girl seated on the middle bunk. "She has rare AB-negative blood. I have a dozen clients in desperate need of organ transplants that match her blood type. *Very* wealthy clients. I expect the auction for her blood and organs will be vigorous and, best of all, lucrative."

Hosseini clapped. "Great news, mistress." Greed glinted in his eyes. "Does this mean my fee will be paid?"

Petrova placed the file back in the holder. She pivoted and turned a steely gaze on the smuggler. "I think you're confusing luck for achievement, so let me make myself clear. I reward success, but I have an *extremely* low tolerance for mistakes. They can often have fatal consequences."

Despite his swarthy complexion, Hosseini paled. He bobbed his head vigorously. "Yes, mistress. I understand."

"Let's be sure you do. You see, that single girl is worth more than all the rest of the rabble you brought me. You bring me another batch like this last one, and," Petrova used two fingers to pantomime scissors, "snip, snip, our relationship is severed."

Petrova leaned closer. "And when I say severed, I mean that literally."

Hosseini's lips and chin trembled. "Ye-yes, mistress," he rasped.

"Good! Here you go." Petrova handed the Iranian a single sheet of paper.

Hosseini hands shook as he took the sheet. "What's this, mistress?"

"My next order. And Farshad?"

"Yes, mistress?"

"*Don't* disappoint me."

By the time Ben returned to Tyler, the fading light had turned the horizon into a panorama of reddish-gold. Rather than going to his apartment, curiosity got the best of him, and he drove back to the old mansion.

In the murky gloom, the mansion's darkened windows looked like giant black eyes from some fearsome creature of the deep. A slither of fear crawled up Ben's back, and he debated whether to return in the morning. After a moment's indecision, he mumbled, "I'm here, so I might as well see if the key works." He started for the front door.

Once inside, Ben tried to flip on the light switch, then realized the wiring was as dated as everything else in the old house. The switch had to be *turned*. He twisted a knob, and light flooded the foyer. He blinked in the sudden brightness. Once his eyes adjusted, he headed for the grandfather clock.

Ben stopped before the clock and dug the key from his pocket. He studied the keyhole for a moment, then inserted the key. It slid in easily. "Yes!"

He tried to turn the key, but it didn't budge. He tried again, harder this time.

It still didn't turn.

He stepped back, lips pinched. *Maybe I didn't set the key in far enough.* He retrieved the key, reinserted it, and pushed harder.

Click.

The faint sound resonated like a gunshot in the quiet foyer. Emboldened, Ben firmly twisted the key. Another *click*, louder this time, rewarded his effort. Before he could celebrate, eye-searing light exploded from the keyhole. Ben backpedaled, covering his eyes. In his haste, his legs became tangled, and he tripped and fell, his head hitting the floor. Stunned, he lay still for a few seconds. He sat up and rubbed his head, but other than a small lump, he appeared to be okay.

Ben returned his attention to the clock. The brilliant radiance had dissipated, but light still glowed from the keyhole. He pushed himself up and returned to the grandfather clock. He leaned closer…and his mouth fell open. The source of light didn't come from the keyhole, but the key! The runic etchings blazed in colorful hues of blue, red, green, and yellow.

Ben reached for the clock panel and gingerly tugged on it.

With a quiet whisper, it swung open. The sight inside caused Ben to immediately doubt his sanity. "What the hell!" he cried.

Rather than a pendulum and weights, a staircase descended from the interior base of the old clock! The stairway spiraled downward and disappeared into shadowy darkness.

I'm seeing things! Ben pinched his cheeks, vigorously shook his head, and rubbed his eyes. But even after taking a second *and* third look, the staircase still remained. *The bump on my head must be worse than I thought.*

He dropped to his hands and knees and looked under the clock.

Nothing but the floor and a few dust bunnies.

Next, he looked behind it. Again, only a solid wall, no stairs. Ben searched the clock from top to bottom, examining every inch. He could find no evidence to explain how a staircase could exist inside the clock.

Ben scratched his head. Either an exception existed to the laws of physics, or he was hallucinating. He didn't like either option, so he got up and ducked his head inside the open clock. He studied the staircase. The wooden steps wound downward in a tight spiral. The stairway had no railing, the narrow, tunnel-like confines leaving no room for a hand rail. The air inside the clock smelled like the attic in his grandparent's house. It carried a musty, stale aroma as if bottled up for years.

Arms crossed, Ben thought furiously. At last, he threw up his hands. He couldn't figure out the paradox inside the old clock. His frustration came with a deeper disappointment. The anomaly inside the clock jeopardized his plan to sell it and use the money to fix up the house and yard. *Who wants to buy a clock straight out of a Twilight Zone episode?*

Maybe it's done with mirrors like the funhouse at a carnival.

The more he thought about it, the more the idea made sense. Hank said Otto Albrecht was an eccentric clockmaker known for his unconventional clocks. He could have made this one with a system of mirrors to create an optical illusion. There was only one way to find out.

Ben stepped into the clock.

He expected the space to be cramped, but instead, the interior was spacious. Despite a thorough examination, he didn't find any mirrors. Ben exited and studied the clock's dimensions. He didn't need a measuring tape to tell him the proportions didn't add up. The interior dimensions far exceeded the exterior.

Ben's frustrations boiled over. *What the hell is going on?*

He re-entered the clock. "Time to get to the bottom of this," he growled. The spiral stairs led somewhere, and he was going to find out!

Ben pulled out his phone, activated the flashlight app, then started down the steps. Coated with a thin layer of dust, the steps angled sharply downward The light also revealed smooth gray walls whose circular shape reminded him of a waterslide chute at a waterpark.

He proceeded only a short distance down the staircase when he experienced an intense feeling of disorientation. He put a hand out to steady himself, but rather than the wall, his hand found only empty space. In the next instant, the stairs beneath his feet moved and transformed from steps to a smooth, slippery surface. Arms flailing and unable to keep his footing, Ben tumbled down the chute, his screams ripped from his mouth as he gained speed.

And into the dark maw of a tunnel.

CHAPTER 7

BEN'S MIND DID MENTAL FLIP-FLOPS AS THE WIND RACED by his ears.

Only a short time earlier, he'd been examining the Otto Albrecht clock. Now he found himself in some *Alice in Wonderland* world fleeing for his life. He considered the possibility he suffered from hallucinations, but after watching Rooster-comb shove a spear through another other-worldly creature, he wasn't anxious to test that theory.

I should have left well enough alone, but no, I just had to follow those damn stairs.

Ben swallowed the bitter recrimination. The life-and-death situation he found himself in pushed aside any second guesses. As if to emphasize this point, his T-rex mount stumbled a few steps before it regained its faltering glide and gallop cadence. Ben glanced over his shoulder.

The distance between himself and Rooster-comb continued to narrow.

Cold fear filled Ben, its icy tendrils making it hard to breathe. He forced himself to return his focus to the distant greenery.

They were close enough that he could make out some detail. Trees, many of them of monstrous size, formed much of the vegetation. Massive trunks rose from the ground and reminded him of the Redwood Forest he once visited as a kid with his parents.

The T-rex thrust its snout into the air and snuffled. An eager honk issued from its mouth, followed by a burst of speed. Something about the forest called to his mount, something powerful enough to overcome the beast's fatigue. Hope replaced the fear that threatened to suffocate Ben.

We're going to make it!

The eagerness of Ben's mount became more pronounced as they drew near the forest. Its honks, now a constant bray, the beast's powerful legs churned in constant motion, and their glide and run speed continued to increase. The wind shrieked past Ben's face, and he struggled to stay seated. He didn't dare glance behind him to check on Rooster-comb's progress for fear of losing his grip on the saddle.

Despite the furious pace and unsteady seating, Ben managed to get a good look at the fast-approaching woodland. A unmistakable demarcation existed between forest and prairie as if a line had been drawn between them. On one side, bushes, ferns, and other plant life formed a dense canopy beneath the enormous trunks, while on the other side, nothing existed but scrub grasses, dry washes, and cacti.

An abrupt realization tore Ben's attention away from the odd pattern of vegetation. *We aren't slowing down.*

They continued to approach the giant trees at breakneck speed!

Closer and closer the thick screen of vegetation approached, and still his mount showed no sign of slowing down. Ben's earlier elation quickly turned to concern. He pulled on the reins and shouted at the beast, with no luck. Their frenzied pace continued. Now only seconds away, Ben ducked behind the T-rex's neck.

They rocketed into the forest.

Within seconds, they went from bright sunlight to murky

gloom. Instead of wind, the sharp sting of leaves and branches whipped Ben's face. The headlong plunge through the dense foliage made it impossible to make out detail or what direction they were headed. The T-rex continued to pound along, Ben's face, arms, and hands a collage of small welts and cuts. Time lost meaning to Ben, his singular focus to hold on until the T-rex tired and slowed down.

A small stream appeared suddenly out of the forest gloom. With an ear-splitting *honk*, the T-Rex came to an abrupt stop, its clawed hind feet finding purchase in the loamy soil. Ben, taken completely by surprise, catapulted from the saddle like a rock from a slingshot.

"*Shiiiiiiiiiit!*"

He flew through the air, somersaulted over the stream, and landed in the middle of a berry-laden bush. Stunned, Ben lay still, his heart beating like a trip-hammer. When he could finally sit up, he found himself tangled in thorny briars. By the time he freed himself from the prickly bush, he had acquired a new set of cuts and scratches. A furious buzzing, like a skill-saw at work, filled the air. It competed with noisy slurps coming from the direction of the stream.

Ben glanced at the brook and discovered the T-rex drinking greedily. Water dripped from its muzzle as the creature looked up and eyed Ben. With a final ill-tempered honk, it turned and fled into the forest gloom. The sight of his only means of transportation vanishing caused something inside Ben to snap.

He savagely kicked the cloying branches of the bramble bush. "Great! Just great!" he bellowed. "What am I supposed to do now?"

The buzzing around him intensified. Motion caught the corner of his eye. "What the—"

Splat. A plump berry bounced off his face, and sticky juice ran down his cheek. *Splat, splat, splat.* In rapid-fire, berries rained on his head and face with unerring accuracy. The bombardment continued unabated until the berry juice dripped from his chin in a sticky-sweet deluge. Ben raised his arms to ward off the salvos and tried to see where the assault of forest fruit came from. He whirled around to get a fix on his attackers, but all he could see were blurs of motion that seemed to come from all directions.

A well-aimed berry made it through the gap in his arms and hit him squarely in the eye. "Yeow!" Ben cried. He stumbled, tripped on a root, and fell with a bone-jarring *thump* onto his butt.

While Ben wiped the berry juice and tears streaming from his eye, the unmistakable sound of giggling came to his ears. He leapt to his feet, spinning in a circle to locate the source of laughter. All he spied were trees and bushes.

"Look, whoever or *whatever* you are," he snarled, "I've had a *very* bad day, so you'd better stop throwing shit at me!"

More giggling answered him, but before he could bark another angry comment, a doll-sized figure whizzed out of the forest and hovered inches from his nose.

"*Gah!*" Ben shouted at the sudden appearance. He fell again and landed on the same bruised backside. The tiny creature zoomed after Ben, and stopped so close it made it impossible to see the miniscule form without becoming cross-eyed. She munched on a purple berry while regarding him with undisguised curiosity.

Ben seriously considered if he had lost his mind. The tiny figure looked like a Barbie Doll with wings. Her translucent wings buzzed like a hummingbird, and she wore a one-piece garment that constantly shifted to match the color of the forest background.

Careful not to make any sudden moves that would trigger another berry bombardment, Ben crept to his feet. The tiny creature followed him inch-by-inch, never leaving her midair position in front of his face. The doll-sized figure—with the exception of her wings—appeared to be a perfect miniature of a human. Her honey-blond hair, cut short in pageboy fashion, framed a heart-shaped face. Green eyes with slight epicanthal folds stared back at him. Although slim, there was no mistaking the feminine curves of her hips and bosom.

"*Grabitz telluh ultah*," Barbie Doll trilled, her voice a melodic tinkle.

"Huh? What?" Ben sputtered.

Barbie Doll studied Ben for a moment then her tiny face brightened. "*Ribbets mara!*" She reached for a pouch at her hip and removed a fistful of dust-sized granules. Before Ben could react, she whipped through the air and scattered the dust on his lips and ears. They tingled as if brushed with a feather.

Ben touched his mouth, then his ears. "What did you do?"

Now seated cross-legged in midair, Barbie Doll said, "I sprinkled prawn dust on you so you could understand me. You're not very smart, are you?"

The sudden comprehension of her speech took a moment or two to sink in. Red-faced, he spluttered, "What? How dare…I mean, who do you think…you have no idea…" Ben angrily gave up trying to form a complete sentence.

"Can't talk very well either, can you?"

Ben, his nerves resembling a skillet of scrambled eggs, exploded. "Look, you-you Tinker Bell from hell. I didn't ask for any of this! One minute I'm inspecting an old clock, the next I'm falling into a Salvador Dali world where some rooster-combed crazy wants to kill me. I'm lucky to even be alive!"

"Not for much longer if the *Taluk* finds you."

"Huh? What do you mean?"

"The *Taluk* is a master tracker, and he's probably following your scent. I imagine you'll end up in his cook pot tonight."

"Co-cook pot?" Ben ran shaking fingers through his hair. "Heh, heh, you're kidding, right?"

"Of course, you could run, but I wouldn't try it. Since your *Chugga* mount ran off, you lost your only chance to escape. You'll only end up being tired when you get caught. Better to face the *Taluk* refreshed and with a clear mind. You *could* fight for your life, but you have no weapons, and it will only anger the *Taluk*. Then, rather than a quick, clean death, he'll toy with you."

Ben stared at the tiny creature who continued to hover around his face like a bothersome gnat. "That's your best advice? Stay here and let the thing chasing me kill then eat me?"

"Yes," Barbie Doll replied, beaming from ear to ear.

The sound of something crashing through the brush galvanized Ben.

"Look, you've got to help me!"

"Me?" Tittering laughter came from Barbie Doll. "You ruined a perfectly good brackleberry bush. Why should I help you?"

The crashing sounds drew closer.

"I'll give you something." Desperate, Ben fished around his pocket and pulled out a few coins.

"*Ooh*," the prawn gushed. In a blink, she landed in his palm. She picked out a shiny dime and held it up. It glinted in the muted light. "Can I have this?"

"Yes!" Ben looked over his shoulder toward the approaching hunter. "Just help me get away from the thing chasing me."

"Whee!" The tiny figure corkscrewed high into the air, then dove back to Ben. She hovered, her hands on either side of his nose. "Names are important and we must have names. What is yours?"

Ben's back itched as the sound of the pursuit drew ever closer. He forced himself to answer. "Ben Hastings."

The prawn mouthed the words as if tasting them. "Hmm, a good name I think."

She pointed at herself. "I'm Pringle."

She grabbed his finger with her hands.

"Let's go, Ben Hastings."

CHAPTER 8

WITH A STRENGTH THAT BELIED HER MINISCULE SIZE, Pringle pulled Ben along in the opposite direction of the pursuing *Talak*.

Ben stumbled along struggling to make progress, his feet and ankles constantly ensnared by roots and brambles. Behind him, the sounds of the chase grew louder.

Pringle dropped Ben's finger and zoomed up to his ear. "Hurry!" she hissed. For the first time, Ben detected concern in the prawn's voice.

"Hey!" he yelped when she grabbed his collar and lifted him into the air. *Buzzzzzzz.* Her wings hummed like a hive of angry bees as she carried him along, his feet barely touching the ground. They zigzagged through the woods, over fallen trees, and down almost invisible forest trails. Pringle set Ben down and flew up into the air. She looked back in the direction of the *Taluk*.

Despite her herculean effort, they were still being pursued. If anything, the crash of something bulling its way through the brush seemed closer.

"Now wh—"

Ben never finished the question. Pringle grabbed his collar in both tiny fists and raised him again into the air. They shot away at an adrenaline-pumping velocity, his feet skimming the tops of the bushes. They careened along so swiftly it made impact with one of the massive trees all but certain. Each time, however, Pringle veered around them at the last second.

After a few more moments of crazed flight, Pringle dropped Ben at the foot of an enormous tree. A titan of the forest, it dwarfed the other trees. Its gnarled trunk—over thirty feet in diameter—climbed so high above the other trees, Ben couldn't see the top.

Hoarse from screaming during the wild ride, Ben leaned against the hoary trunk. "Wha-what now?" he croaked.

"Use the key," she answered.

"What key? What are you talking about?"

"The Taluk is almost upon us. *Use the key!*"

A familiar honk split the air. *Rooster-comb's riding mount!* An eager guttural shout followed. The nearness of the cry caused a butt-puckering panic in Ben.

In the next moment, Pringle plunged into the pocket of his pants. She squirmed around, then emerged holding the key to the grandfather clock.

"*Use. The. Key.*" She emphasized each word as if Ben were the village idiot. She dropped the key into his hand. Numb, he stared at it, unsure what to do.

With an irritated squeak, Pringle zoomed to the tree trunk and pointed at a keyhole cleverly camouflaged by the lichen-covered bark. Ben rushed to the tree, fumbled to insert the key, then turned it. A *click* rewarded his effort.

Nothing happened.

Ben froze in terror at Rooster-comb's triumphant shout. Pringle broke his paralysis when she picked him up, and tossed him directly at the tree! With no time to raise his arms to protect himself, Ben braced for impact, expecting his head to crack against the hard wood.

Instead, he sailed *through* the tree trunk.

"*Oof.*" He belly-flopped onto a hard surface in total darkness. When he could finally catch his breath, he staggered to his feet, tripped on something, and pitched forward. Ben's head struck a hard object, and stars exploded in his head.

He passed out.

Ben awoke with his face pressed against a hard, cold surface.

He groaned and sat up. Pain throbbed from his temple. He gently probed the area with his fingers and found a lump the size of a golf ball. He staggered to his feet and looked around with bleary eyes.

Gloom surrounded him, but a soft luminescence glowed from the...walls? The memory of Pringle tossing him into the tree came rushing back.

Where the hell am I?

The faint luminescence revealed dim shapes spaced within a large area. Ben carefully threaded his way around them and discovered the objects to be a table and chairs. One chair lay overturned, probably the one he tripped over. He reached for the wall and ran his fingers over the coarse, irregular surface. *Wood.* There could be no doubt. *I'm inside the tree!*

A bright light flared to life from a sconce mounted on the wall above his head. This started a chain reaction, with one torch after another blazing to life. Their combined light revealed the circular contours of an enormous hollow. Crafted from the living wood of the tree, delicate glass petals enclosed each torch so that they looked like fiery flowers.

A sense of intense weariness filled Ben. The rapid sequence of events seemed like a nightmare he couldn't wake up from. None of it could be real.

Could it?

He set the overturned chair upright, and collapsed onto it.

Frustration and anger boiled over inside him. He struck the table with his fist and roared, "*Where am I, and what is this damn place?*"

"You're in a Wizard's Hutch. You don't know much, do you?" said a voice in his ear.

"Yah!" Ben cried toppling off the chair.

He rolled onto all fours and spotted Pringle.

"Stop doing that!" he shouted.

"If you don't want questions answered, why do you ask them?"

Ben snorted, dusted himself off, righted the chair *again*, and sat down. Pringle hovered close to his nose. He pushed her away.

"Personal space!" he snapped. "You don't need to be right in my face."

Pringle tittered. "You are funny, Ben Hastings. How have you survived this long?"

"Look, I'm not from…wherever this crazy world is. Believe it or not, we don't go around trying to skewer people with spears and eat them."

Pringle zoomed closer. "Ooh, really? Where—"

"Personal space!"

"—are you from, Ben Hastings?" Pringle continued unfazed.

Ben eyed Pringle. "I'll make a deal with you. If you move away and give me some breathing room, I'll tell you." Pringle flew backward a foot or two, and Ben sighed in relief.

"That's better. I'm from Texas in the United States. That's on the planet Earth." The last part immediately made him feel foolish. It was like he had just recited a line from a low-budget, science fiction movie.

"Okay, here's a question for you. I know we are in a Wizard's whatchamacallit, but where is this place, this-this world?"

Pringle shook her head. "You really don't know much, do you?"

"Yeah, I know. You've already told me a bunch of times. Just answer the question."

Pringle buzzed up to Ben. "This is the great forest of Almeera. Everyone knows that."

"Yeah, great, so next question. *What* are you?"

"A prawn. Prawns are Children of the Forest. But everyone knows that too." Pringle shook her head sadly. "Poor Ben Hastings. You've been damaged. You're like one of my brother prawns. He was sleeping when an acorn fell and hit him on the head. Now he sits on a brightfire bush for hours and begs the butterflies to pollinate him."

Heat flushed Ben's face. "Now, look. I'm not crazy!"

Pringle clapped. "Oh, good!"

Ben took a deep breath. He couldn't believe his situation. He had a PhD in History, and yet this escapee from a Disney movie was lecturing *him*. The absurdity struck him as so hilarious he began to chuckle. The chuckles quickly transitioned to hysterical laughter. This served to sharpen the throb of pain in his head. He grabbed his head and moaned.

Pringle, concern etched across her tiny face, buzzed up to Ben and examined the lump. She reached into her pouch and removed a glistening substance. She softly rubbed it on the bump. Sparkles of light glittered from the salve, and Ben felt immediate relief. He straightened in amazement.

"What did you do?"

Pringle beamed. "Rubbed your hurt with *alactrus* paste. It grows everywhere in the forest and is good for all sorts of bumps and bruises."

Her comment caused Ben to pause. For the first time, he studied Pringle in a different light. Despite being childishly blunt, she had not only saved his life from Rooster-comb, she had also found this refuge, and provided a salve for the welt on his head. In short, he owed her his life. Maybe instead of irritation, he needed to display another kind of emotion.

Gratitude.

CHAPTER 9

BEN CLOSED HIS EYES. *GET A HOLD OF YOURSELF.*
He opened them and forced himself to smile. "Thank you, Pringle. You saved my life."

He gestured toward the table. "Can you, uh, land here and just stay still?" In a blink, Pringle stood upon the wooden surface.

"Wow. You can really move fast."

Pringle wiggled a finger at him. "No, Ben Hastings. *This* is fast."

Zip, zip, zip, zip, zip, zip.

Pringle circled the room half-a-dozen times before Ben could take his next breath. A high-pitched whine—like a mosquito on steroids—was the only evidence of her passage. The next thing he knew, she had returned to the same spot on the table. She giggled at his expression.

"You don't know anything about prawns, do you, Ben Hastings?"

This time, the smile tugging at Ben's face was genuine. "No, I guess I don't."

As he studied her tiny figure, other details about Pringle's appearance came to light. She stood about eight inches tall with no shoes. A vine tied about her waist secured her pouch. The pouch looked like a leaf sewn together with gossamer thread—like a strand from a spider's web. Pringle's short hair exposed ears with pointed tips. Feminine curves and a shallow bosom gave her the look of a girl on the precipice of adolescence.

"What are you looking at?" Pringle asked.

Embarrassed, Ben struggled to reply. "Well, you see…I've never seen…that is to say, I've never met, uh, anyone like you before."

Pringle whizzed to the tip of Ben's nose. "You've never seen a prawn before? You've never even *heard* of a prawn?"

Ben sighed and gently pushed her hovering form away. "I'm afraid so. And before you say 'Poor Ben Hastings' again, I admit I don't know anything about your world. I need you to teach me. Can you do that?"

Pringle squealed with delight. "Yes, Ben Hastings. I will teach you! This is going to be fun!" She did cartwheels in the air in a blur of arms and legs. In the next moment, she landed on his shoulder beside his ear. "What do you want to know?"

Ben pointed at the table, and Pringle zipped back to her former position. "Thanks," he said. "Give me a minute to think."

Pringle's cheerful attitude reminded him of a child. In fact, everything about her behavior could be described as childish. She seemed utterly carefree without a single worry.

"How old are you?" he asked.

Pringle's tiny face frowned. "What do you mean?"

"Your age. Are you ten, fifteen, twenty years old?"

Her frown deepened. "What is age, Ben Hastings?"

"You know. The passage of time like days, weeks, months or years."

Pringle shook her head. "The sun goes down, and the sun comes up. Is that what you mean, Ben Hastings?"

Stunned, Ben leaned back in the chair. The concept of time seemed completely foreign to Pringle. Minutes, hours, and years were meaningless to her.

Another thought struck him. "Do prawns die?"

Pringle laughed. "Of course not. You are funny, Ben Hastings."

"But you must have been born, right?"

Pringle stretched out lengthwise and hovered. Chin cupped in both hands, she asked, "What is *born*, Ben Hastings?"

Ben stared at Pringle and considered how to reply. The more he thought about it, the less inclined he was to answer her question. He'd have to explain a host of things—including where babies came from.

Best to ignore the question and change the subject—quickly!

"Uh, never mind." He waved at the hollow. "You called this a Wizard's Hutch. What is it?"

Pringle giggled. "You don't know any—"

"Yes, Yes," Ben interjected. "I don't know anything. How about we skip that part, and you just answer my questions?"

"But you have the *devron* key, Ben Hastings."

"The...what?"

"You used the key to enter the Wizard's Hutch. If you have the key, you must know where we are." With that, Pringle sat and dangled her legs over the table's edge.

Ben blinked. "Huh? What kind of key is that? What does it do?"

"A *devron* key is used by travelers to move from one place to another. It contains powerful magic unique to whoever possesses it. But everyone knows—"

"Pringle! I'm not everyone, so stop saying it!"

With great effort, Ben reined in his frustration and considered her explanation. *A key that allowed someone to travel from one place to another? How far? How distant?*

"Does it open doors to other worlds? Other dimensions?"

Pringle somersaulted to her feet. "What's a world? What's a dimension?"

Ben ground his teeth in frustration. *This is like talking to a kindergartener.* Despite his irritation with Pringle, one thing was certain—this entire mess centered around the key.

He should have paid closer attention to Hank Harper's cryptic comment. *Be careful with the key. You never know what forces are at work.* But how could he have known what the diminutive shopkeeper meant? His exasperation evaporated when a horrible thought struck him.

"Where's the key?" he blurted.

Pringle, now twirling in midair like a ballerina, answered, "In the keyhole where you left it."

Ben shot to his feet, and his chair catapulted to the floor with a *bang.* "The *Taluk!* What if he finds the key? He'll use it to come after me!" Ben spun around, searching every corner and crevice in the hollow.

Pringle's musical laughter echoed off the walls. "The *Taluk* has already found the key and tried to use it."

"What? I need to hide!" Ben jabbered.

"And the key hurled the *Taluk* across the glade." Pringle giggled. "He won't try that again."

Ben blinked. "What? I don't understand."

"Only you can use the key, Ben Hastings. Anyone else will be repelled by its magic. But everyone knows that." The matter settled, Pringle returned to the table and began to perform a series of backflips.

Relief flooded Ben—until another thought brought his respite to an abrupt end.

"If the key is outside the tree and I'm on the inside, then how..."

Ben whirled to face Pringle.

"Then how am I supposed to get out of here?"

CHAPTER 10

SILENCE FILLED THE HOLLOW.

Ben pointed at Pringle. "Answer me. How the hell do I get out of this hobbit hole?"

For the first time, the little prawn, rather than her usual hyperactive movement, remained still. Finally, she flitted over to Ben.

"I don't know, Ben Hastings."

"Great! Just great! You mean I'm going to be a prisoner forever in this, this—"

"—Wizard's Hutch," Pringle added.

Ben's temper boiled over. Deposited in a bizarro world by the grandfather clock from hell, chased like a hunted animal, *thrown* into a tree hollow by a creature small enough to fit into his pocket, and now he finds there's no way out! His frayed nerves snapped.

With a howl, he picked up a fallen chair and hurled it. It struck the wall of the Wizard's Hutch with a sharp *crack* and splintered into pieces. He chose another chair and launched it. He roared in satisfaction as the chair exploded into broken fragments.

He jumped when a chair flew by him and smashed to pieces against the rigid interior of the tree. He glanced over his shoulder where Pringle clapped her hands in delight.

"Whee! This is fun!" She buzzed over to a side table, picked it up, and launched it against the wall.

This is too ridiculous! Ben couldn't help himself. A snort escaped his lips that quickly grew to uncontrollable laughter. Tears streamed down his face, and he staggered to the lone undamaged chair and plopped down. Pringle landed on his shoulder, her melodic laughter joining his. The hysterical hilarity served to calm Ben's nerves and soothe his tattered emotions. Drained, he sat back and tried to catch his breath.

"You are funny, Ben Hastings!" Pringle said.

"We make quite a pair, don't we, Pringle?"

Pringle placed her hands on his cheek and nuzzled against him, her body a sliver of warmth against his skin. She whispered into his ear, "Yes we do, Ben Hastings."

A scraping noise came from the mound of splintered chairs. Ben glanced at the wreckage and stiffened. "What the hell?" he choked out.

The pile of debris is moving!

Pieces and splinters of wood rose into the air. As if going through a sorting process, they separated into individual clusters of broken rubble. A dry swish—like dead leaves blown by the wind—filled the hollow.

Before Ben could process the incredible sight, the levitating bits and pieces rushed together with a loud *pop!* In an instant, each shattered chair returned to its whole, undamaged state. With a *thump*, they dropped to the floor. *Screeeech!* The chairs slid along the floor and returned to their original positions around the table.

The whole process started and finished so quickly, that the last chair skimmed to a stop beside Ben before he could react.

He shot to his feet and pointed a shaking finger at the chairs. "What—what happened?"

Pringle laughed. "The magic of the Wizard's Hutch."

She whizzed to the nearest chair and picked it up. "Now we can do it again, Ben Hastings!" she gushed.

"No!" Ben cried before Pringle could hurl the piece of furniture. "Just put the chair down."

Disappointed, Pringle let the chair drop to the floor. It glided back to its place at the table.

"No one, I mean no one, would believe this," Ben mumbled.

"Why?" Pringle asked. "Don't you have Wizard Hutches in your forests?"

Ben, resigned to the finality of his situation, dropped back into the chair. He patted the table. Pringle landed and sat cross-legged, her eyes bright with anticipation. "Okay, here's how things work in my forest, uh, I mean, world," he said.

He launched into how he ended up in Almeera. He tried to explain the differences between the two worlds, particularly the absence of *magic* on earth. The effort to simplify his description so Pringle would understand was maddening, and a headache began to throb at his temple. After twenty minutes, he slumped back and rubbed his eyes. "That's the best I can do. You have any questions?"

"You mean your forest has no magic?" Pringle asked in disbelief. She buzzed to his head and patted it. "Poor, Ben Hastings."

"World, not forest," he corrected her. "And I'm afraid not. At least not in the sense you think it works. We have what we call science and laws of physics which control everything."

Pringle cast a look of pity at Ben. She flitted to his shoulder, and sat down with her back against his neck. Legs stretched out in front of her, she said, "Don't worry, Ben Hastings, I'll stay with you."

"Thanks, Pringle, but I'm going to find a way out of this tree. Maybe there's an ax in here I can use to chop my way out."

Pringle stood up, placed both tiny hands on his cheek, and kissed him. "I don't know what an ax is, Ben Hastings, but I will help you find one."

Pringle's kiss, soft as the touch of a feather, left Ben's skin tingling. Despite being trapped like a bug in a jar, her offer touched him. The little forest prawn was definitely beginning to grow on him.

It took no leap of intuition to see that living in a world without magic was something beyond the comprehension of the little prawn. He didn't want to waste more time discussing it. With Pringle riding on his shoulder, he began a thorough investigation of the Wizard's Hutch.

Several smaller chambers led from the main hollow. One room, filled with tools, sealed jars, and casks, was obviously used for storage. Cubbyholes, carved from the living wood of the tree, contained different sets of implements. Flat shelves also grew from the walls. They held clear vials and jars that contained a variety of the preserved remains of plants, powders, and other...*things*.

One jar contained eyeballs of various sizes. When the eyeballs moved to follow Ben's progress, he almost jumped out of his skin. He fought the urge to look back to see if they were still watching him, then forced himself to continue his inspection.

A small table perched in the middle of the room. On its scarred surface rested empty glass containers that resembled laboratory beakers. Thin glass tubes connected some of the beakers, and a pestle and mortar sat next to them. The entire room and its contents looked like the lair of a mad scientist—which reminded Ben anew of the shattered chairs reassembling themselves.

He decided not to touch anything.

Ben resumed his exploration and came upon a library. Arranged from floor to ceiling were tiers of books accessed by a wheeled wooden ladder. A flat table sprouted from the middle of the floor like a mushroom. Two comfortable chairs, covered in a green-tinged leather, sat beside the table.

As Ben approached the books, the ladder trembled, then rolled along the floor to stop beside him. He waited a moment or two, but when the ladder made no more movement, he reapproached the books and cautiously reached for one. The pages of the leather-bound book consisted of thick vellum inscribed in an unfamiliar language. He chose a few more books at random and realized they all contained the same strange script.

One book stood out from the rest because of its distinctive red binding. Curious, Ben took it off the shelf. When he opened the book, it growled loudly at him. "Hey!" Ben cried. He dropped it to the floor where it continued to snap and snarl at him. With great care, he used the toe of his shoe to flip the cover over and close the book. The growling stopped. Ben sighed with relief and placed it back on the shelf.

I'd better not open any more books. At this rate, he might need to make a list of do's and don'ts just to navigate around the Wizard's Hutch.

Pringle remained strangely silent during Ben's exploration. *Maybe she's still in shock I come from a world without magic.* Although grateful he didn't have to endure her heart-stopping appearances at the tip of his nose, Ben found he missed her super-charged effervescence.

He shrugged and continued his exploration.

In the last room, Ben discovered a kitchen. More storage cubbyholes were arranged alongside the wall, and they contained a variety of pots, pans, and other cooking implements. Carved wooden mugs and bowls lay scattered across a dining table—as if someone had left in a hurry.

A wooden basin protruded from the circular wall of the hollow. Ben's eyes widened in recognition. A sink! A wooden spout protruded from the wall above the sink, and a hole in the bottom allowed water to drain. Ben could find no faucet handles, but when he ran his hands around the spout, a thin stream of water erupted from it—more proof of the magic of Pringle's world.

A square object made of gray rock sat next to the sink. It stood four feet tall with three circular disks of clear crystal inlaid on the top. They resembled burners on a stove. Ben repeated the motion he used on the sink and moved his hand over them. Heat immediately rose from the crystal disks. "Okay, I've found a wizardly sink and stove," he muttered, "what else is in here?"

An open doorway was the only other item of interest in the room. Ben hoped it led to a food pantry, but when he entered, the temperature dropped precipitously. He shivered and hurried out. "Make that a sink, stove, *and* fridge."

While Ben considered what to do next, his stomach growled—a reminder he'd had nothing to eat since early that morning. He searched every storage area in the room, but the wizard's kitchen was as empty of food as his stomach. A chilling thought occurred to him. *I might starve to death before I can find a way out of this damn place.*

"What are we going to do for food?" he asked Pringle.

Pringle, her earlier reticence gone, laughed and launched herself into the air. She hovered before Ben. "The great forest is all around us. It has all the food we could ever eat."

"Yes, but that's out there, and we're in here. We can't get out, so how are we supposed to gather anything?"

"Like this!" Pringle shot toward the wall of the Wizard's Hutch.

"Stop!" Ben cried. "You're going to hurt yourself!"

A second later, Pringle barreled into the wall.

And disappeared through it.

CHAPTER II

AFTER A MOMENT OF BAFFLED SILENCE, BEN RUSHED TO the location Pringle had used to exit the tree, and examined it.

He pushed and prodded at the area, but his inspection revealed only hard, unyielding wood.

"Damn it! Everything about this world is upside down and backwards!" He beat at the wall with his fists until the pain made him stop. He stepped back and forced himself to take deep, even breaths. When he finally reined in his frustration, he reapproached the area and went over every inch. He even tried inspecting it from different angles to see if the section Pringle disappeared through had any subtle irregularities.

Nothing. Just the same coarse wood.

Ben threw himself back into the chair. He drummed his fingers on the table, the only disturbance in the thick silence of the Wizard's Hutch. As irritating and unpredictable as Pringle could be, he already missed the little pixie's musical laughter.

Ben pushed himself up, and wandered aimlessly about the Wizard's Hutch until he found himself back in the library. Wary of the growling tome, he made sure to avoid the books as he made a slow circuit of the room. Unsure what to do next, Ben stopped and leaned against a section of the library wall.

And fell into another hidden room.

With a shout, Ben stumbled, arms flailing. His shoulder slammed against something solid. "Ow!" He whirled, and fists raised, crouched in a defensive position. Heart racing, Ben looked about. "What the—"

Light flared from wall-mounted sconces. They illuminated a narrow corridor that rose straight up like a giant conduit pipe. The torches also revealed another doorway in the wall of the library he tumbled through. It wavered like the hazy outline of a mirage. He rubbed his eyes and looked again, but the door continued to flicker as if not quite solid. Ben poked his finger at the mirage, and his hand passed through easily. Next, he shoved his entire arm through. Emboldened, he stepped through the doorway and found himself back in the library. He turned back, but only solid wood presented itself. He poked at it again, and when his hand passed through the wall, he walked back through it.

"This place has more secret passages than a Spielberg movie."

Except the passageway wasn't exactly hidden. The wizard who created the hutch must've been able to see it, and even Pringle found a way out of the hollow. *So I'm the only one who can't see the freaking doors.*

Thump!

Thump!

Thump!

Flat panels of wood—*steps*—slid from the sides of the wall. They spiraled upward following the curved bole of the massive tree. By this time, nothing surprised Ben. If it started raining gummy bears, he doubted he would give it a second thought.

The steps, spaced evenly apart, were about a foot wide and two feet in length. He shrugged. "Well, it's not the yellow-brick road, but what the hell." Ben stepped on the first tread. It held him easily, and he made his way up the stairs.

The stairway led to a second level and another suite of rooms. "*Hmm*. What do we have here?"

A hurried exploration revealed several bedrooms. The first two had small beds with a chest at the foot of each. Ben opened one to find that it held sheets, pillows, and other bedding materials. Each room also had a closet—a crude nook carved from the wood. The closets contained a ridge of wood upon which folded bedclothes and robes rested. Ben rubbed the material of one of the robes between his fingers, surprised at its softness.

The last bedroom proved to be much larger than the previous two. The bed—a four poster affair—could easily accommodate any NBA or NFL player. Ben discovered clothes hanging from pegs in the room's large closet. The wizard's clothing—tunics, pants, and robes—ranged from dark gray to a tan-brown.

Ben looked at his stained and torn shirt and jeans, then at the wizard's clothing. *Why not?* He stripped and tried on a pair of the pants and a tunic. Even on Ben's 6'3" frame, the pants drooped a bit long, while the tunic fit loosely. Whoever owned the Wizard's Hutch must have been taller and stouter than Ben.

Through an exit adjacent to the bedroom, he entered a wizardly version of a bathroom. A small oval sink protruded from the wall with a cubicle located beside it. The stall, made of wood like everything else, had numerous tiny holes that perforated the top, and a drain-hole in the floor.

Because the kitchen stove and faucet were motion-activated, Ben waved his hand beneath the perforations. Streams of lukewarm water poured out. Ben whooped and danced around the wizard's bathroom. "We got us a shower, boys!"

A squat structure with a water-filled basin and wooden seat rose from the floor next to the shower. Ben needed no further scrutiny to know he'd found the toilet.

He went back to the bedroom, sat on the edge of the bed, and did a quick inventory. The Wizard's Hutch had a library, kitchen, bedroom, bathroom, books, clothes and linens. His prison had all the comforts of home.

Except food.

At least he'd be clean and well-rested when he died of starvation.

Ben shrugged off the wizard's clothes and headed for the shower. Folded towels lay on a nearby shelf, and as Ben reached for one of the towels, the wall beside the shelf clouded over. Moments later, it clarified into an oval mirror. His reflection displayed an unflattering image. Twigs and leaves poked from his matted hair, and his entire body was covered with scratches and abrasions, some still oozing blood. Blue-black bruises checkered his face and neck, his lower lip was split, and dark circles edged his eyes.

He looked like an accident victim in ER.

His looks weren't going to improve no matter how long he stood before the mirror, so he stepped into the shower. A brown square of what he hoped was soap lay in a small recess within the shower. He grabbed it and sniffed, pleased by the aroma of sandalwood and cloves.

He waved his hand and water streamed from the ceiling. Ben vigorously lathered up, but when he tried to transfer the bar to his other hand, it slipped out and squirted to the floor. Before he could pick it up, the soap rose into the air, swooped around him, and began to scrub his back. It felt like a soapy massage. Ben closed his eyes and relaxed while the bar made its way over every square inch of his body.

Until it reached his groin.

"Hey!" Ben grabbed the bar and held it while he rinsed off. He stepped out of the stall and placed the soap back in the shower.

Before he could dry off, one of the towels flew into the air. It soared toward him like a magic carpet, wrapped itself around him, and began to rub him dry. When it traveled below his waist, he grabbed the towel and finished drying off. He attempted to drop the towel to the floor, but it floated to the shower drain where it flapped like a flag in a stiff breeze. A moment later, the towel folded itself and returned to the shelf.

Ben ran his hand over the towel. *Bone dry. Who needs dry cleaning when you have this place?*

Ben put the wizard's clothing back on, then stood before the mirror. He chuckled at the sight. The tan-colored tunic and pants made him look like some sort of deranged Jedi knight. *All I need is a light saber, and I'm ready to battle a Sith.*

He left the bathroom and lay on the bed to test the mattress. It felt glorious, a perfect balance of softness and firmness. He stretched out and put his arms behind his head. The bed molded itself to his lanky frame, and within minutes, he became drowsy. The physical, mental, and emotional exhaustion of his rollercoaster day caught up with him all at once.

Ben fell into a deep and unbroken sleep.

Chapter 12

Hosseini maneuvered his black Mercedes S-Class sedan to a strategic location in the parking lot. He parked and waited.

From his viewpoint through the tinted windows of the sedan, he could see the flow of clientele into the main entrance of *Bodies in Motion*, an upscale fitness center. He'd googled the fitness center and discovered it had its own Water Bar that served vitamin and mineral water, as well as a "Spirit Pool" for meditation. Hosseini snorted. Only in the United States would you find such opulence for weak-minded fools. His phone chimed, and he glanced at the text.

She's leaving.

A few moments later, a pretty blond dressed in a black sports top with matching yoga pants exited the building. The athletic attire clung to the young woman's curves like a second skin. She tossed her gym bag into a BMW convertible and drove away.

Hosseini nodded with approval. *Just the kind of product Petrova wants.*

A young man in a sweat-soaked tank top left the fitness center. He stopped, looked around, then made his way to the Mercedes.

Hosseini powered the passenger window down. "Get in, Bashir."

Bashir nodded, opened the door and slid into the seat. A younger, slimmer version of Hosseini, he had a mane of curly black hair. "What do you think?" he asked.

"She's exactly what we're looking for. What do you know about her?"

Bashir smiled. "A typical American whore. I bought her a mineral water and she told me her life's story. Her father's some rich lawyer, and she works for him as a part-time secretary. Right now she's furious with her boyfriend because he won't return her phone calls or texts."

Bashir added, "I'm sorry, Boss. The chances of her being a virgin are zero."

Hosseini shrugged. "Virgins are overrated. The sheiks and princes have more money than common sense. Why waste time with screaming and crying when you can have an experienced concubine?"

Bashir nodded, a troubled look on his face. "Why are we considering this, Boss? It's one thing to snatch poor immigrants or women and children in refugee camps—no one's going to miss them—but to take an American here in her own country is going to cause trouble. Her father's a lawyer, and the blowback will be—"

The meaty *slap* of Hosseini's hand across Bashir's face echoed in the closed confines of the sedan. "I'll do the thinking, so keep your mouth shut!" he snarled.

Bashir, eyes bright with tears of pain, held his hand to his face and nodded.

"My life, your life, we're all at risk, so let me make our position with Petrova clear," Hosseini hissed. "She's threatened to remove my balls and nail them to the wall if I don't start delivering a better product."

Hosseini sat back in the seat and smoothed his shirt. "What do you know about the Russian bitch?"

Hand still on his face, Bashir mumbled, "Not much, Boss."

"Well, let me educate you. Petrova doesn't bluff. She has the money and muscle to carry out whatever she orders. If she says she's going to do something, it's a done deal. *And* she's a big believer in a scorched earth policy that delivers a message. Do you know what that means?"

Bashir shook his head.

"It means everyone in our operation will be taken out, even the middlemen we use. No one will be spared."

Bashir paled. "She'll kill us all?"

"Yes, you fool. So if the choice is between the greater risk in a snatch or the wrath of Petrova, I'll gamble we won't get caught. Do I make myself clear?"

"Yes, Boss."

"Good!" Hosseini tossed Bashir a wad of bills. "Buy a membership and be there every time the whore shows up. Find out everything you can about her, especially her address, then text it to me. I'll set up the abduction and delivery to Petrova. Any questions?"

Bashir shook his head. He opened the car door and got out. Before he could turn to leave, Hosseini leaned across the seat. "Don't fail me, Bashir. I can cause accidents too. Painful ones."

The window closed, and Hosseini drove off.

Ben woke with a start.

After a moment or two of disorientation, the memories of the previous day rushed back. He forced himself to close his eyes and control his panicked breathing. When his wildly beating heart finally slowed to normal, he turned his head and looked around.

The light had dimmed to the point he could barely make out the contours of the bedroom. As if cued by his slight movement, the sconce torches flared to life.

More magic, Ben thought, yawning. *If I could bottle it, I could make a fortune when I get back to Texas.* The thought served to remind him anew of his crushing reality—trapped with no food and no way out. Any residual sleep immediately fled.

Ben tried to sit up but then realized something warm lay on his chest. He looked down, and his mouth fell open.

There, curled up like a cat, rested the slumbering form of Pringle.

Ben's movements woke the pixie. She stood, stretched lazily, then sprang into the air and drifted before Ben's astonished eyes.

"I'm hungry, Ben Hastings!"

Ben swallowed. "But…but how…how did you get back into the hutch?"

Pringle regarded Ben with a look he'd become all too familiar with. Quickly, he added, "Remember, I don't know anything."

"I just flew through the doorway the Devron key opened."

Ben swung his legs off the bed and stood up. He straightened his borrowed clothes and thought about what the little prawn said.

"If you can go in and out through the door, why can't I?"

With tiny brows furrowed, Pringle considered Ben's question. At last, she spread her arms and said, "I don't know, Ben Hastings. Prawns are creatures of the forest, and the magic of Almeera has always been part of us. Maybe you can't see doorways because your world has no magic."

Sadness dripped from Pringle's voice, the concept of a magicless world something Ben knew she found difficult to fathom. However, her comment gave him an idea.

"Are there more magical doorways in this tree?" he asked.

Pringle's face brightened. "Yes!" she cried. "Follow me!" She sped from the bedroom, Ben racing after her.

The corridor connecting the bedrooms followed the circular contours of the gigantic tree. Ben tore around a curve and skidded to a stop. The passageway came to a dead-end at yet another featureless wall. Pringle pointed at it. "Here, Ben Hastings, here!"

Having already fallen through one wall, Ben knew the sight of solid wood meant nothing. In the world of Almeera, appearances could be deceiving, so he eagerly darted to the wall and examined it. Careful not to pick up any splinters on the coarse wood, Ben ran his fingers over the hard surface.

His hand disappeared through it!

Ben, waving his hands in front of him like a blind man, carefully made his way through the invisible entrance. Once on the other side, he discovered he stood at the bottom of an enormous hollow. The familiar sconces flickered on one by one to give a clear picture of what lay within the cavity. They circled upward in a dizzying spiral that eventually disappeared from sight.

Ben craned his neck in an unsuccessful attempt to see where the lights led. "How high does this place go?" he whispered. Before he could puzzle it out further, the scrape of wood penetrated the silence of the hollow..

Thump!

Thump!

Thump!

Ben whirled. Another set of wooden steps slid out of the tree wall. In the absolute silence of the enormous cavity, the whispered movement rumbled like the sound of an avalanche.

Ben experienced vertigo even on a stepladder, so the sight of the stairs twisting upward to disappear into the great height of the tree caused him to quickly look away.

"They must go up 10-12 stories," he muttered. Curiosity competed with his fear of heights. "Wonder what's up there?" he added.

"I'll find out, Ben Hastings!" Pringle cried.

She shot upward. "*Wheee!*"

While he waited for Pringle to return, Ben worked up the courage to test the bottommost steps. They were the same dimensions as the other stairs he'd discovered with no outside handrail. After going up the stairs a short way, Ben made the mistake of looking down. He broke out in a cold sweat and with his back plastered against the wall, he inched his way back down. He heaved an enormous sigh of relief when his feet touched the solid floor.

Pringle's voice hailed him from above.

"Ben Hastings!" Ben spied Pringle hurtling toward him. She stopped inches from his face. "There's a scrying chamber up there!" she gushed.

"What-what's a *scrying* chamber?" he asked.

She ignored his question and bobbed up and down. "Let's go!"

"What? Up there? Are you crazy?"

"Yes. Let's go!" Pringle repeated and tugged on Ben's sleeve.

"Absolutely not! I got dizzy just walking up a few of those steps. There's no way I—

"Hey!" Ben's panicked cry echoed in the silent hollow as Pringle, impatient, grabbed Ben's collar in a firm grip, and heaved him off his feet.

Together, they rocketed upward.

CHAPTER 13

THE SPIRALING LIGHTS AND STEPS WHIZZED BY IN a blur as Pringle shot upward, Ben's terrified screams echoing behind them.

After an excruciating trip of heart-stopping seconds, they reached a smaller platform high in the hollow. Pringle deposited him onto the landing, and he scuttled like a crab away from the edge.

On the verge of hyperventilating, Ben tried to get his breathing under control. He pointed a shaking finger at Pringle.

"Are you *NUTS?*" he screeched. "You could have killed me!"

"But I thought you wanted to see the wizard's scrying chamber."

"Look, I don't even know what a 'scrying' chamber is!" Ben shouted. "Why would I want to see one?"

Pringle zipped up to Ben's nose and shook a tiny finger at him. "You asked me to show you other doorways, Ben Hastings, and I did." She crossed her arms, and turned her back to Ben.

Teeth clenched, Ben strained to rein in his temper. When he managed to regain his composure, he stood up. Back against the wall, hands flat on the hard wood, he did his best to emulate a fly and sidle even farther away from the ledge. When he reached a safe distance, he bent over in relief. Pringle's mid-air position remained unchanged, her back still to Ben.

"Okay, I'm sorry I shouted at you," Ben said. "I don't handle stressful situations well. But since we're up here, we might as well look at the scrying chamber."

"Yes!" Pringle shouted. She flew in dizzying circles around his head.

"However," Ben added, "before I take one more step, we need to have a new rule."

Pringle cocked her head. "What is a rule, Ben Hastings?"

Ben wanted to scream but told himself, *Small steps, Ben, small steps.* "It means, uh, an agreement or understanding."

Pringle beamed. "Okay, Ben Hastings."

Relieved, he said, "Here's the new rule. Never pick me up and carry me through the air again!"

Pringle sniffed. "That's a stupid rule."

Ben fought for patience. "You may think it's stupid, but people in my world don't like to be snatched up and carried like a sack of potatoes."

"What are potatoes?"

"*Aargh!*" Ben wanted to pull his hair out. "Enough with the questions! Do we have an agreement or not?"

"Yes." Pringle flew to his shoulder and sat, legs dangling. She reached up and tugged his ear. "But it's still stupid."

Ben refused to respond and turned his attention to the landing. It contained an arched entryway, the area beyond cast in dim shadow. Curious, despite Pringle's heart-stopping transport, Ben slid along the tree wall to the entrance. He passed through the entry and stopped. With the sheer drop-off now out of his direct sight, he felt comfortable enough to push away from the wall and move on.

Sconces flickered on, illuminating a small chamber. The sight that greeted Ben—a circular basin and a single chair—was disappointing. *I survived a terrifying mid-air ride for this?* He moved into the room for a closer inspection.

Like everything else in the Wizard's Hutch, the basin and chair were wooden. Bowl-shaped, the basin rose several feet from the floor and reminded Ben of an old-fashioned washtub. He searched the rest of the chamber, but it contained no other objects. Stumped, Ben sat in the chair. *What the hell makes this place so special?*

He decided Pringle's exuberance must have been a massive overreaction, but then noticed a slight gleam within the bowl. He leaned closer, and with a start, realized it wasn't empty.

Some sort of liquid filled the basin!

Ben moved within inches of the pool. He sniffed but couldn't detect any odor, so he dipped a finger into the pool and tasted it.

Water. Ordinary water.

So clear to be almost invisible, the water cast no reflection of Ben or the flickering light of the torches. He sat back and frowned. *All this hype for a tubful of water?* His irritation with Pringle for leading him on this fool's errand itched like a bad rash. He started to stand…then stopped.

Prints of some kind were molded into the top of the basin.

He half-expected the prints to parody some alien caricature of paws or fingers, but they looked ordinary—like human hands. Ben compared his hands to those on the wooden rim. *Not a perfect fit, but close.* He carefully placed each hand into the molds. The act forced Ben forward over the placid pool.

A moment or two passed. Nothing happened. *I must look like an idiot.* He'd had enough, but before he could remove his hands, a tiny ripple disturbed the water. Bubbles rose and percolated to the surface. Motes of light followed, quickly filling the pool with a pulsing luminescence. A kaleidoscope of colors swirled and churned within the basin. The mosaic of light abruptly coalesced into a picture-sharp image of the forest canopy.

Ben gasped at the sudden transformation of the pool. The

forest, a perfect 3D image, would put any IMAX theater to shame. He could see *and* hear the wind rustle the leaves, while the boughs moved and creaked. The representation, so real it felt like he floated just above the trees, made high definition seem hopelessly bland.

Any slight movement of Ben's fingers caused the image to swoop up, down, or sideways. By experimenting, he discovered he could control the direction and speed of the *scrying*. Soon, he hurtled above the treetops, the forest passing by at a dizzying pace. The woodland ended, and a broad expanse of scrub trees and grasses appeared. He immediately recognized the land across which Rooster-comb had pursued him.

Ben decided he'd try to find the location where he'd been deposited into Almeera.

A bead of sweat formed on his forehead. It traced an irritating path down his cheek. Distracted, he swiped at the droplet. The pool's image tilted crazily and accelerated in a zigzag course. Ben quickly returned his hand, but the careening images caused his head to spin. The disconnect between his eyes and brain made it seem like he rode a death-defying rollercoaster, and the sudden loops and rolls caused his vertigo to return with a vengeance. Ben became so disoriented his eyes rolled back into his head.

He pitched off the chair and onto the floor.

Ben lay still, his eyes closed until the spinning in his head stopped. When he finally opened them, Pringle hovered above him, worry on her small face.

She buzzed closer. "Are you well, Ben Hastings?"

With a groan, Ben struggled to his knees and used the chair to pull himself up. "I guess this scrying thing takes some getting used to."

Pringle watched Ben closely as he stood and seated himself again in the scrying chair. When he leaned forward to place his hands in the handprints, Pringle shot forward and pushed against his cheek.

"Do you think it wise to continue, Ben Hastings?"

Ben liked the feel of Pringle's warm little form touching his face. He knew it was crazy, but she was the closest thing to a friend he had on this world. When he collapsed to the floor, it shook the little prawn. Her concern touched something deep inside him. Oddly enough, he couldn't say he'd ever felt that way with Cara. *When's the last time she worried about anyone but herself?*

"Maybe you're right. Maybe I should try again later." A loud growl came from his stomach. He groaned. "If I don't find something to eat soon, I'll starve to death."

"But there's lots of food. I brought it last night while you were sleeping."

Her announcement elicited another long, rumbling growl from Ben's stomach. "Food? Where?" he demanded.

"On the big table where you entered the Wizard's Hutch."

Ben shot to his feet. "You mean it's been there this whole time, and you're just now telling me?"

"You asked me if there were more doorways and—"

"Stop! We've already been over this." Ben's frustration with the little pixie warred with his intense hunger. Then a more chilling thought caused Ben to stumble back against the wall.

How am I going to get back down?

CHAPTER 14

BEN'S MIND ENGAGED IN A FIERCE WAR WITH HIS BELLY. His terror of heights kept him rooted in place, while his stomach, now rumbling like an active volcano, relentlessly pushed him toward the steps. He thought of his last meal at Burger King—*have it your way, hamburger, fries, and a shake*—and the growling rose to a fever pitch.

Just the thought of fast food started him salivating like Pavlov's dog. Hunger overcame fear, and he began to inch along the wall. He exited the scrying chamber, but halted at the sight of Pringle drifting above the landing. Beyond her, the yawning hollow of the huge tree seemed as big as an ocean. A chill ran down his spine and his chest constricted.

There's no way I go down those steps.

Fear and hunger continued to grip him like a vise. Unable to ignore the sharp pangs of hunger anymore, Ben blurted, "Pringle, you have my permission to carry me back down!"

"But you said not to."

"I-I changed my mind. But promise you won't drop me!"

Pringle's musical laughter filled the air. "I would never do that, Ben Hastings." She picked him up by the collar, carried him to the edge, and they plunged downward.

Ben never saw their descent. His eyes, screwed so tightly shut it felt like they'd found a new home at the back of his skull, blacked out the entire trip. When Pringle released him and his feet touched the floor of the hollow, he dropped to his hands and knees gibbering with relief.

Pringle giggled. "You're funny, Ben Hastings."

A loud, continuous growl issued from his stomach. "Food, Pringle. Lead me to the food!"

The little prawn whirred away with Ben in hot pursuit. They shot through the magical doorway, down the short flight of steps, past the bedrooms, kitchen, and library, and back into the original room he'd been thrown into. He skidded to a stop at the sight of the repast before him. The table—every inch of it—groaned under the feast Pringle had gathered from the forest.

Fruit, nuts, berries, tubers, and vegetables of every description and variety lay in mounds on the table. Some looked familiar, others completely alien. All looked delicious.

He attacked the bounty with wild abandon.

Sated, Ben lay on the floor. Streaks of red and purple juice stained his lips and chin. He'd stuffed himself until he could eat no more, his stomach so tight and full, he could drum a melody on it. With a satisfied groan, he sat up.

Brraapp! Ben's explosive belch bounced off the walls. "Maybe I ate too much."

Pringle sat on the table, her legs dangling over the edge. She stood up, grabbed two round, purple berries, and flew to Ben.

She hovered, juggling the berries. "Let's play." She tossed one berry, then the other high into the air.

Zip, zip. She streaked after the berries, caught them, then returned to Ben. He blinked, constantly amazed at how fast the little pixie could move.

But Ben needed to focus on the problem at hand—how to get escape the Wizard's Hutch. He waved at the pixie. "I'm sorry, Pringle, but I need to find a way back home."

Disappointment tinged Pringle's voice. "Okay, Ben Hastings." She resumed juggling, adding melons and nuts, the cavalcade of blends forming a colorful arc.

Ben's thoughts returned to the scrying chamber. *If I can find where the grandfather clock dropped me into this world, maybe I can use the same door, gate, or whatever the hell it is to take me back.*

The possibility a portal existed in the same place, although a longshot, was all he had. He could use the scrying pool to search for it, but even if he found the gateway, he still had to find a way out of the damn hutch. And, of course, it meant Pringle carting him up to the scrying chamber. His butt puckered at the thought of another high altitude trip.

Ben had to act before he lost his courage. "Can you take me back to the scrying chamber?"

Pringle, still juggling, zipped up to his face. "Yes. It will be fun."

Sticky juice covered Ben's face and clothes. "I'm going to take a shower first and change into clean clothes, uh, robes. Then we can go."

He made his way back to the wizard's bedroom, stripped, and stepped into the shower stall. A wave of his hand started the cascade of water, and he grabbed the soap. The bar wriggled out of his hand and started scrubbing his chest. Ben closed his eyes enjoying the soapy massage.

"Whee!"

Ben's eyes shot open. Pringle circled his head like a crazed firefly, spraying water in all directions. She stopped, formed a soap bubble in one hand, and blew on it. The bubble expanded to the size of a softball, and floated into the air. Pringle lay across the bubble and used her wings to propel it around the shower.

"What the hell are you doing?" Ben shouted.

"Having fun. Prawns always dance in the rain," she replied.

The soap bubble rolled over and over, with Pringle somehow clinging on.

"But I'm naked, I don't have any clothes—"

Ben squawked as the soap reached his groin. He grabbed the bar while trying to cover himself.

Pringle buzzed up to his nose. Water dripped from her face and chin. "What is naked, Ben Hastings?"

This isn't happening. I'm asleep and dreaming I'm part of some cheesy sitcom.

"You look funny, Ben Hastings. Your face is all twisted up. Did you eat a sour berry?"

Ben started to reply, then snapped his mouth shut.

Pringle didn't have a stitch of clothing on either.

"Go!" he roared. "Out of the shower! I'll explain later."

He immediately regretted his outburst. The little prawn's shocked expression was one he was all too familiar with.

Hurt.

She streaked out of the stall.

Ben waved and turned off the shower. He poked his head out and Pringle was nowhere in sight. The coast clear, he stepped out and quickly toweled off. When he reached for his clothes, he discovered they were spotless. He held them up to his nose and sniffed. *Clean and fresh.* Self-cleaning clothes—more benefits of the wizard's magic. He dressed and went to search for Pringle.

He found her on the bed, knees pulled up to her chest. Tiny streaks of tears ran down her cheeks. The sight of the little sprite in such a condition caused Ben's heart to plummet.

He knelt before her. "I'm sorry, Pringle. I'm an asshole for shouting at you."

"What's an asshole, Ben Hastings?" she sniffled.

Ben chuckled. "Me, for yelling at you. I'd give you a hug but you're not big enough." He gently brushed the tears from her face with a knuckle.

Pringle wrapped her arms around his finger, and squeezed. "I can give hugs, Ben Hastings." His skin tingled where she touched him.

She looked up at him, and for a moment, their gazes locked. "I feel different when I'm with you, Ben Hastings," she said. "Why is that?"

Ben smiled. "You ask too many questions, but I do have one for you."

Pringle beamed and leapt into the air. "What? What is it?"

"Are you ready to carry me back to the scrying chamber?"

CHAPTER 15

THE SECOND GRAVITY-DEFYING TRIP TO THE uppermost chamber didn't terrify Ben nearly as much as the first. Whether better prepared this time or just too tired to care, he didn't know, but when Pringle set him down on the landing, he wasted no time scrambling away from the chasm and into the scrying chamber.

The pool, mirror-smooth, appeared exactly the same as the first time. With Pringle perched on his shoulder, he sat in the chair, took a deep breath, and placed his hands in the imprints. Like before, the water began to roil, then burst into a display of color and light. The aerial display of the forest appeared.

Ben paused. *How do I get back to where Rooster-comb tried to kill me—where I fell into this world?* The memory of the fierce fighting and Rooster-comb's leering face still chilled his blood. A ripple spread across the pool, and a prairie replaced the forest. The landscape of scrub trees and grasses rushed by in a blur as if Ben had pushed a fast-forward button. Then the flashing images stopped abruptly. Far below lay an empty encampment.

Ben blinked, unsure of what just happened. *Do I just 'think' of a place, and the scrying pool takes me there?* He temporarily put the question aside and moved on to his next problem—how to get closer. Deciding to experiment, he made small adjustments to the placement of his fingers.

The abandoned camp moved closer.

"Yes!" After more testing, Ben found he could move nearer, farther away, up, down, and sideways. "It's like a video game!" he cried. He grinned at Pringle. "I'm an Apex Predator on *Apex Legends*. This is gonna be a piece of cake."

He turned back to the pool before she could ask what a piece of cake was. He moved closer, the camp roughly arranged in a circle. Swirling wind caused eddies of dust, the tent flaps waving in the breeze like flags.

Deserted. The entire camp lay empty of life. Ben decided to zoom closer. Dead bodies lay about the abandoned camp like discarded marionettes.

The gruesome sight caused him to jerk back and almost lose contact with the scrying pool. After a moment to settle his rattled nerves, he resumed his search. Rodent-like animals moved about the site gorging themselves on the bodies of the other-worldly creatures. Flapping bat-like wings, the only interruption to their orgy of feasting came when they squawked at fellow scavengers who ventured too close. Sickened, Ben turned his attention to the rest of the camp.

He zipped along but found only more empty tents. Overturned carts and debris lay everywhere. Empty trunks, discarded clothing, and broken weapons were strewn about as if hastily appraised and tossed aside. More searching revealed little of interest, so Ben returned to his aerial view above the camp.

Maybe the abandoned camp is the remains of a caravan. And Rooster-comb led the raiders that attacked and plundered it.

"Too bad that ugly bastard's carcass isn't one of the dead," he muttered angrily.

"Your face is twisted up again, Ben Hastings," Pringle spoke into his ear.

"I know, I know," he quickly answered. "The thing that chased me, the Taluk, is responsible for all this. I wish I could get my hands around his—"

The scrying pool rippled then resolved into the cruel image of Rooster-comb.

"What the hell!" Ben yelped. The scene tilted crazily as Ben's head snapped back, his hands losing contact with the imprints.

He spent the next few minutes in a struggle to reestablish control, and to avoid the return of his vertigo. After he recovered from the Taluk's sudden appearance, he decided the scrying pool must work the same way with a person or creature. *All I have to do is think of them, and the scrying pool takes me to their location.*

He immediately tested the theory by fixing the image of Rooster-comb in his mind. The pool clouded over, then resolved to display the brutal creature's face. "Yeah, I see you, you piece of shit!" he spat in triumph.

"What's a piece of shit, Ben Hastings?"

"You're looking at it," Ben replied. He made a mental note to watch his language around the forest prawn, then moved higher for a better view.

Rooster-comb rode one of the T-rexes, a long line of similarly mounted riders snaking behind him. A group of captives, tied to each other by leather thongs around their necks, trudged along with heads bent low and eyes downcast. Similar in appearance to the squat creature speared and killed by Rooster-comb, the prisoners moved in single file. If one fell, they were dragged and slowly strangled until they could regain their feet. Their number included smaller versions of the creatures, undoubtedly females and children. Forced to carry the booty pillaged from the caravan, the backs of the captives bowed under their heavy burdens.

The cruel sight angered Ben. Pringle shifted on his shoulder with a quiet sob. He turned, and her face was buried in the nape of his neck. "What happened, Ben Hastings?" her muffled voice asked. "Why are the fingerlings treated so?"

It took him a moment to realize by "fingerlings," she meant

the children. In her idyllic forest environment, Pringle probably never witnessed such barbarity. And now he'd provided her with a front-row seat.

"Don't look. You shouldn't see this."

Ben's anger continued to burn. *There must be something I can do.*

A child slowly staggered along under its heavy load. With an angry cry, a raider rode down the line of prisoners and savagely whipped the small creature. The child's agonized cry rang out as clearly as if it originated within the scrying chamber. Even though the juvenile looked no more human than a horny toad, Ben's fury raged at the sight of the mistreatment.

Think, dammit, think!

An idea came to him. If *he* heard the child's cry, then maybe...

Ben maneuvered nearer to the rider, then homed in on the ear hole of the raider's T-rex. He moved so close he could count the mount's fine ear hairs, then sucked in a lungful of air. "HEY!" he bellowed.

The T-rex reacted like scalding acid had been poured into its ear. With a honk of pain and fear, it leaped high into the air. Caught by surprise, the raider catapulted from the saddle end-over-end, and face-planted into the ground. It lay unmoving. When the T-rex's clawed feet hit the ground, it took off at a dead run. Other mounted raiders and those on foot were knocked down like bowling pins in the spooked creature's crazed attempt to escape.

Pringle's voice cheered, "Whee! Do it again, Ben Hastings!"

Buoyed by his success, Ben went to the next mounted raider and shouted into his mount's ear. He repeated this with each rider until the scene resembled a bounce house gone mad. A stampede of bucking, braying, T-rexes pitched raiders into the air like ping-pong balls. An unlucky few with a foot caught in the stirrup, were dragged away screaming.

Into the confusion and chaos rode a familiar swatch of purple.

Rooster-comb!

Somehow, the murderous Taluk had managed to keep his skittish T-rex under control. He stood up in the stirrups, and waved a lance, bellowing at his fellow raiders in an attempt to regain control. Ben grinned.

The timing couldn't be more perfect.

With laser-like accuracy, Ben zeroed in on the ear hole of Rooster-comb's T-rex. However, Ben reserved a special surprise for Rooster-comb.

"Watch this," he said to Pringle.

Ben pursed his lips. *Phhuuwweeeeeeet!*

The whistle, so loud and piercing Pringle clapped her hands to her ears, blasted off the walls of the scrying chamber.

With a terrified honk, Rooster-comb's T-Rex exploded upward like a cannonball. When its feet hit the ground, the T-rex took off bucking and snorting. The panicked creature blindly collided with anything in the way of its headlong rush to escape. A few of the bucked raiders had regained their feet only to be flattened again by the T-rex.

As for Rooster-comb, the effect was like being launched from a missile tube. He flew through the air in a long, parabolic arc, and hit the ground with an audible *crunch*. Ben shouted in triumph, "Take that, you shit-eating bastard!"

He turned his attention from the unmoving Rooster-comb to the prisoners. Despite the uproar, they stood around listlessly. Too confused and battered to seize the moment, they didn't move. Ben knew if they didn't act soon, their only chance to escape would evaporate.

He moved along the line of prisoners and shouted, "You're free! Run! Run for your lives!" Galvanized by his unseen voice, the captives began to stir.

A trickle of movement ran down the line of tethered prisoners. Then one plucked a knife from the belt of a fallen raider. The creature hacked through its tether, and moved to help the others. This produced a chain reaction, with the newly liberated sawing through the leather bonds of other captives. When all were freed, they fled from the caravan. A few dazed raiders tried to stop them but were quickly overwhelmed and disposed of. Some of the former prisoners took the time for revenge against their captors. They grabbed fallen weapons and paused long enough in their escape to stab and slash at any stunned marauder within reach.

With no desire to see more carnage, Ben turned his attention to a theory he wanted to try. If the magic of the *Devron* key could open doors from distant places like Tyler, Texas, maybe the scrying pool could do the same.

Ben closed his eyes and concentrated on a location he knew well. Satisfied he'd fixed the site in his mind, he opened them. The water-filled basin no longer carried the scene of Rooster-comb and the captives. Instead, a cloudy film covered the water. A few moments passed with no change, and Ben despaired he'd reached a dead-end. Then a light grew within the basin. It dimmed, brightened, then dimmed again like a smart TV trying to connect to a weak digital signal.

The light winked out.

Ben shook his head. "Well, it was worth a—"

A brilliant radiance exploded from the pool. When Ben's vision cleared from the searing light, his jaw dropped.

The crystal-clear image of a townhouse appeared…*Cara's* townhouse!

Ben's triumphant expression morphed into puzzlement. A maroon Lexis sat in the driveway next to Cara's car. The Lexis seemed familiar and tugged at Ben's memory. Then the door to the townhouse opened.

Out stepped Bronson Smith.

The chemistry professor always parked his Lexus next to Ben's VW in the faculty parking lot. No wonder it looked familiar. That jogged another piece of Ben's memory. Smith had shown interest—unusual interest—in Cara at the last faculty mixer.

Dapper as usual, Smith wore sharply creased dress slacks

and an expensive powder blue polo shirt. A fashionable growth of stubble adorned the otherwise clean lines of his face. Ben always thought of Smith as a vain asshole more comfortable on the cover of an L.L. Bean catalog than in a college classroom.

However surprised Ben might have been at the sight of Smith leaving Cara's townhouse, nothing prepared him for what happened next.

Before Smith could head to his car, Cara appeared at the door dressed only in a thin silk robe untied and partially open. She wrapped an arm around Smith's waist and pulled him toward her.

They shared a long, passionate kiss.

CHAPTER 16

BEN BLINKED, HIS MIND FUMBLING TO PROCESS THE scene of a half-naked Cara kissing Smith. *It's almost like they, they...*

Comprehension smacked him like a knockout punch. "They spent the night together!" he shouted.

Ben leaped to his feet, the image in the pool winking out. "That preening bastard! He's trying to steal Cara! Wait till I get back. I'll shove Smith's styling gel so far down his throat, he'll shit hair products for a month!"

Pringle launched into the air and buzzed back and forth before his face. "What's wrong, Ben Hastings?"

Ben stabbed a finger at the now placid scrying pool. "Bronson Smith's what's wrong. He slept with *my* girlfriend."

"I spent the night with you, Ben Hastings," Pringle gushed. "You're warm! Maybe they wanted to keep warm."

A harsh laugh left Ben. "Oh, I'm sure they produced heat. Sex has a way of doing that."

"What's sex, Ben Hastings?"

Ben groaned. *Why can't I learn to keep my mouth shut?* He threw up his hands. "It means, uh, mating. Yes, that's it. Mating."

He waited for Pringle to ask what mating is, but instead, the little forest sprite nodded. "Are you mated, Ben Hastings?"

"Yes, I mean no, I mean…maybe." Ben clenched his fists, fingernails digging into his flesh. "Cara didn't want us to live together. She wanted to get married. But I—I kept dragging my feet. Now it might be too late."

He dropped heavily into the scrying chair. "My whole life has been turned inside out since I dropped into this world. Cara's probably called and texted me a hundred times, but I can't answer. She must think I've ignored her and decided to pay me back. Maybe even break it off."

He slammed his fist onto the chair's arm. "And here I am stuck in this wizard's tree, with no way out and no way to get back home." He slumped, face in his hands.

"But, Ben Hastings—"

"And even if I could find a way back, how would I ever explain it to Cara?"

"But—"

"She'd think I made the whole thing up or worse, that I'm crazy."

"But—"

"I'm screwed no matter what I say or do."

"BEN HASTINGS!" Pringle shouted.

"What?" Ben snapped. "Can't you see my life's dissolving right before my eyes?"

"All you need is the devron key and a gate to place it in. The key's magic will return you to your world."

Ben snorted. "Now why didn't I think of that? Use the key to escape? *Hmm*, let's see. Maybe if I *had* the key, but the key is outside the wizard's hutch…*and I'm inside!*"

"I can bring it to you."

Ben stared at Pringle. He swallowed. "You can?"

"Yes," she answered, beaming.

He slowly pushed himself up. "Why in the name of all that's

holy didn't you tell me sooner?" His voice rose. "Why didn't you get the key right from the start?"

"You didn't ask, Ben Hastings."

Ben felt like his eyes would explode right out of their sockets. "*Gaahh!*" he roared. He stalked around the room, looking for something to throw and smash against the wall, but the chamber held only a chair and the scrying pool.

Pringle followed Ben, trilling, "*Screeeeeeee,*" the sound like a summer cicada on steroids. She stopped in front of Ben's nose, her tiny cheeks flushed pink.

"This is fun! Let's make some more noises."

Ben couldn't help it. He started chuckling. Ever since he'd met Pringle, no matter how low his life seemed to have sunk or how dire the circumstance, she could still make him laugh.

He started yowling like a wolf.

Pringle joined him, their voices reverberating in unison. A short time later, breathless, Ben sat down. Back against the wall, his knees drawn up, he watched Pringle zing around the chamber in happy loop-de-loops. She landed on his knee and did a handstand.

"You never have a bad day, do you, Pringle?"

"Prawns have fun. And you should too, Ben Hastings," Pringle answered while flipping back to her feet.

Ben smiled. "Yeah, you're right, but it's not as easy for me." He reached out and tickled her stomach. Pringle giggled and wrapped her arms around his finger.

"Sometimes I wish you were bigger," Ben mused.

Pringle shot up to his face. Rather than her usual cherubic expression, she wore a serious look. "Wishes are powerful things, Ben Hastings. Be careful what you wish for."

Ben shrugged. "I'll take that under advisement." He stood up and dusted off his borrowed wizard's clothes. "Right now, what I wish for is the key and a way home."

In a blink, Pringle streaked out of the scrying chamber. Her absence left the room even emptier. *How can such a little prawn fill such a large hole?*

"Do you mean this room or your heart?" he whispered.

Ben gave an emphatic shake of his head. "I've got to get out of here. Now I'm talking to myself."

Before he could muse on it further, Pringle zoomed through the arched doorway. She dropped something into his hand. His eyes widened.

It's the damn key!

The runes on the skeleton key glinted in colors of red, blue, green, and gold. Ben held it up and examined every inch. It was undoubtedly the same key, the one used to open the grandfather clock and to enter the wizard's hutch.

"You did it!" he crowed. "You got the key." Pringle beamed at Ben's happy shout.

"Now what do I do?" he asked.

"Use the key to open the gate."

Ben hesitated. "Okay. What does the gate look like? Better yet, where is it?"

Pringle spread her hands. "I don't know where it is, Ben Hastings, but it should look like the gate you used to travel to Almeera."

"You mean the gate is another grandfather clock?"

"What is a—"

"Never mind," Ben quickly interjected.

A harsh laugh left his lips. "Unbelievable. I have the key, but now I need a gate. It's like being a cast member from *Groundhog Day*. No matter how many pieces I gather, I start over in the same place every day."

Dejected, he stared at the floor. A thin layer of dust covered the base of the scrying chamber. An idea came to him, and he knelt on the floor. He used his finger to draw the rough outline of the grandfather clock in the dust. He filled in the clockface with Roman numerals and the clock hands. Next, he drew the base and sketched the pendulum and weights. Finished, he stood and wiped his hands on his robe.

"That's what we're looking for."

Pringle hovered above the likeness of the clock, the wind from her wings stirring the dust. She turned and rocketed from the room.

Ben had barely settled down to wait when Pringle returned. Without a word, she grabbed his collar and lifted him off his feet. A strangled, "Hey!" left his lips as they skimmed over the landing and plummeted in a stomach-dropping descent. Rather than release Ben when they reached the bottom of the hollow, Pringle continued to carry him. They careened down passages and through the magical doors until they reached the library. She released him and zipped to a section of the library wall next to the bookcase.

She buzzed up and down, unable to contain her excitement. "Here it is, Ben Hastings. The clock is here," she said, pointing.

Heart hammering like an angry blacksmith, Ben staggered to the nearest chair and collapsed into it. "I-I told you to ask before picking me up again," he gasped.

"But I found what you seek."

The comment immediately captured Ben's attention. He got up and studied the wall. It looked just like the rest of the hollow's interior—a rough, wood surface.

"I don't see—"

He spied the faint outline of a minute hand. He shifted his position, never taking his eyes off the wall. Other parts—he pendulum, clockface, and hour hand—swam into view. He kept moving, but the grandfather clock wouldn't clarify into a clear image. Then he realized why.

The clock's been carved to look like an autostereogram or Magic Eye. I have to look past it. He stepped back and focused on an imaginary point past the section of wall.

A crystal-clear image snapped into view. The clock resembled a man dressed in robes with a tall, peaked hat and a long flowing beard. The man's 'face' contained strange numerals spaced evenly apart, with the big and little hands rotating from the nose. Part of the robe's belt, the pendulum, swung back and forth. The man's arms were spread wide, the palms turned outward. A dark symmetrical shape marked the middle of the palm of the left hand.

Ben drew in a sharp breath of recognition.

The keyhole.

CHAPTER 17

BEN APPROACHED THE KEYHOLE. CAREFULLY, HE PLACED the key in the slot and turned.

Click.

The bottom panel of the clock swung open with a whispered *swish.* Ben poked his head inside. A staircase, identical to the one inside his Otto Albrecht clock, appeared. Only these stairs led *up*, not down.

Ben rocked back on his heels, thinking. *I fell into this world. To return must mean I have to travel back in the opposite direction. I gotta go up.*

He returned to the room with the remains of the food Pringle had gathered. He filled his pockets with the larger fruits, then rushed back to the open gateway. "I've got food and the key," he said to Pringle. "I can always come back if the stairs lead to the wrong place."

She moved to hover between Ben and the gate. "Don't go, Ben Hastings. Stay here, and we can have fun every day." Her mournful expression caused a lump in his throat.

He shook his head. "I don't belong here, Pringle. This is your world, not mine, and I need to go home."

Tears streaked down Pringle's face for the second time since the little prawn rocketed into his life. Ben wished again that she was big enough to hug.

"I'm going to miss you, Pringle. You saved my life and you've been a good friend to me. I won't forget you."

Pringle flashed up to him and plastered herself across his cheek. His skin tingled from the damp spot left by her tears. She drifted back and placed both tiny hands on his face.

She leaned in and kissed his lips. Like a triple shot of expresso, the sensation traveled through his body like an electric jolt.

"I will miss you too, Ben Hastings." She twisted her hands. "I've never felt this way. I don't know what to do."

Ben knew all too well the emotion Pringle felt. Sadness. *Another toxic gift I've left her. I need to get out of here before I ruin things even more.*

He entered the clock. Once inside, he turned and waved one last time at Pringle. The door began to close as he made his way to the foot of the staircase. Just before the panel shut completely, a streak of motion shot through the crack.

And disappeared into one of Ben's fruit-filled pockets.

Ben trudged up the staircase.

He'd been at it for almost an hour, and his aching legs screamed for relief. He stopped and sat down on a stairstep. Unlike his wild slip-and-slide ride into Almeera, the trip back had to be done the hard way—one step at a time. Muted light emanated from the stairs, but gave no clue how much farther he needed to go. Fortunately, the tunnel-like confines of the winding staircase didn't allow a downward view, so his vertigo never returned.

With a groan, he stood and resumed his climb up the stairs.

After another fifteen minutes of travel, a steady drip of sweat from his chin, Ben considered going back. The endless staircase made it seem pointless to continue. He stopped and leaned against the curved wall.

"Keep going, Ben," he muttered. "Don't give up now."

With more determination than he felt, Ben pushed away and continued his climb. After another five minutes of travel, he noticed a subtle change in the light. It seemed brighter. Invigorated, he picked up his pace. With each step, the illumination grew stronger. He rushed up the staircase, rounded a curve, and stumbled onto a landing. Bright light leaked out around the edges of a four-sided object.

A door!

Ben released a huge sigh of relief. He rushed to the door, searched for the keyhole, and found it halfway up the panel. With a shaking hand, he removed the key from his pocket and inserted it.

Click.

The door swung open. Brilliant light invaded the stairwell, blinding Ben. "Yeow!" he cried. After traveling in semi-darkness for so long, the effect was like having a powerful searchlight trained on him.

He stumbled out and waited for his vision to clear.

When the spots cleared from his eyes, he straightened and looked around. Large picture windows covered one wall, and abundant sunlight filled the room. Through the glass, he spied leaf-filled branches of trees swaying gently in the breeze. Beneath the picture windows, another staircase stretched downward.

This must be an upper floor of some building.

Ranks of wooden storage cases filled the room. Arranged in tidy rows, they were all crammed with books. Ben moved in for a closer inspection and discovered some of them were locked glass display cases. Inside the display case, the books—many yellowed with age—had notecards posted beside them with the title and price. Ben recognized a few of the them, like Winston Churchill's *History of the English Speaking Peoples.*

Damn. It's a first edition. He gulped at the listed $6000 price.

Another edition, Edward Gibbon's, *Decline and Fall of the Roman Empire,* had a scribbled price of $8,500. Yet another, George Washington Carver's, *The Man Who Overcame,* carried a $500 price tag. A musty smell clung to the entire room.

"What is this place?" he breathed.

"Don't move! I have a gun, and I know how to use it!"

Ben whirled. Facing him was a young black man around six feet tall with a round, pudgy build. He wore gray Under Armour joggers and a sweat shirt. Hand inside the pocket of the sweat top, he poked something at Ben through the fabric.

"What's with the clothes? Did you get lost on your way to a Star Wars Convention?" The shop owner shoved his hidden weapon higher. "Not that it matters because we're closed. How'd you get past me downstairs?"

Ben gaped at the young man. "What is this place? Where am I?" he demanded.

"Well, it's not Tatooine, and you're trespassing. I have every right to shoot you."

Ben gestured at the 'gun'. "You realize putting a finger in your pocket and pretending it's a gun is the oldest dodge in the books, don't you?"

The store owner jabbed the unseen weapon at Ben. "I'm warning you."

Ben chuckled. "I'm sorry, Dude, but I can't help thinking all you need now is your finger to stick out a hole to complete the cliche."

"I don't find anything funny about a stranger breaking into my bookstore."

Ben held his arms out wide. "Look, my name's Ben, and I don't want any trouble. I just want to get back home."

"And where's home?"

"Tyler, Texas."

"Well, Ben—if that's really your name—you're a long way from there because Jefferson is over an hour away from Tyler."

He thrust the 'gun' farther out. "And you still haven't answered my question. How did you get past me *and* my locked doors?"

"You wouldn't believe me if I told you. You'd think I'm crazy."

"How 'bout we let the police decide just how crazy you are?" The store owner fished a cell phone from his other pocket.

"No, wait!" Ben cried. He turned to point at where he entered the bookstore…and stopped.

A large, ornately carved grandfather clock stood against the wall, the bottom panel open. The intricately sculpted wood had an immediate familiarity. *Another Otto Albrecht clock!*

He cleared his throat. "I've got a grandfather clock just like yours. When the lower panel's unlocked, there are stairs inside that lead to another world."

"Oh, so Dorothy and Toto are going to join us too?" the shop owner quipped. "And you're right. I do think you're crazy."

"Now, look—"

Ben got no farther because the young man's jaw dropped. He pointed a shaking finger, "What, what…" His face went slack, and his eyes rolled back. *Thump.* The bookstore owner fainted and slumped to the floor.

"Why did he do that?" Ben spun around at the sound of the voice.

Pringle hovered clapping. "Is this a new game, Ben Hastings?"

CHAPTER 18

BEN'S ATTENTION VACILLATED FROM THE UNCONSCIOUS shop owner to Pringle. His stunned mind spun in a fruitless effort to reconcile the rapid sequence of events.

"What, how," he sputtered, "*why* are you here?" he finally managed to ask.

"I hid in your pocket," Pringle quipped happily. "Now we can have more fun."

"No! You should have stayed—"

A moan interrupted Ben. The young man on the floor stirred and sat up. He rubbed his eyes. "Wow, I've got to cut back on the monster energy drinks. I thought I saw—"

He squeaked at the sight of Pringle flying above Ben's shoulder. *Thump*. He'd fainted again.

"Does everyone in your world sleep so easily, Ben Hastings?" she asked.

Ben shook his head. *This whole ludicrous scene is straight out of Comedy Central.* He pulled his tattered emotions together and gestured to Pringle. She perched on the palm of his hand.

He pointed at the unconscious bookstore owner. "That guy's never seen a real fairy—at least not one in the flesh. You scared him." He held up a hand before Pringle could speak. "And on earth, we call prawns *fairies*."

"But I wouldn't hurt him, Ben Hastings."

"I know, but we gotta do something different, or he'll pass out every time he sees you."

Ben tapped his lips. "Okay, let's try this. I'll bring him around, and you hide behind me. When I've got him prepped to see you, I'll put a hand behind my back, and you stand in it like you are now. Then I'll slowly move my hand to the front and show you to him. I'll do all the talking, and for God's sake, no matter what, *don't* swoop up to the tip of his nose, or he'll fall out again."

Pringle buzzed up and down in agreement, then zoomed behind Ben's back.

Ben patted the young man's face. After a moment or two, he groaned and opened his eyes. Ben helped him up.

"Thanks," he said. "I keep seeing things." His eyes narrowed. "Say, you haven't slipped me fentanyl or something have you?"

"No, and you aren't seeing things either," Ben retorted. "Get a hold of yourself so I can show you something. Can you keep from passing out again?"

The bookstore owner nodded.

Ben reached behind his back, and brought Pringle forward. She danced in his palm with an ear-to-ear smile.

"You-you mean it's real?" the shop owner gasped. "I'm not delusional?"

"Yes, *she's* real. Pringle, say hello to—" Ben stopped. "I'm sorry, I don't know your name."

"Archimedes Jones," the young man answered. "Although everyone calls me Archie."

"That's," Ben paused, "quite a name. Pringle, say hello to Archie."

"Hello!" Pringle sprang into the air and hovered between the two men.

"I can't believe I'm seeing this," Archie whispered.

"In the words of *Bachman Turner Overdrive*, 'You ain't seen nothing yet'. Follow me." Ben turned and went to stand beside the open grandfather clock. Archie hesitated, then trailed after Ben.

"How'd you know I'm a classic rock fan?"

"I didn't, but I felt inspired," Ben quipped, then motioned for him to look inside the clock.

Archie poked his head inside. "*What the hell?*" he exploded.

"My exact sentiment the first time I saw the staircase. But go ahead, step in and check it out. Look for hidden data projectors, mirrors, or anything that could display a false image."

Archie disappeared inside. He emerged a few minutes later shaking his head. "Either we're both suffering the same delusions, or the stairs and Pringle are real."

"Good." Ben took the key from his pocket, shut the panel, and locked it. He turned to Archie.

"Do you have somewhere we can talk?"

Archie nodded. "Let's go to my office."

He started down the stairs, Ben close behind. When Pringle didn't follow, Ben frowned. "What's the matter? C'mon."

"You said not to swoop, Ben Hastings."

Ben chuckled. "We're okay now. Swoop all you want."

"Wheeeee!" Pringle jetted around the room, then hurtled down the staircase past Archie.

"She has, uh, quite a bit of energy, doesn't she?"

"You have no idea."

They reached the first floor, and made their way to an office at the back of the store. Several file cabinets stood sentinel along one wall, with stacked boxes against another wall. Archie's desk sat at the back of the office looking like a garage sale reject. A pair of scratched and blemished chairs rested in front of the desk. Mounted on the wall behind the second-hand furniture were framed pictures and diplomas.

Archie collapsed into a wheeled office chair behind the desk, the worn springs squeaking in protest. He gestured for Ben to take one of the chairs. Ben sat down, Pringle settling on his shoulder. "Now I've got a few questions for you," Archie said. "Let's start with why you're dressed like a Jedi knight and what exactly *is* Pringle."

Ben sighed. "It's a long, unbelievable story, but here it is." Ben explained how he came into possession of the Otto Albrecht grandfather clock, how he bought the key from Hank Harper, and what happened when he unlocked the clock. He described his descent into the world of Almeera, being chased by Roostercomb, and how he met Pringle and found the wizard's hutch. He pointedly left out discovering the scrying chamber.

"If I hadn't seen Pringle and the inside of the clock with my own eyes, I'd say you are either an escapee from a rubber room or a writer trying out themes for your next sci-fi/fantasy novel."

Archie leaned forward on his elbows. "Can I see the key?"

Ben reached into his pocket and handed it to Archie. He held the key up to the light, turning it to catch the colorful hieroglyphs etched in red, blue, green, and gold. "These are runes, probably Germanic in origin."

Ben frowned. "How do you know so much about runes?"

Archie laughed and handed the key back. "Dude, I own a bookstore, and I read a lot."

"Okay," Ben said, pocketing the key, "if you don't mind me asking, what's with the rare and expensive first-edition books?"

"Would you believe I'm a world-class thief and I stole them?"

"No."

Archie smiled. "Well, seeing that you showed me your fairy, I guess its only fair I tell you more about myself." He stood up and pointed at a framed diploma on the wall. "University of Texas. Go 'Horns. Besides reading, I've always loved math and working with numbers. So, I received my degree, became an actuary, and went right to work for a large insurance company. Turns out, pouring over actuarial estimates is just as dry and boring as everyone said it would be. I hated going to work. Then I got lucky."

Archie pointed at another framed picture. It held only two

objects—a lottery ticket and a picture of a grinning Archie holding a giant cardboard check.

"I was coming home from a tedious insurance conference over equally dull actuarial projections, when I stopped at a convenience store for gas and an energy drink. I bought a lottery ticket and found out a week later I had the winning ticket." Archie took the picture off the wall and handed it to Ben.

Ben blinked. The amount on the check was 50 million dollars.

"I took the lump sum, so after taxes, I received almost thirty million," Archie continued. "Got my picture on the front page of the Austin paper, had my face plastered all over the internet, and was a rock star for months. Someone discovered my cell number, and it rang nonstop with people and businesses begging for money. I had to get away from Austin, the traffic, and the hectic pace of life to someplace simpler and slower. So, I quit my job and moved to Jefferson. I bought The Black Swan Bookstore, then indulged in my other passion—collecting books, particularly first editions."

"You're a…millionaire?" Ben asked, incredulous.

"Yep, which is why I can offer you a hundred thousand dollars for your key."

CHAPTER 19

BEN'S MOUTH WENT DRY.

A hundred grand. He could pay off his student loans, the mortgage on his new house, and fix it up properly. It might even be enough to win Cara back—if he even wanted her back. Her liaison with Smith, his near death in an alternate world at the hands of a purple-combed monster, made his previous priorities seem trivial, even foolish.

What about Pringle?

What would happen to her, her forest and world if others learned about Almeera? In his mind's eye he could see the giant trees cut down and whole sections of the forest bulldozed for subdivisions, golf courses, and strip malls. Pringle's brother and sister fairies would be dispossessed and scattered. Worse, some might be captured for 'study' like a new species of insect.

Pringle sprang from his shoulder and hovered before him. "Ben Hastings, your face is twisted up again."

That sealed it for Ben. Although Pringle's world contained bloodthirsty creatures like Rooster-comb, it was also home to prawns and other harmless magical creatures. He'd melt the key and burn the grandfather clock before he allowed them to be victims of 'development.'

"I'm sorry, Archie. The key's not for sale."

"How about two hundred thousand?"

Ben shook his head. "Not for any price. It's too dangerous."

Archie threw up his hands. "Okay, what about returning to Pringle's world so I can see it?"

"Absolutely not!" Ben shot to his feet. "You don't understand. This isn't a game, a safari to see the wild animals. I barely escaped with my life, and I wouldn't go back for *any* amount!"

"Then how's Pringle going to return?"

"I, um, she'll, uh, I can...I don't know," he admitted.

Pringle zipped to Archie's desk and landed, the wind from her wings scattering papers. "I don't want to go back, Archie Jones. I'm having too much fun with Ben Hastings."

Archie eyed Pringle. "How about lending me Pringle for a while? Name your price."

Ben glared at Archie. "I don't own her. She was supposed to stay in her world, but hitched a ride in my pocket instead. As an African-American, I'm sure you can appreciate Pringle's right to make her own decisions. How would you like it if I asked to borrow *you* for a few days?"

Archie held up his hands. "Okay, okay, I get it. Stupid question that never should have been asked. It's just that I find this fascinating, an actual fairy tale come true."

"Do your fairy tales include brutes with purple coxcombs? Because if they don't, you don't have a clue what you're talking about!"

"I don't make apologies for being inquisitive, Ben. I'm just curious."

Ben's temper ebbed. "I'm sorry. It's just that I've been through a lot. Sometimes I wonder if I *am* crazy and all this stuff is some fevered delusion."

Archie laughed. "Well, if you're suffering from visions, it would be the first time in history that two different people shared the same hallucination."

"I suppose you're right."

Archie straightened and leaned forward. "So…now what?"

The question caught Ben off guard. *What am I going to do now?* Return to his old life, his job at the university? But what about Pringle? Did he take her with him, or try to return her to Almeera? Just the thought of going back caused a shiver of fear to race up his spine. Then there was Cara. Were they through? Did he try to repair their relationship? And he still owned an old mansion in desperate need of repair.

In short, nothing much had changed. He faced the same challenges as before with one exception.

Pringle.

Ben sighed. "Can you take me, I mean us, back to Tyler? I can pay you for your trouble once I get back home."

Archie shrugged. "No problem, but don't worry about paying me. You know I don't need the money. However, I would like to continue our association."

"I don't know—"

"Your secret's safe with me," Archie quickly interjected. "I won't tell anyone about Pringle or Almeera. Like I said, I'm just curious."

"Well I guess if I can't trust a former actuary and millionaire lottery winner, then who can I trust?" Ben joked.

Archie grinned. "My thoughts exactly."

He stood up and thrust out his hand. "Partners in crime then?"

With a firm grip, Ben shook Archie's hand. He followed the bookstore owner out of his office and they exited a side door into a garage. A meticulously restored red and white Corvette convertible sat in the space. Archie hit a button and the garage door rolled up. Sunlight spilled in and glinted off the car's spotless chrome.

Ben whistled. "Wow. The original American muscle car. What year?"

Archie ran his hand lovingly across the hood. "She's a '64 hardtop but I leave the top off during good weather. Nothing like rolling down the highway with the wind in your hair."

They got into the 'Vette, and Archie started the car. *Vroom.* A throaty roar filled the garage as he backed out. As they pulled onto the road, Ben got his first clear look at The Black Swan. Painted white, the Victorian-era structure stood two stories high, its gabled roof sharply pitched. Its black shutters and trim gave the old house an eye-catching contrast.

Archie noticed Ben's interest and said, "The original house was built in 1855 by a wealthy steamboat captain when Jefferson was an important Texas port. Lots of history, but unfortunately, it's changed hands a bunch of times the past forty or fifty years. When I bought it, I tried to restore as much of the original architecture as possible. My only nod to modernity was to remodel a few of the back rooms into an apartment and kitchenette."

Ben glanced at Archie. "I can't figure you out. Why live in a cramped apartment in an old house when you can afford whatever you want?"

"Because this *is* what I want. I love Jefferson, its diversity, and the relaxed pace of life. Why complicate things with a big house and all the things I'd have to keep up with?"

The irony of the bookstore owner's comment compared to Ben's situation was not lost on him. *Wait till you see my Munster's Mansion. You'll laugh your ass off all the way back to Jefferson.*

"Your face is twisted again, Ben Hastings."

"It's okay, Pringle, I—"

He suddenly realized the little prawn wasn't inside the car. She flew beside the speeding Corvette, easily keeping pace.

"Stop that! Get inside the car!" he shouted.

"Why, Ben Hastings? This is fun."

"Because people might see you, and you might hit something."

Pringle zipped into the seat beside him. Arms folded, her lip stuck out, she said, "This is *not* fun!"

Ben blinked. Besides the first time he met her when she pelted him with berries, he'd never seen her angry.

"I just don't want you to get hurt, Pringle."

Archie looked at Ben. "Why don't you let her buzz around since we're out of the city? There's not much traffic on these rural roads."

"Are you crazy? She could end up like a bug on a windshield."

"You *did* say she comes from a forest. Seems to me a fairy living in a place filled with trees is used to navigating around things."

The memory flashed through his mind of Pringle carrying him at breakneck speed as they fled from Rooster-comb. Every time a collision with a tree seemed imminent, she veered off. *Maybe she has some kind of fairy radar.*

"You do have a point," he admitted.

"*Wheeeee!*" Pringle sprang into the air and flew in circles around the speeding car.

"Thanks, Archie," Ben grumbled. "Now I'll never get her back into the car." He glanced at the speedometer. "We're going sixty-five?"

"Yep. Speed limit's seventy, but I always go five miles under." He winked at Ben. "You know, just to be on the safe side, being a black man and all, driving a sportscar."

"I didn't mean to imply—" Ben stopped at Archie's wide smile.

"You really need to loosen up," Archie chuckled.

Irritated, Ben changed the subject. "How'd you get a name like Archimedes?"

"My dad teaches chemistry and physics at Trinity Valley Community College, and my mother's a high school counselor. Archimedes is considered the Father of Mathematics, so my parents named me after him."

"Must have made introductions, uh, interesting for you."

"Only to white people. Black folks never question my name." Ben's face warmed. "Oh, sorry."

Archie laughed. "Gotcha again. Man this is fun, and we still have another hour before we reach Tyler."

Archie's good humor was infectious. Soon they engaged in

an easy conversation that lasted until they neared Tyler and the traffic thickened.

Ben released a sharp whistle, then gestured at Pringle. "You have to get in the car now."

She zipped up to him, and he shook his head at the disapproval on her face. "No one must see you. They won't understand. In fact, you're going to have to hide in my pocket just like you did when I left Almeera."

"But I don't want to, Ben Hastings."

"I know, but you need to trust me until I can figure something out."

Pringle crossed her arms. By the sour look on her tiny face, Ben didn't trust she'd do what he asked.

Then with a buzz like an angry bee, she slipped into his pocket.

CHAPTER 20

THE 'VETTE TURNED ONTO THE RESIDENTIAL STREET leading to Ben's house.

When they reached the end of the cul-de-sac, Archie pulled up behind Ben's VW. He killed the engine, studied the old mansion, then turned to Ben.

"You're kidding me."

Ben shook his head. "Nope. It's the only thing the real estate agent showed me that I could afford."

"Freddy Krueger would love this place. Tell me you didn't sign the papers."

"Like I said, everything else was out of my price range."

"This moldy dump is proof of that. On the bright side, you can always rent your house out at Halloween."

"Very funny. Do you want to see the Otto Albrecht clock or not?"

Archie got out of the Corvette. "Lead on, Kemosabe."

They walked to the front gate, but before he could open it, an angry voice called out, "Mr. Hastings, you have some explaining to do!"

Ben's face dropped at the sight of Maude Thorne hurrying

toward him. She shook a finger at him. "You said you were going to do something about this jungle you call a yard."

"I'm working on it, Maude."

"Really? Because I haven't seen you or anyone else around here for days. Is that your idea of 'working on it'?"

She pointed at his clothing. "And what's this? Do you belong to a cult?"

Archie stepped forward and stuck out his hand. "Archie Jones, ma'am. And you are?"

Maude eyed his hand like it was a poisonous serpent. Reluctantly, she took it. "Maude Thorne, President of the HOA."

Archie pumped her hand vigorously. "I own a landscaping business, and Mr. Hastings contacted me about cleaning up his lot. We were just about to tour the place."

Maude withdrew her hand. She looked at Archie's car and then back at him. Her eyes narrowed. "Most landscapers drive trucks. I've never seen one driving a vintage sportscar. That's what drug dealers use."

"You mean you know a bunch of drug dealers?"

Maude's face reddened. "No. Of course not! I just, I mean, I wasn't implying—"

She spun and stormed away. Halfway to her house, she turned and spat, "Get your yard cleaned up, Hastings, or it will be the first thing I bring up at the next HOA meeting!" She entered her house and slammed the door.

Ben chuckled and slapped Archie on the back. "Thanks. She's been on my back since I bought the place."

"No problem. I'm generally a live and let live kind of guy, but if I had a house next to Maude's, I'd be the one ringing her doorbell to leave a flaming bag of dog poop."

He gestured at Ben. "C'mon. I'm sure she's looking. We better walk around and act like I'm studying your yard."

As they wandered around the overgrown lot, Pringle poked

her head out of Ben's pocket. "Is this the forest you live in, Ben Hastings?"

Ben gave a harsh laugh. "Yeah, I guess it does look a bit like the woods." He shook his head. "It'll take me weeks to clean it all up, but I'm sure Maude will call an HOA meeting long before then."

"You make the HOA sound like something from the Spanish Inquisition," Archie said. "What's she going to do? Stretch you out on the rack?"

"You met her. There's no telling what she's capable of." Ben kicked at a clump of weeds. "Let's go back. I think we've put on a convincing show." They turned and headed for the old mansion.

When they reached the steps, Ben trudged up and tried the front door.

Locked.

"Dammit! I left my keys inside. This place is built like a fort, and short of breaking a window, I don't know how we'll get in."

"Let me try, Ben Hastings."

Before Ben could object, Pringle launched into the air. She reached into her pouch and removed a handful of a glittering substance. She sprinkled the dust on the door from top to bottom..

"Cool!" Archie exclaimed. "Fairy dust."

Finished, Pringle zoomed back to Ben and sat on his shoulder. "Uh, okay. What now?"

"I should think that would be obvious," the door said.

Ben yelped and took a step back. A mouth, nose, and eyes appeared on the wooden surface, and the door frowned. "I'm waiting."

Ben gulped. "What?"

The door rolled its eyes. "Okay, here's a clue. I'm supposed to shut and…"

"Um, open?"

"Winner, winner, chicken dinner to the quick-thinking gentleman!" the door cried. It swung open.

Archie whooped in delight. "A smartass smart door. I gotta get me one of those too."

Speechless, Ben sidled past the door and into the mansion. Archie followed, and they stood in the darkened interior.

"*Harrumph.*"

"Oh." Ben gestured at the open door. "Uh, I guess you can shut."

"Your brilliance continues to amaze me!"

Slam.

Ben's lips pressed together. "First Maude, and now a door that insults people. This day's getting better and better."

"Strictly speaking, I only disrespected you," the door replied.

Ben whirled. "How'd you like me to find some termites and sprinkle them on you just like Pringle did with her dust?"

"You wouldn't dare!"

"Just as soon as I can find my phone, I'm going to order some nice juicy Amazon jungle termites that can turn wood into Swiss cheese!"

"My apologies, magnificent sir," the door quivered. "I shall endeavor to be more polite."

"That's more like it."

Archie patted Ben on the shoulder. "Way to put the furniture in its place."

"Damn straight." Ben smoothed his robe. "Now, let's go find the grandfather clock."

Pringle led the way and zoomed to the base of the staircase. The door panel to the old clock stood open as Ben had left it. He twisted the old-fashioned light switch on the wall, and light from an ancient chandelier flooded the room. He searched the area around the clock for his phone. Not finding it, he and Archie went inside the clock. After another thorough search, they still couldn't locate the cell.

When Archie approached the downward spiraling stairs, Ben barked, "Stop! Unless you want a one-way trip to your worst nightmare, don't take another step!"

Archie froze. He carefully backed up. "You could've told me that before we went inside the clock," he groused.

Ben waved off the comment. "Well, now you know." He gestured at Pringle, and she zoomed up to him. "Can you fly down the stairs and search for my phone? It's a square thing and not very big."

Bzzzipp! She jetted down the stairs. A few moments later, she returned with Ben's phone and dropped it in his hand. "It lay on one of the steps, Ben Hastings."

Ben released a shaky breath. "I thought it might have fallen with me into Almeera." He followed Archie out of the grandfather clock, then shut the panel and locked it. "Now, for what I've been dreading."

Archie raised an eyebrow. "What's that?"

"I've got to call Cara."

CHAPTER 21

ZELKOVA PETROVA APPRAISED HOSSEINI'S LATEST DELIVERY of human cargo through the two-way glass. The ragged group of refugees clung to each other in shared fear and misery. Most looked like they hadn't eaten a decent meal in weeks.

Nostrils flaring, she whirled on Hosseini. "You call this an improvement? They can barely stand, you idiot!"

Like morning dew, sweat beaded on Hosseini's forehead. "Think of their potential, Mistress. Once they're cleaned up, fed, and given a fresh change of clothes, they'll be much more appealing."

Petrova grabbed a fistful of Hosseini's expensive silk shirt and jerked him to within inches of her face. "I don't run a charity. I sell a product," she hissed. "Your suggestion takes time *and* money, neither of which I'm willing to invest. If I wanted the kind of rabble you're bringing me, I'd just snatch homeless vermin off the street."

She nodded, and a hulking form stepped forward. "Georgi, I think Farshad has a hearing problem. See if you can help him with that."

The massive bodyguard smiled, his white teeth gleaming like piano keys. "My pleasure." He reached into his pocket and pulled out a knife. *Flick.* A sharp, four-inch blade sprang from the switchblade. "Which ear shall I remove first?"

All color drained from the smuggler's face. He fell to his knees. "Mercy, Mistress, mercy!"

Petrova knelt to eye-level with Hosseini. "I started whoring at twelve. Mercy was beaten out of me long ago. So, unless you can provide me with a younger, healthier product, I think our association has come to an end."

She stood and gestured at Ivanov.

"No! I have just the person you need!" Hosseini cried.

Petrova held up her hand to stop Ivanov. "Speak!" she snapped at the smuggler. "And be quick about it!"

Hosseini struggled to his feet. "I've got the perfect woman. She's young and beautiful and will bring you a fortune!" He ripped his phone from his pocket, tapped keys, and opened his camera app. "See, here's pictures of her."

Petrova studied the images. "Then why isn't she here instead of this third-world shit you've brought me?"

"Because there's more risk, and I've had to plan more carefully." Sweat now rained from Hosseini's face in a steady deluge. "It's taken more time, but I can bring her to you within the week."

Petrova smiled. She draped an arm around the smuggler's neck. "See how easy this is? You give me what I want," she tightened her arm in a viselike grip until Hosseini gagged and struggled to draw a breath, "and you get what you want."

She released him and shoved him away. "Have the woman to me by the end of the week," she snarled, "or I'll have Georgi carve pieces from you, starting with your balls!"

"Yes, Mistress," Hosseini croaked.

He fled from the room.

Ben stared morosely at his phone.

He sat with Archie in the kitchen, the only place with a modern plug he trusted not to fry his phone charger. Since the battery had died days ago, he'd been forced to recharge the cell. Apprehension filled his mind while he waited. *How will I explain any of this to Cara? She'll think I'm either nuts or lying.*

On top of everything else, Pringle constantly distracted him. The little prawn's insatiable curiosity drove her to fly around inspecting everything. She had peppered him with questions:

What's this, Ben Hastings?

A lampstand and light.

What's this, Ben Hastings?

The electrical cord you plug the lamp in with.

And so it went, endless queries about anything new Pringle had never seen—which was pretty much everything. He caught a break when he accidentally turned on the ceiling fan while looking for the light switch. Distracted, Pringle swooped up to the fan and began chasing the blades.

Archie finally spoke. "You don't really want to call your girlfriend, do you?"

"Why do you say that?"

He pointed at the cell. "Because you have thirty percent battery, more than enough to make a call."

Ben gave a bitter shake of his head. "I don't know what to say. I can't tell her the truth."

"You mean like an old grandfather clock transported you to a new world with monsters and fairies? And that you barely escaped with your life before you found another clock and made your way back? Oh, and that you brought back a prawn named Pringle?"

"Yeah. Something like that."

Archie slapped his knee. "Damn, Ben. Your goose is cooked, you're dead in the water, down for the count. I bet I can come up with a hundred more cliché's."

"Thanks," Ben grumbled. "You're a real fount of encouragement." He sighed. "I guess it doesn't matter anyway. I might have already lost her."

"Why?"

Ben launched into how he'd found the scrying pool and seen Bronson Smith leaving Cara's townhouse.

"You mean you can just think of someone or someplace, and this scrying thing can find them like a Google search?" Archie blurted.

Ben nodded.

"Why didn't you tell this earlier?"

Ben shrugged. "I don't know. Maybe because you'd think I'm crazy."

"Normally I'd say you *are* crazy with a capital 'C', but since I've seen a flying fairy and a talking door, I'll take your word for it."

Archie chuckled. "Anyway, you're missing the obvious solution to your problem."

"Yeah? And what would it be?"

"Lie. Make something up Cara *will* believe."

"Like what?"

"How should I know? She's your girlfriend…although I don't know why you bother."

Ben frowned. "What do you mean?"

"Look, she slept with another guy while you were dodging monsters in Almeera, and yet you're worried she won't believe you? You really think *that's* the problem?"

"You don't understand."

"I'm sure I don't. I mean, I've heard of 'open' relationships, but if all it takes is a few days absence for Cara to hook up with someone else, then you're better off without her."

"So now you're an actuary *and* a relationship counselor?" Ben snapped.

Pringle zipped up to Ben and landed on his shoulder. "I've slept with Ben Hastings," she announced. "He's warm." She hugged his cheek.

Heat rose in Ben's face. "It's not what you think," he hastily interjected.

"Really? What am I thinking?"

"You know. You think there's something, something like…" Ben stopped and glared at Archie. "The door's not the only smartass in this mansion."

Archie, laughing so hard he had to lean against the kitchen counter, fought to catch his breath. "Sorry," he finally managed to say, "but I haven't had this much fun in years."

He pushed away from the counter. "Anyway, back to what I suggested earlier. If your girlfriend won't believe the truth, make something up."

Ben tapped his lips. "That's not a bad idea. I could tell her I spent the time trying to fix the place up and surprise her."

"Ben Hastings?"

He ignored Pringle and continued. "But you've seen the mansion. Although I had the first floor professionally cleaned, it still looks like a dump."

"Ben Hastings?"

"But it's a big place, and I could say it's taken a lot of time and effort just to get it to look like it does now."

"BEN HASTINGS!"

"What is it?" Ben cried. "Can't you see I'm talking to Archie?"

"What's a girlfriend?"

Ben blinked. "It's, uh, someone you care about, someone you like a lot."

Pringle sprang into the air and hovered before Ben's face.

"Can I be your girlfriend too?"

CHAPTER 22

THE SILENCE THAT FOLLOWED LAY LIKE A THICK blanket.

Ben finally found his tongue. "Um…what?"

"I like you, Ben Hastings. We have fun!" Pringle twirled merrily in the air, then stilled. "You like me too don't you, Ben Hastings?"

Ben cast a desperate glance at Archie.

He held up his hands. "Don't look at me. You're the one with a fairy sidekick."

"She doesn't understand." Ben stepped closer to Archie. "I don't want to hurt her feelings," he hissed into his ear.

Archie glanced at Pringle, who bobbed excitedly up and down. "I think that ship's already left port, Ben. You need to tell her something."

Ben swallowed. *What choice do I have?* "Yes, you can be my girlfriend—"

"*Whee!* I'm Ben Hastings's girlfriend too!" Pringle cried. She jetted around him in dizzying circles, moving so fast a high-pitched whine, like turbines on a jet engine, filled the room.

Pringle slowed abruptly. She drifted closer, nuzzled his cheek, then moved to his lips.

She kissed him.

A bolt of adrenaline surged through Ben. When Pringle glided back far enough he could see her without turning cross-eyed, she wore an expression he'd never seen on her before.

Thoughtful.

On the free-spirited prawn, such a change couldn't be more stark, like the difference between night and day.

"I feel strange, Ben Hastings. Is that part of being a girlfriend?"

Ben tried to find his tongue. *Damn if I don't feel something too.*

Archie cleared his throat. "Uh, Ben? You going to answer Pringle?"

The rush of heat to Ben's face forced his brain to engage. "Well, uh, yes, I guess it is. A girlfriend's supposed to, you know, like her boyfriend."

"Yay! Ben Hastings is my boyfriend!" She whizzed around then stopped. "What's a boyfriend, Ben Hastings?"

"Really walked into that one, didn't you?" Archie quipped. "Want me to take this one for you?"

"Uh, I, er, I think…" Ben stopped, at a loss for words.

"I'll take that as a yes," Archie said. He turned to Pringle. "A boyfriend and girlfriend are two people who like each other."

"Whee!" Pringle whooped. She zipped to Ben's shoulder and sat. "Ben Hastings is my boyfriend, Archie Jones," she proudly stated.

"I can see that."

Ben scowled at Archie. "Thanks for nothing. What am I going to do now?"

Archie laughed. "That's easy. What you planned to do before."

Still fuming, Ben answered, "And what's my plan again?"

"Call your *other* girlfriend."

Ben went outside on the porch to make the call. He told Pringle to stay inside with Archie. The last thing he needed was the little prawn distracting him or, worse, being spotted by Maude. The curtains on her house twitched even as he took the cell from his pocket.

She must spend the whole day spying on her neighbors.

He went to his contacts, his finger poised above Cara's number. He took a deep breath.

And punched her number.

After a few rings, the call ended. Puzzled, he tried again. Again, the call dropped after a few rings. After a third try ended the same way, he pocketed the phone.

His shoulders slumped. "She knows from caller ID it's me, and she's ending my calls," he mumbled.

He turned to go back into the mansion when his cell trilled. His hand shot into his pocket and grabbed the phone, almost dropping it in his haste. Cara's image and number appeared on the cell.

"Cara!" he answered.

"The only reason I'm calling back is to say what a mean, miserable bastard you are!"

Click. The call ended.

Ben stared at the cell. Before he could completely process what had just happened, it rang again.

"Hello?"

"You don't answer my calls or texts for days? What's wrong with you?"

"Let me—"

Click.

A moment passed and it rang again.

"He-hello?"

"I worried myself sick thinking something bad had happened to you."

"I know, but—"

Click.

The cell rang again. Ben answered.

"I thought you loved me, but no one treats someone they love like that!"

Click.

Ben waited, and his phone rang. This time when he answered, he blurted, "Cara, don't hang up! Give me a chance to explain!"

Silence answered him, but thankfully, she didn't hang up. Finally, she snapped, "Okay. Explain!"

Ben released a pent-up sigh of relief. "Can we meet somewhere to talk instead of over the phone?"

A long pause followed. "Very well," she answered at last. "Meet me at Longino's. I'm going to need a bottle of wine to get through whatever you have to say."

Click.

"Problems with the boyfriend?" Bashir asked.

Cara angrily stuffed her towel and bottle of Iceberg water into her bag. "He drops out of sight for days, doesn't call or text, doesn't answer *my* calls or texts, and then expects me to carry on as if nothing happened?"

She slung the bag over her shoulder. "To hell with that!"

Around them, the rattle of weights and hum of treadmills merged with the grunts of other men and women at *Bodies in Motion.*

"So what are you going to do?"

Cara paused. "I don't know. Hear him out, I suppose. I love him. Or at least I thought I did."

She spun and headed for the exit.

Bashir pulled out his cell and sent a one word text—*Go.* He ran to catch up with Cara. "Wait!" he called out.

She stopped, and Bashir caught up with her. "Let me carry your bag." He flashed her a smile. "It's the least I can do for someone with boyfriend problems."

Cara returned his smile and handed him her bag.

They exited the gym and headed across the parking lot to Cara's car. Bashir put her bag in the back seat. He gestured to her. "Let me show you something before you leave."

Cara paused. "What is it?"

"A surprise." Bashir grinned. "I promise you'll like it." He headed for an isolated corner of the parking lot. A line of trees partially blocked Cara's view. After a moment's hesitation, she hurried after him.

She caught up with him just as he reached a black Ford truck. He opened the passenger door and rummaged around. "Damn, I know it's here somewhere."

Curiosity drove Cara to move closer. She leaned forward to get a better view. "What are you looking for?"

"Aha! Here it is!" Bashir cried. He held something in his hand, but his body shielded Cara from getting a clear view.

"What is it?"

"This." He held a folded white cloth. A pungent odor rose from it.

Before she could move, he clamped the chloroform-soaked rag over her mouth and nose. After a brief struggle, she slumped, unconscious. Bashir caught her before she fell to the ground. Seconds later, a black Mercedes sedan roared up to the truck. With a squeal of brakes, it stopped beside the truck. The trunk lid popped open.

Hosseini emerged from the car and scanned the area. "Good! No one's around. Quickly, now! Let's get her into the trunk."

They carried Cara around to the back of the sedan and dropped her into the trunk. While Hosseini gagged her, Bashir took a pair of zip ties from his pocket and secured her wrists and ankles. Finished, Hosseini slammed the lid.

The entire kidnapping took less than five minutes.

Hosseini gestured at Bashir. "You sure the security cameras aren't working?"

Bashir grinned and nodded. "The entire security system is

down. I chatted up the girl working the desk, and she said it hasn't worked in weeks. I don't think they're in a hurry to spend the money to fix it."

Hosseini snorted. "Arrogant Americans. More worried about profit than their own safety." He fixed Bashir with a steely gaze. "Someone is sure to have seen you leave with the woman regardless of whether the security cameras are working or not. How do you plan to explain that?"

Bashir's grin widened. "By giving the authorities a suspect they're sure has something to do with her disappearance."

"Who?"

"Her boyfriend. She's furious with him and kept hanging up on him. When the cops question me, I'll tell them they had a huge fight. A check of her cell will confirm a log of their calls to each other, and the time-stamp on the calls will coincide with her disappearance. That makes boyfriend suspect number one."

Hosseini gave a grudging nod. "I like it. Go back and resume your workout. When the police question you, just keep your cool and point them straight to her boyfriend."

"Yes, sir." Bashir jogged back to the fitness center.

Hosseini got into the Mercedes and drove around the corner, making sure to take a circuitous route away from *Bodies in Motion* and any patrons who might see his car. An enormous weight slipped off his shoulders.

I finally got what the Russian bitch wanted.

CHAPTER 23

BEN GLANCED AT HIS PHONE.

Cara was late.

Seated at a corner table in Longino's, an untouched bottle of Cabernet Sauvignon resting in a bucket of ice beside him, he chose the secluded location because he wanted no interruptions. He planned to tell Cara a colorful tale of partial truths and outright lies, something he wasn't proud of. But when a lie is far more believable than the truth, he had no other option.

Impatient, he called. When the call went to voice mail, he tried texting. When he received no reply, anger crept its way into his mind.

Did she stand me up?

He motioned to the waiter and pointed at his wineglass. The waiter, dressed in black pants and shirt, a crisp white apron tied around his waist, decanted the bottle and poured out a small amount for him to taste. Ben shook his head. "I'm sure the wine's fine. Just fill it up." The waiter shrugged and filled the glass halfway.

"Are you ready to order, sir?"

"No, I'm still waiting for someone."

"Very good." The waiter looked at Ben, then returned to the kitchen.

Even he thinks I've been stood up.

The trill of his phone interrupted his thoughts.

He grabbed the cell without glancing at the caller ID. "Cara! Where the hell are you?"

"Sorry, dude, it's Archie."

"Oh. What is it?"

"Pringle's hungry, and I know zilch about the care and feeding of fairies."

Ben sat back. "I don't know much either, but she likes sweet stuff like fruits and berries."

"You know, hummingbirds sip nectar," Archie said. "Their metabolism is so high they have to eat about half their body weight every ten to fifteen minutes."

"Why are you telling me this?"

"Because Pringle moves and flies like a hummingbird. I bet her metabolism is similar, and she needs to eat a lot."

Concern for Pringle temporarily pushed his irritation with Cara aside. "I haven't been in the mansion long enough to stock much food. I do have a bunch of sugar packets for my coffee. They're in a box on the kitchen counter."

"Okay. I'll mix some with water, and see if Pringle will drink it."

"Thanks. I'll stop by Walmart on the way home and get some groceries."

Ben clicked off.

Thirty minutes and half a bottle of wine later, Ben decided Cara was a no-show. His irritation, a slow boil before, now turned into full-blown anger. He paid for the wine and stormed out of the restaurant.

He started the VW, but his cell rang before he could drive away. He snatched it off the console. "What!"

"Whoa, dude. Cara never showed, huh?"

"No! So, what is it, Archie?"

"You still plan to stop and get groceries?"

123

"I said I would, didn't I?"

"No need to get all smartass on me."

Ben took a deep breath. "Okay, I'm sorry. Yes, I'm stopping at Walmart."

"Then you need to plan on buying more sugar. A lot more."

"Why?"

"Let's just say you were right about Pringle liking sweet stuff." Archie paused, "And Ben?"

"Yes."

"Don't blame me. Pringle went through all the sugar packets before I could stop her."

Uneasiness replaced Ben's anger. "What aren't you telling me?"

"You have to see this for yourself. Just get here as soon as you can."

"Why? What's going on?"

"I repeat. Get back here asap. And whatever you do, *don't* forget the sugar!"

Ben drove as fast as the old van would go.

He stopped at the nearest Walmart and rushed inside. He went to the grocery section, and began tossing items into his shopping cart. When he reached the aisle containing the sugar, he hesitated, then grabbed a half-dozen one pound bags of sugar. He hurried to the self-checkout, bagged and paid for his purchases, then sped out of the store to the van.

Archie's cryptic comments produced a level of anxiety in Ben that he could barely contain. *Is something wrong with Pringle? Has something happened to her?*

The little prawn had touched something deep inside him. If anything happened to her, he would never forgive himself.

The VW's engine whined as he pushed the pedal to the floor.

Cara groaned and her eyes fluttered open.

At first, she found it hard to focus. Her vision swam, and when she attempted to sit up, she became so dizzy she thought she might pass out. Gamely, she grit her teeth and pushed herself up. After a moment the dizziness passed. She looked around.

She sat on a bunk bed in a small room. A toilet, stainless steel sink, and shower occupied the back of the room. A window and door sat in the front. The bare, unadorned walls, were painted hospital white.

Fear crept into her mind. *Where am I?*

She stood, went to the sink, and splashed water on her face to clear her befuddled mind. The door opened as she reached for paper towels to dry her face.

"Good. You're awake."

Cara whirled. A tall woman entered the room with one of the largest men she had ever seen by her side. Glossy black hair framed the woman's face, and she regarded Cara with icy-blue eyes.

"For once, that fool Hosseini got it right." She smirked at the huge man. "I guess we'll let him live…for now."

"For now," the man repeated with a cruel smile.

Anger flared within Cara. "Where the hell am I?" she demanded. "By the time my father finishes with you, you'll be lucky to own a toothbrush!"

"First lesson," the woman said motioning to the big man, "is to speak only when told to."

The massive bodyguard moved with startling quickness, and one meaty hand grabbed Cara's neck. She gurgled, unable to breathe, and scrabbled at his hand in an impotent attempt to free his grip.

"Careful, Georgi. We can't have any bruises."

"Yes, Mistress." He released Cara and stepped back.

Cara fell to her knees, gagging. She massaged her throat in an attempt to regain her breath.

"Now, do we have an understanding?" Petrova asked.

Eyes filled with tears, Cara nodded.

"Good. Get up."

Cara stumbled to her feet.

"Take off your clothes."

"What? You must be kidding?" Cara blurted.

The big man moved toward her.

"No! Please, I'll do it!" she cried.

The huge bodyguard stepped back.

Tears now falling freely, Cara stripped. She tossed her clothing on the bed and stood naked. She closed her eyes and repeated a desperate mantra in her mind. *This isn't happening, this isn't happening, this isn't—*

"Tits are a little small," the woman's voice said, interrupting her. Cara opened her eyes. Her captor was inspecting her as if she were a heifer at a livestock sale. "But other than that, she'll fetch an excellent price at auction."

She pointed at the bed. "Sit!" Cara scrambled to the bed, then tried to cover herself with her hands.

Petrova smirked at her attempts at modesty. "You'll address me as 'Mistress.' You'll be sold to the highest bidder and end up as someone's concubine, probably a sheik with more oil money than he knows what to do with. You'll find it can be a hard life or an easy one, depending on how you adapt. If you please your owner, you'll be kept comfortable. If you fight or resist, you'll be beaten into submission."

Petrova paused. "In the meantime, until the auction, I expect complete obedience. I know ways of inflicting pain that won't mar your beauty, so *don't* test me."

She gestured to Georgi. He handed Cara a plastic bag.

"The bag contains toiletries. You'll wash, brush your teeth, and otherwise keep yourself clean and neat." She pointed at a camera bubble mounted in the corner of the room. "You'll be monitored twenty-four hours a day, so again, don't test me."

She turned, and with Georgi close behind, left the room. The door shut behind them, its lock engaging with an audible *click*.

Cara buried her face in her hands and wept.

CHAPTER 24

BEN LEAPED OUT BEFORE THE VAN HAD BARELY ROLLED to a stop.

He snatched the grocery bags, dashed through the gate, and up the steps. He grabbed the doorknob.

"Greetings, oh magnificent master. Your brilliance shines brighter—"

"Open up before I kick your wooden ass!" Ben barked.

"There's no need for such coarse rudeness," the door grumbled and swung open.

Ben ran into the empty foyer. "Archie!" he cried.

"In the kitchen."

Ben raced down the hall and burst through the doorway. He skidded to a stop.

Pringle sat on the counter next to a pile of empty sugar packets, Archie at the kitchen table a short distance away.

"Hi, Ben Hastings!" she greeted him merrily. "I'm hungry."

The grocery bags dropped from Ben's hands. "What? How?" he babbled.

The little prawn, once not much bigger than a small bird, had increased to the size of a chihuahua.

He turned to Archie. "What happened?" he demanded.

"It's not my fault," Archie blurted. "All I did was mix some of the sugar packets with water and give it to Pringle. She drank it and asked for more. How was I supposed to know she'd sprout up like a magic beanstalk?"

Ben studied the empty stack of sugar packets. "How is she still hungry?"

"If I were an expert in fairy physiology, I might have an explanation, but since I'm not, your guess is as good as mine."

One of the sacks of sugar had tumbled from the grocery bag onto the floor. Pringle's eyes widened. She swooped down and snatched it up. Before Ben could stop her, she ripped it open and poured the contents down her throat. Within seconds, she had swallowed the entire sack of sugar. She then zipped to the sink, turned on the faucet, and gulped down water.

Buurrrp. "That's good, Ben Hastings. Can I have some more?"

"No!" he cried. "You've had enough." He hastily gathered up the rest of the sugar bags and placed them in the pantry. He shook a finger at Pringle. "No more."

"But I'm still hungry, Ben Hastings."

"How? You just ate a pound of sugar."

"Prawns are always hungry, Ben Hastings."

Archie cleared his throat. "It could be her, ah, growth spurt. The bigger she gets, the more calories she needs to fuel her metabolism."

"Says the guy who just admitted he knows nothing about fairies," Ben snapped.

Archie shrugged. "Just basic science. If Pringle's metabolism is on speed dial, then it follows she'll need more food."

Ben held up his hand to stop Archie from saying more. "Pringle, you haven't seen the rest of the mansion. Why don't you go look around?"

She zipped up to Ben. "What's a mansion, Ben Hastings?"

Pringle's tendency to suddenly hover within inches of his face was bad enough when she was tiny, but her new, larger size made it even more unnerving.

"It-it's like a hutch but it belongs to me instead of a wizard."

"Whee!" She shot out of the kitchen.

Ben paced back and forth, his concern for Pringle growing. He ran his hands through his hair. "We may have started a reaction in Pringle we can't stop."

"You mean like that old Sci-fi movie, *Attack of the 50 Foot Woman?*"

The image of a giant Pringle buzzing through the air like an aerial King Kong coursed through Ben's mind. *I can't let that happen.*

"Why did I ever open that damn clock—"

Ben stopped pacing. "Wait! The key! The guy I bought it from said something about being careful with it, like it was some kind of mystical object. I thought he was joking, so I didn't take him seriously."

Archie sat straighter. "He did? Then he must know something. Who is he?"

"I don't remember his name, but he owns a store filled with a bunch of old stuff."

Ben whipped out his phone and scrolled through his calls. "Hank Harper! That's it! His name is Hank Harper, and the store is *Harper's Antiques and Oddities.*"

"We have to go see him," Archie said. "Where's his store located?"

"Mt. Pleasant."

"Let's go."

Ben hesitated. "What is it?" Archie asked.

"You'll like Hank, but he's, uh, little."

"What, he's real short?"

"Well, yes, in a way. He's a dwarf."

"One of the little people?" Archie rubbed his hands together. "Man, this just gets better and better. I can't wait to meet him."

They started for the door, but Ben stopped. "Wait. What are we going to do with Pringle?"

"Take her with us."

Ben shook his head. "That was easy when she fit in my pocket. She's too big to hide now."

"You got a suitcase or something?"

"Are you kidding? I'm *not* putting Pringle in a suitcase!"

They stood for a moment, undecided on what to do next. Then Ben snapped his fingers. "I've got it! I have a backpack I use to carry my books and papers to my classes at the university. I bet she'll fit in it."

He ran out of the kitchen and rummaged through some boxes beside the staircase. "Got it." He pulled out a tan backpack, held it aloft, and inspected it. "I think it'll do."

"Pringle!" he called.

Buzzip. She appeared beside him a split second later. "Here I am, Ben Hastings."

He hitched the backpack onto his shoulders. "See if you can fit inside this."

She dived into the pack, then poked her head out. "It tickles," she giggled.

Ben breathed a sigh of relief. "Okay, we're going on a trip, but like before, people can't see you."

"Why, Ben Hastings?"

"Like I told you, in my world, no one's ever seen a forest prawn. They won't understand."

"Okay, Ben Hastings." She disappeared into the pack.

Ben signaled Archie. "Let's go."

Maude Thorne swung open the gate, then marched up the steps to the front door of the mansion. She tried to keep the smile off her face but couldn't help the feeling of satisfaction. She'd show that hippie professor and his drug-dealing friend who the *real* authority was on this block.

In her hand was a folded piece of paper she planned to personally deliver to Hastings. She wanted to see his face when he looked at it and saw the agenda for the next HOA meeting. Top of the list, and the first item up for discussion, was Hastings' failure to keep a neat and tidy yard as per HOA rules.

She raised her hand, but before she could knock, a voice said, "State your business, please."

Maude stumbled back. She scanned the area around the door but could see no camera or speaker.

"Madame, are you hard of hearing? I said state your business!"

Maude drew in a sharp breath. *The door has a face!* Its mouth moved as it said, "Hello? Knock, knock, anyone home?"

Maude dropped the agenda, and ran away screaming.

The door swung open, and Ben and Archie hurried out.

Ben heard screaming and spotted Maude racing away like her girdle was on fire. "What's up with her?"

Archie bent over and picked up a piece of paper lying on the porch. He unfolded and scanned it. "Don't know, but maybe it has something to do with this." He handed the paper to Ben.

Ben looked it over and swore. "She's put me on the next HOA meeting for not cleaning up my yard."

Archie studied the overgrown lot and said, "It does have a Jumanji-like look. They could've filmed the movie here."

"Funny, but I can handle only one crisis at a time. I'll deal with Maude after we see Hank Harper."

They hurried to Archie's car and started for Mt. Pleasant.

CHAPTER 25

THEY REACHED MT. PLEASANT BY LATE AFTERNOON. Most of the downtown area was empty, and Archie found a parking place in front of Hank Harper's store. Ben hitched the backpack up on his shoulders, and they went inside.

The tinkle of the bell on the door announced their presence. A voice called from the back of the store, "Be there in a minute."

Archie looked around with wide-eyed wonder, and Ben chuckled at his reaction. "You look like a kid in a candy store."

Archie pointed at the display window. "That's a genuine Lionel train and track," he said in hushed awe. "I wonder if it's a complete set?"

"It is, and I also have the original box it came in," a jovial voice announced. Hank stood a few feet away. "Welcome to Harper's Antiques and Oddities. What can I do for you?"

"Hey, Hank," Ben said. "I don't know if you remember me, but—"

"You bought a key to an Otto Albrecht clock from me," Hank finished for him. "Did it work?"

"Yes. Too well I'm afraid."

Hank frowned. "I see. You must have used it or you wouldn't be here. Remember, I *did* say be careful with the key."

"Yeah, well you didn't quite define what 'being careful' meant, Hank."

Hank crossed his arms. "So, what happened?"

Ben looked at Archie. "What do you think?"

He shrugged. "Your call, dude."

If I tell him everything he'll think I'm nuts. But I need answers, and Hank might be the only one who can provide them. Ben slipped off the backpack.

"This happened. Pringle, come out and say hello to Hank Harper."

Pringle shot out of the pack and hovered beside Ben. "Hello, Hank Harper. I'm Ben Hasting's girlfriend," she gushed. "I'm hungry. Do you have any sugar?"

Hank's eyes widened. "Oh, my."

Ben felt his face flush. "I can explain. It's not what you think."

Hank held up his hand. "Quick. To the back of the store before anyone sees the forest prawn."

He rushed to lock the store's entrance, then turned the store sign to *Closed*. He hurried back, and motioned them through a door and into another large room. One wall held a floor-to-ceiling bookcase with a locked glass front, while boxes were stacked against another wall. A table and chairs occupied the center of the room. Hank motioned for them to take a seat.

"Now, tell me what happened. Start from the beginning and leave nothing out."

When Ben finished his tale, he felt drained but strangely satisfied, as if a great weight had been removed from his shoulders. Hank, for his part, listened attentively with few questions. Throughout the entire account, the diminutive shopkeeper remained stoic.

"Anyone want a beer?" Hank asked.

Ben blinked. The last response he expected was to be offered a beer. "You mean, you don't have more questions? You believe me?"

"Of course. Why wouldn't I?"

"Because it sounds crazy even to me, and *I* was there."

Hank smiled. "Ah, the proverbial 'crazy,' a term often misused by those who simply don't understand. Be right back."

Hank left and returned with three ice-cold bottles of Corona. He handed them out and then held something up for Pringle to see.

She zipped up to him. "Oooh, what is it, Hank Harper?"

"A sucker." He handed her a cherry-flavored Tootsie-Pop. "It should last you a long time."

Pringle took the sucker from Hank and popped it in her mouth. She flashed a delighted smile at him. "It's good, Hank Harper." She flew back to the stack of boxes and sat, her concentration on the sucker.

Hank took a long pull from the Corona. "You've really stepped into a pile, Ben. You managed to not only travel to another world, but you brought back a fairy creature. Pringle doesn't belong in our world."

"I know, Hank, but in my defense, I didn't plan to take a trip through an enchanted clock to Almeera, and I sure as *hell* didn't intend to bring Pringle back here with me. So can we skip the blame game and get to what matters *now*. Namely, what to do about Pringle? Every time she eats something, especially anything with sugar, she gets bigger."

"Why don't you just send her back?" Hank asked.

"You mean just open the clock and—"

"No!"

Pringle's sucker dangled in one hand. Her face held a determined look. "I *will* stay with Ben Hastings."

For the second time, Ben was struck by a distinctly unfairy-like reaction from Pringle. *Something's happening with her that has nothing to do with her size.*

Pringle zoomed up to Ben. "Do you hear me, Ben Hastings? I want to stay with you."

Ben swallowed his surprise. "Uh, okay, Pringle. No one's going to force you to go back."

Her face brightened, and she flew back to her perch on the box, licking the sucker. "I'm sleepy," she announced. She placed the Tootsie-Pop in her mouth, curled up on the box, and within seconds, fell asleep.

Archie looked at Pringle, then turned back to Ben. "What just happened? One minute she's a fun-loving little fairy, the next, all serious and stubborn."

Ben spread his hands. "I-I don't know."

"I'm afraid the longer Pringle stays here, the more she becomes part of our world and less of hers," Hank said.

Ben ran his hand through his hair. "Are you sure?"

"Not absolutely, but I usually have a pretty good feel about these things."

"Speaking of which," Archie interjected, "how is it you seem to have such an extensive knowledge of the arcane and unusual? For example, how'd you know Pringle was a forest prawn?"

Hank chuckled. "Let's just say the fairy folk are an interest of mine."

"Seems like more than just an interest," Archie persisted.

Hank sighed. "I've learned a good deal in my life, mostly by keeping an open mind on things many would consider superstitious claptrap. Take fairies, for example. Ancient scripts document sightings of fairies that pre-date the Babylonian Empire, but does anyone believe them? Of course not. I, however, choose to consider anything possible until proven one-hundred percent otherwise."

Hank took another pull from the Corona. "That said, I may have a few books which could shed some light on Pringle's condition."

He put his beer down and pushed a four-foot stepstool to the bookcase. He took a ring of keys from his pocket, chose one, then unlocked the case and slid the glass back. He climbed up the ladder and perused the books.

"Ah, here it is."

He dragged a thick volume from the case, climbed down, and carried it to the table. Boiled leather formed the cover of the ancient book. It had been engraved to form a scene of frolicking forest creatures.

Ben leaned closer and realized the creatures included fairies like Pringle, elvish folk with pointed hats and ears, and a satyr with a pipe at his lips, playing while the others danced.

"I-I've seen books like this," Archie said in reverent awe, "but only in pictures, never an actual copy."

"It's just a book," Ben remarked. "Not the holy grail."

"You don't understand. The carved leather covering is a dead giveaway that the book is old, very old." He glanced at Hank. "May I?"

Hank nodded and Archie carefully opened the book. He leaned closer, careful not to touch the yellowed pages. "Vellum." He looked up at Hank. "10th century?"

"Close, but I think even earlier, 9th century. You'll notice the inscriptions are in Latin. A monk probably did both the illustrations and the writing."

Ben blinked. "You mean this book is over a thousand years old?"

Hank nodded. He donned a pair of white cotton gloves, then carefully turned the pages. He stopped at a page with a beautifully illustrated arch of stone. Garlanded in vines with blue, red, and yellow flowers, the interior of the arch displayed a woodland scene of giant trees.

Just like Almeera, Ben thought. But what caused the breath to catch in Ben's throat was the figure that hovered within the arch—a tiny, winged creature with arms folded and a mischievous look on her face.

A forest prawn just like Pringle.

CHAPTER 26

"HOW-HOW CAN THAT BE?" BEN GULPED. He glanced at Pringle's slumbering form. "The fairy in the picture looks just like Pringle."

Hank nodded. "Yes, but there may not be many variations in forest prawns. They might all look the same."

"I say that all the time about white people," Archie joked. At Ben's sour look, he quickly added, "but there *is* a remarkable resemblance."

Hank traced a glove-clad finger along the Latin script, silently mouthing the words. Unable to control his curiosity, Ben blurted, "What's it say?"

Hank held up his hand and continued reading. When he finished, he sighed and sat back. "Nothing good, I'm afraid. Roughly translated, the arch of stone represents a door or gateway, a transition point between worlds. Somehow, Otto Albrecht managed to create gateways within some of his clocks. We may never know how or why, but that's not what's important."

Ben didn't like the look on Hank's face. "Then what is?"

Hank pointed at the script under the illustration. "*Separare semper debent regna magica et hominum.* The Latin translates to, 'Separate must always be the realms of magic and men.'"

A shaky laugh left Ben. "So magic and real life don't mix. Not a big deal, right?"

Hank carefully closed the book. "It means what I said before." He glanced at Pringle, still fast asleep. "She doesn't belong here, Ben. Sooner or later, she may reach a point where she *can't* go back. The changes in her will be permanent."

Silence fell over the room. Guilt and concern for Pringle warred within Ben. "How long?" he asked. "How long before she changes so completely, she won't be able to return to Almeera?"

Hank drummed his fingers on the tabletop. "I don't know. It could be days, weeks, or even months. But you're still not seeing the bigger problem."

A harsh snort left Ben. "Really? What can top Pringle being stranded here?"

"She's attached to you," Hank said. "Whatever the two of you experienced together in Almeera, it's formed a bond that may be difficult to break. Pringle won't willingly go back to her world. Not without you."

She saved my life, kept me from starving, and never left my side. He couldn't stop the sudden rush of tears that came to his eyes. "She doesn't deserve this and it's my fault."

Hank pushed away from the table and approached Ben. He laid a hand on his arm. "There's still time to figure something out. In the meantime, help Pringle adapt while she's here. That's the best advice I can give."

Ben swiped at his eyes. "But what about her size? What if she keeps growing?"

Hank chuckled. "I don't think you have to worry about that. Yes, she'll probably continue to grow, but remember, she's becoming part of *our* world. That means her growth will be limited to the size of a normal woman."

Normal.

Ben shook his head. Nothing in his life had been "normal" since he used the key to open the enchanted grandfather clock—and the prospects for normal seemed dim for his immediate future.

He got up and retrieved his backpack. He gestured to Archie. "I guess it's time to leave." He reached out and shook Hank's hand. "Thanks for your help. Can I call if I have more questions?"

Hank gripped Ben's hand firmly. "Of course. I'll continue to research and see what I can find. Maybe there's a solution we're just not seeing yet."

"Thanks." Although Ben appreciated Hank's continued help, he knew the store owner didn't think an alternate solution was likely.

"Er, Hank?" Archie said.

"Yes?"

"Would you entertain an offer for your book?"

Hank smiled. "Sorry, but all these books are part of my personal collection. They're not for sale."

Archie grinned. "I figured that. Oh, well. I had to take a shot."

"But you're welcome to come by any time and look at my collection."

"I may take you up on that."

Ben, only half-listening, stood over Pringle's sleeping form. She lay curled like a cat with her head pillowed in her hands, her face a picture of blissful serenity. The sucker jutting from her mouth somehow made the scene even more endearing to Ben.

A powerful tug pulled at Ben's heart. He reached out and brushed a strand of honey-brown hair away from her face.

"Ben?"

Startled, he glanced over his shoulder to discover Archie beside him. "You ready to go?"

"Uh, yeah." He gently scooped Pringle up. She opened her eyes and met his gaze.

"Are we going home, Ben Hastings?"

"Yes."

Pringle raised her arms and stretched languidly, then leaped in the air and hovered before Hank. "Goodbye, Hank Harper. You have a good hutch."

Hank's eyes sparkled. "I'm sure we'll meet again, Pringle. But before you go, I have something for you." He pulled his hand from behind his back and held up a grape-flavored Tootsie-Pop.

"Whee!" She grabbed the sucker and jammed it in her mouth to join the other partially eaten Tootsie-Pop. After making several dizzying loops around the room, she swooped into the backpack Ben had hoisted onto his shoulders.

Hank handed a bag of suckers to Ben. "Take these. They'll last awhile and help curb her hunger."

Ben took the bag. "Thanks, Hank...for everything."

They threaded their way through the store. When they reached the front door, Hank unlocked it and held it open for them. Archie exited first but when Ben followed, Hank stopped him with a tug on his arm.

"Some things are meant to be, Ben. And if that's true, they have a way of working out."

He gave Ben a final wave, then shut and locked the door.

The diminutive shopkeeper's comment circled Ben's mind all the way back to Tyler.

Ben turned onto the residential street that led to his old mansion.

The setting sun supplied a dim illumination that revealed a police car parked behind Archie's 'Vette. When they exited the van, a policewoman got out of the patrol car and met them.

"Are you Ben Hastings?" she asked.

"Yes." Puzzled, Ben asked, "Is something wrong?"

"Mr. Hastings, we received a complaint—"

"I called the police!" a voice echoed in the dying light. Maude Thorne stormed up and shook a finger at Ben.

"Thought you were clever, huh? Scaring me with your stupid special effects. What did you think, that I would forget the violation of HOA rules concerning your yard? Well, I can tell you I'm made of sterner stuff. I don't scare easily!"

"Mrs. Thorne, I'll ask the questions," the policewoman said.

"Go ahead. Ask him about the threats his door made!"

The policewoman held up her hand. "Mrs. Thorne, I will ask the questions!"

She turned back to Ben. "I'm sorry, Mr. Hastings. I don't have a search warrant, nor am I going to request one, but I think we can clear this up if you will show me your front door."

Archie rolled his eyes. "Really, officer? A door that mugs people? Don't you have better things to do with your time?"

The policewoman shrugged. "I'm just trying to defuse a situation."

"Hey, it's okay," Ben said. "Just let me put up my pack and you can look all you want to." He opened the gate and started for the steps.

Frantic, Maude waved her arms. "Don't let him leave! Don't let him out of your sight!"

"Mrs. Thorne, please! I told you to let me do the investigation. You need to go back to your home," the policewoman ordered.

"Well, I never. Your police chief will hear about this!" Maude spun on her heel and stalked away.

Ben hurried up the steps and fought the urge to look over his shoulder. When he reached the door, a greeting boomed out. "Welcome magnificent, sir! How was—"

"Shut the hell up!" Ben hissed.

"My, someone didn't get a hug today," the door grumbled.

"Listen, someone's going to come and inspect you. Don't do anything and don't say a word. Act like a normal door."

"Act like a door? I don't know. My acting skills are a bit rusty."

"I read somewhere that when termites eat, they make a scratching sound like fingernails against wood."

"And my lips are sealed, oh resplendent sir. A normal door it is."

Ben sighed. One problem down and one huge problem to go.

What to do about Pringle.

CHAPTER 27

THE POLICE OFFICER PERFORMED A CURSORY examination of the door.

Ben could tell the search was for Maude's benefit, like a parent looking under a child's bed for monsters.

Duty done, she thanked Ben and left.

They went inside, and Pringle shot out of the backpack like a missile. She hovered before them. "I'm hungry, Ben Hastings."

Ben blinked. *Is she bigger?* The dim light in the foyer made it difficult to tell. *Has she grown in the time it took us to drive back from Mt. Pleasant?*

Ben reached for the bag of Tootsie-Pops in his pocket and pulled out a sucker. He removed the wrapper and handed it to Pringle. "Here you go."

Her eyes lit up and she snatched the sucker. "Whee!" she sang, popping it in her mouth. She whirled in circles and then settled on Ben's shoulder.

Ben grunted. She *definitely* weighed more.

"What are you going to do now?" Archie asked.

Since Ben exited the clock in Archie's store, his life had moved at breakneck speed with little time for planning or thought.

Ben ran his fingers through his hair. "I don't know. Take it one day at a time, I guess."

Day!

Realization hit Ben that he didn't know what day it was, much less how much time had passed since he fell through the grandfather clock and into Almeera. Fleeing from Rooster-comb, trapped in a wizard's hutch, finding his way back via Archie's clock, his life had moved so fast he'd barely had time to take a breath, much less think about time.

"What day is it?" he blurted.

"It's Monday, dude. Why?"

Ben did a rapid calculation in his mind. He entered the clock on Friday, spent maybe two days in the wizard's hutch, then exited the clock in Archie's store today. If he counted Friday, he'd spent three days in Almeera. That meant the time *there* paralleled the time *here.*

He heaved a huge sigh of relief. *The university is still on spring break.* The last thing he needed was to jeopardize his professorship because he failed to show up to teach his classes.

"Just trying to figure out how much time I lost in Almeera," he told Archie. "Did you see on Maude's agenda when the HOA meeting is being held?"

"I think it said this Thursday. I don't remember the time."

"Dammit! I haven't even owned this place for a week, and she's already trying to get me blacklisted."

"What troubles you, Ben Hastings?" Pringle asked. She launched into the air and clutched his face with both hands. Her green eyes studied him. "Are you hungry too?"

Through all their harrowing experiences together in Almeera, Pringle had never questioned him like that. *Why now?* Did it mean her emotional maturity increased with her size? There were too many unknowns going on with Pringle, and his sense of helplessness threatened to swallow him up. With great effort, he pushed his frustration aside.

Ben shook his head. "No, I'm not hungry, just tired. It's nothing a good night's sleep can't fix."

He turned to Archie and held out his hand. "Thanks for everything. I don't know how I can ever repay you."

Archie gripped his hand. "Actually, there *is* a way you can repay me."

Ben narrowed his eyes. "And that is?"

"You can let me see this through with you."

"What do you mean? With Pringle, Maude, or the damn clock?"

"I mean all of it."

Ben spread his hands. "But why? You just met me, and besides, you're a millionaire with your own rare books store. You can do anything you want. Why be involved in my problems?"

"At the risk of sounding like Hank, do you have any beer?"

"Yeah, in the kitchen."

"Then get me one and I'll tell you why."

They made their way to the kitchen and Ben took two cans of Shiner from the 60's era refrigerator. They sat at the kitchen table, and Ben popped the tab on both cans. He handed one to Archie, then took a long swallow, and wiped his mouth with the back of his hand. He gestured at Archie. "Okay, shoot."

Archie settled back in the chair and fiddled with the can. "You ever see a movie or TV show where one of the actors is at work in an office cubicle? And he's surrounded by a dozen other people in cubicles?"

"Sure. Everyone has."

"Well, that was my life. Straight out of college, I took a job revising actuarial tables with a major insurance company. After a few months, I knew I'd made a mistake. I felt like a hamster in a cage running on one of those wheels. No matter how fast I ran, I never made any progress."

Archie took a drink of the beer. "Well, you already know by a stroke of luck, I won a multi-million-dollar lottery. I quit, moved to Jefferson, bought the Black Swan, and yadda, yadda, you know the rest. So my life is rocking along, but after a while, I feel like I'm in a rut again. The cage is bigger, the wheel easier to turn, but I still feel trapped. And that's when I realized the old adage is true. Money can't buy you happiness, only temporary fulfillment."

He took another sip. "So, just when I feel like my life is headed for another dead end, something remarkable happens."

Intrigued, Ben leaned forward. "What?"

"You and Pringle come out of that old clock. My life went from boring to supercharged in an instant. Then I got to meet Hank, a mysterious antique store-owner who knows more about ancient books than I'll ever know."

Archie ticked off the fingers on his hand. "In the space of just a few hours, I discovered an alternate world exists, saw an honest-to-God fairy, and learned I own an enchanted grandfather clock. I can't imagine what the next few days may have in store."

He put the beer down and looked Ben in the eye. "What I'm saying is I don't want to go back to boring. Let me help you with Pringle. Hell, I'll even help you with the nosy neighbor next door. I'll do whatever I can, just don't shut me out."

The hint of desperation in Archie's voice touched a nerve inside Ben. Besides, other than Hank, who else could he talk to about Pringle? He couldn't share her existence with anyone else, and Archie understood his predicament.

Ben raised his beer. "To friendships and fairies."

With a grin, Archie bumped his can against Ben's. "Friendships and fairies."

Archie stood. "I'll pay Hank another visit tomorrow and take a look at that book again. I'll stop here on my way back."

Ben walked him to the door. "Thanks, Archie."

"Nah. You got that wrong, dude. Thank *you* for trusting me."

They shook hands and Ben said, "Open sesame," to the door.

"Oh, please. What a tired cliché," the door grumbled as it swung open.

Pringle zoomed up and planted a kiss on Archie's cheek. He touched his face. "What's that for?"

"For helping my Ben Hastings."

A wide smile split Archie's face. "Kissed by a fairy. What a way to end the day."

He walked to his car, waved, and drove away.

Bone-tired, Ben made his way to take a shower and prepare for bed. He made sure to firmly tell Pringle to stay out of the shower before he did. He could barely keep his eyes open when he emerged from the shower, dried off and changed into shorts and a T-shirt.

Pringle followed him as he threw the covers back and got into bed. She hovered above him, settled on the bed's end, and curled into a ball. Ben yawned. "Night, Pringle."

He turned off the bedside light, then lay back, asleep almost before his head hit the pillow.

A few hours later, Pringle stirred. She flew into the air and stopped above Ben's head. "I'm hungry, Ben Hastings." Other than a murmur, her comment went unanswered.

After a moment, she shot out of the room, down the stairs, and into the kitchen. She circled once before stopping by the pantry. She opened the pantry door and clapped at the sight of the stacked bags of sugar. She grabbed one and ripped open the top. A cascade of sugar poured into her mouth. Soon she had emptied the sack. After gulping down water from the faucet, she returned to the pantry.

There were four more bags of sugar.

CHAPTER 28

BEN AWOKE FROM A DREAMLESS SLEEP, YAWNED, AND looked at his bedside clock. *Eight a.m.* He'd slept for twelve straight hours, not a record for him, but something he hadn't done since his undergraduate days.

Arms behind his head, he thought about the day ahead. He supposed he'd try to call Cara again. Maybe she would have cooled off enough to talk. Even by her standards, standing him up yesterday was a petulant act. If she meant to tell him off, she wouldn't have missed the opportunity to do it face-to-face.

He shook his head. A week ago, Cara's rebuff would have been devastating. But now…now he didn't know how he felt anymore. He snorted bitterly. *I guess near-death experiences have a way of changing one's perspective.* This led to an even more unsettling thought. *Did I ever love her?*

What a contrast to Pringle. While Cara had expectations he might never be able to meet, Pringle didn't ask for anything—except sugar. Thoughts of her caused him to smile. What would it have been like if he had met someone like Pringle instead of Cara? A non-fairy version, of course, adult-sized and more mature.

He stretched. *Why not wish for the moon for all the good it'll do?*

Pringle's warm weight lay on his feet at the end of the bed.

He wriggled them out from under her. She stirred, stood up on the mattress, and stretched. "Hi, Ben Hastings."

Ben took one look—and bolted out of bed. He pointed a shaking finger. "Wha-what?" he garbled.

Pringle stood well over five feet tall!

Her hair now flowed past her shoulders. Her one-piece garment—molded to her frame like a second skin—revealed soft curves and full breasts. Gone was the lean, adolescent figure.

Instead, a young woman stood at the end of his bed.

Her sparkling jade eyes regarded him with concern. "Are you hurt, Ben Hastings?"

She flew toward him, the wind from her larger wings causing the bedsheets to flap like sails on a catamaran.

"What did you do?" Ben cried.

Pringle landed beside him. "I was hungry, Ben Hastings. I told you, but you were asleep."

Ben's mind raced, all vestiges of slumber gone. "Oh, no!" he choked.

He rushed out of the bedroom and down the stairs. Bursting through the kitchen door, he skidded to a stop.

Five empty sacks of sugar lay scattered on the floor.

"She ate them all," he whispered. "Every single bag."

Pringle landed beside Ben, the bags swirling. He turned and gripped her shoulders. "You weren't supposed to eat all the sugar! I could have given you a sucker—"

He bit off the comment. "What am I saying? It's too late now."

Ben collapsed in a kitchen chair. He grabbed his hair with both hands. "Great! Just great! What am I going to do now?"

Pringle scooted onto the table and dangled her legs. "I'm not hungry anymore, Ben Hastings."

Her comment reminded him of what Hank had said—the longer Pringle remained with him, the more she would become part of his world. Fueled by the sugar, her overnight growth spurt transformed her to a normal size. No wonder she wasn't hungry anymore.

Ben sat straighter and studied Pringle. She looked right back, smiling. Her larger size magnified everything about her. Her clear, emerald-green eyes looked as big as the ocean, her silky hair a cascade of golden brown. The pointed tips of her ears flared out from under her hair, and when combined with the slight epicanthic folds of her eyes, gave her a stunning, exotic look.

For the first time, Ben detected a scent given off by Pringle, a mix of warm summer rain and a freshness of soil and forest. He took a deep breath of the intoxicating fragrance.

"Why do you look at me so strangely, Ben Hastings?" she asked.

Taken aback, Ben groped for an answer. "Because—because you're beautiful, Pringle."

"Ooh, really?" She paused. "What does beautiful mean, Ben Hastings?"

I'm just sinking deeper and deeper, he groaned. Again, he searched for a way to answer her. "It means you're like a pretty flower, pleasing to look at," he managed to say.

Pringle wrinkled her nose. "Is pretty a good thing, Ben Hastings?"

He closed his eyes. *Why can't I learn to keep my mouth shut?*

With a sigh, he said, "Most of the time, yes."

She leaned toward him until their faces were inches apart. "Do you find me pleasing, Ben Hastings?"

Ben froze and wished he could be a thousand miles away. He swallowed and said, "Uh, yes. Yes, I do."

She moved closer until their lips met. Her kiss tasted like cinnamon and wildflowers. It took his breath away. He fought the overwhelming urge to pull her close and kiss her again. Instead, he gently pushed her away.

"I feel so strange, Ben Hastings. What is happening to me?"

You're having a crash course in going from fairy to woman in a single day, and your hormones have gone from zero to a hundred miles per hour. Welcome to earth!

He had no way of knowing how long Pringle's emotional roll-ercoaster ride would last. He *did* know there was no way in hell he could explain it to her.

"You're just going to have to hang in there for a while. Sooner or later, you'll understand."

She reached out and stroked his cheek. "Alright, Ben Hastings."

Her touch, warm and smooth, left his skin tingling. He cleared his throat. "Uh, Pringle, can you get my phone? It's the little square thing I left on the table beside the bed."

She brightened. "Whee!" Pringle shot out of the kitchen, the empty sugar sacks swirling in her jet stream.

He shook his head. *And just like that, she's back to being a fun-loving fairy.*

She returned seconds later and dropped the phone in Ben's hand. Buffeted by the wind of her return, his hair swirled around his face. Curious, he touched a wing.

Pringle giggled. "That tickles, Ben Hastings."

Made of a tough, translucent membrane, a network of veins ran like tributaries throughout her wings. Now at rest, the wings—attached between her shoulder blades—folded across the small of her back. She shivered as he continued to run his hand across them.

"Prawns don't like their wings to be touched, Ben Hastings. But I like it when you do it."

Ben snatched his hand back. "Oh. Sorry."

He fumbled with his cell and punched a contact number. Archie's cheery voice answered. "Hey, Ben!"

Pringle's sharp ears picked up the sound of Archie's voice. She darted forward and pushed her face next to the cell. "Hello, Archie Jones! I'm not hungry anymore, and Ben Hastings said I was beautiful."

Ben snatched the phone back. "I'm going to talk to Archie, okay?"

"Alright, Ben Hastings."

As Ben walked away, he could feel his face turn red. "Uh, it's not what you think."

"Oh, I can think of a lot of things. What's going on?"

"Pringle's grown to a full-sized woman, *that's* what's going on. While I was asleep last night, she snuck back to the kitchen and raided the pantry. She ate the rest of the sugar, every single bag."

"No shit? What are you going to do now?"

"Why do you think I'm calling you? You said you didn't want to go back to boring, well here's your chance to jump in. Gimme some advice!"

After a long pause, Archie asked, "How's she acting?"

"One minute, like the normal Pringle, the next, more…mature. It's hard to explain."

"Do you think she can behave herself if you take her to the store?"

"I have no idea. Why?"

"Because the last I checked, Pringle's wardrobe consisted of a single Tarzan and Jane unisuit. If she's going to pass for a normal person, she needs normal clothes."

"Take Pringle shopping? You can't be serious. There's no telling how she'll react with a bunch of people and all kind of different sights and sounds around her."

"She listens to you, doesn't she?"

"Yeah. Well, most of the time anyway."

"Then sit her down and explain what you're going to do and why. She may be a forest prawn from another world, but she's not stupid, Ben. At some point, you're going to have to trust her."

Ben ran his fingers through his hair. Maybe Archie was right. Besides, he couldn't treat Pringle like a prisoner and hide her forever. "Okay. I don't guess I have a choice."

"Good. I'm going to head your way later today, and you can tell me all about it."

Ben clicked off, then turned and went back to the kitchen. Pringle was doing a handstand, and her eyes lit up when she saw Ben. She flipped to her feet. "Is Archie Jones coming? I like him."

Ben nodded. He sat on the table and patted the area next to him. Pringle extended her wings, fluttered into the air, and alighted next to him. Ben opened his mouth, then abruptly stopped. The sight of her flying caused him to realize what should have been obvious from the beginning. He couldn't take Pringle to the store. He couldn't take her anywhere. A part of her anatomy made it impossible.

Her wings.

CHAPTER 29

BEN BURIED HIS FACE IN HIS HANDS. "WHY IS everything so hard?" he moaned. "Why can't something work out, just once?"

Pringle put her arm across his shoulders. "Lots of things are soft, Ben Hastings. Leaves, feathers, and flowers." She pointed at her chest. "Even me."

Ben sat up. "I'm not talking about things that are—"

He threw up his hands. "Never mind. Thanks, Pringle, but the problem is your wings. I can't take you anywhere. The first time someone sees your wings, especially if you try to use them, they'll run off screaming."

"Why would anyone be frightened of my wings, Ben Hastings?"

"Because in my world, only certain creatures like birds and insects have wings."

"How strange." She twisted to face him. "But I can hide them, Ben Hastings."

"How? If I have you put a shirt over them, it'll make you look weird, like some kind of a hunchback."

"I don't know what a hunchback is, Ben Hastings, but I can do this."

Pringle twirled and stopped, her back to Ben. He blinked, rubbed his eyes, then blinked again.

Her wings had disappeared!

"What—where did your wings go?" he stammered.

Pringle peered over her shoulder at him. "I still have them, Ben Hastings."

He reached out and carefully touched her back. His hand brushed against the smooth surface of a wing. He moved closer, his eyes just inches from his fingers. Only where they touched could he see any visible surface of her wings.

"Camouflage," he breathed. "You're using camouflage to hide your wings."

"What's camouflage, Ben Hastings?"

In a rush, like a fog lifting, it all made sense to him. Pringle was a creature of the forest, and like any woodland creature, she and all her fellow prawns could blend in with their environment. Their bodies might even automatically change to mimic their surroundings without conscious thought.

He ignored her question and asked, "Can you disguise your whole body?"

The words had barely left his lips when Pringle disappeared. He squinted and tried to locate her, but the only indication of her presence was a slight blurring of what appeared to be thin air.

"Wow."

She reappeared right in front of him and wrapped her arms around his waist. Her face just inches from his lips, she asked, "Does this please you, Ben Hastings? Can we go now?"

Ben swallowed. Her warm body pressed firmly against him, stirred a reaction he needed to stop. *Think of kittens, puppies, cotton candy, walks in the park, anything but where your mind's headed.*

He pushed her away. "Sure. But you can't wear what you've got on now. Until we can get you new clothes, I'll see if I have something that'll work."

Ben turned and hurried up the stairs to his room. He

rummaged through his closet and grabbed a brown, long-sleeved flannel shirt. He hesitated, then dug a pair of jogging shorts out of a drawer.

"Pringle!" he called.

She buzzed through the door and landed beside him. "Here I am, Ben Hastings."

He handed her the shirt. "Put this on."

Pringle put the shirt on backward, so Ben had to take it off and help her slip it on correctly. He buttoned it up, then moved back to scrutinize the fit. He turned her around so he could see where she needed holes cut through the fabric for her wings—and was pleasantly surprised to discover it was unnecessary. The way her wings lay against her back didn't cause the hump he feared. Pleased, he handed her the shorts.

Again, Pringle put the clothing on backward. With a sigh, he slipped the shorts off, turned them around, and handed them back to her. Even after cinching the drawstring as tight as it allowed, the shorts still hung from her waist like wet laundry on a clothesline. Fortunately, the long shirt draped from her shoulders like a dress and covered most of the shorts.

None of Ben's shoes would fit Pringle, so he dug through his sock drawer and pulled out a pair of bright blue, Sonic the Hedgehog socks. A Christmas stocking stuffer his parents had given him one year when he was a kid, he'd kept them for sentimental reasons. Sonic's image was emblazoned on each sock, and they came complete with toes. Pringle sat on the bed while he put them on each of her feet.

He stood back to examine his work. The mismatched, ill-fitting clothing, when combined with her blue-toed socks, made her look like a bad Andy Warhol print.

He shrugged. *Nothing I can do about it. I just need to get her to a store, buy some clothes and shoes, and she can wear them out.*

Pringle pulled out her pouch so it dangled over the shorts. "Are these my clothes, Ben Hastings?"

"Yes, but they're only temporary. We'll get you better stuff at the store."

He spent the next fifteen minutes going over the do's and don'ts. Chief among them was to keep her wings camouflaged and *not* to fly. Satisfied he'd covered all the most important points, they made their way down the stairs. The door swung open. "Have a nice day, magnificent master."

Ben stifled a retort, and they headed for the VW. Once in the van, he helped Pringle with her seatbelt. He started the van and clutched the wheel but hesitated when an eerie feeling gripped him. He sensed he'd reached a line, a boundary, and once past it, his life would never be the same. He glanced at Pringle, and she looked back with a happy smile.

He put the van in gear and pulled away.

Cara jumped as the door to her room opened.

Georgi entered and tossed a bag on the bunk bed. Unsure what to do, she just stared at it. Mumbling something in Russian, he snatched up the bag and dumped the contents on the bed. Clothing and a make-up kit tumbled out.

"Get dressed and pretty yourself up. Make sure you look as good as possible." His last words carried an underlying threat if she didn't.

Cara scrambled to pick up the clothing, a black dress, black lace bra and panties, and a pair of black stiletto heels. She started to undress, then stopped.

Georgi hadn't moved.

He grinned, his expression like a shark preparing to feast. "Better get used to taking off your clothes, girl."

She continued to undress, then put on the panties, bra, and dress. Last, she slipped on the stilettos. She smoothed the short, tight dress, picked up the make-up kit, and moved to the mirror.

Georgi glanced at the large gold watch on his wrist. "Hurry! We're running out of time."

Cara put on the make-up as quickly as possible, and lastly, applied a bright, blood-colored shade of red lipstick. Done, she turned and Georgi gripped her elbow. "Come with me."

He led her down a corridor lined with locked rooms like her own. They reached a heavy metal door with a keypad. Georgi tapped in a code followed by the metallic sound of a lock releasing. The door swung open, and they entered a large room in the shape of an octagon. A dozen glass-cased cubicles lined the wall, all facing the middle of the room where digital cameras—one for each compartment—were located.

Georgi punched a button beside one of the glass booths. With a *whisk*, it slid open. He shoved Cara. "Get in."

She stumbled into the oval chamber. Other than the glass facing and smooth, curved walls, the compartment was empty.

Georgi leaned in. He pointed at the ceiling to a recessed speaker. "You'll be instructed what to do. Follow the instructions with *no* hesitation." He moved closer, his eyes hard shards of flint. "Am I clear?"

Fear filled Cara. She stumbled back. "Ye-yes, I understand."

Georgi grinned. The act somehow made him seem even more intimidating. He punched the button again, and the glass panel slid shut. The size and absolute quiet inside the cubicle had a coffin-like quality, and she struggled to quell her growing anxiety.

A voice crackled from the speaker above, one Cara recognized immediately—the tall mistress, Georgi's boss.

"Gentlemen, as you know, today is the preliminary to the final auction to be held Saturday. We'll show you our merchandise, and you have the next three days to determine the price you're willing to pay. All sales are final, but as always, we guarantee the quality of our product."

The speaker shut off.

Cara's blood ran cold. Until now, she'd locked herself in a corner of her mind, a safe space where only fantasy existed.

This is all a bad nightmare that I'll wake up from.

Daddy will have an army of police and private security teams looking for me.

Somehow, I'll find a way to escape.

All these illusionary possibilities collapsed to dust in her mind. She didn't even have the release of crying. If she ruined her make-up, Georgi would beat her.

"Face the glass," the voice from the speaker ordered. "Turn slowly so the clients can view every part of you."

Cara complied.

"Good. Now *very* slowly take off the dress but leave the panties and bra on. We don't want to unwrap the entire package—not yet. Better to give the clients a taste and let their imagination fill-in the rest. Once you've removed the dress, twirl in a leisurely fashion to give them a full view."

Humiliated past the point of caring, Cara followed the instructions with robot-like efficiency.

Afterward, she stood listlessly, waiting for further instructions. "Very good," the mistress's voice finally said. "You've attracted more interest than we've had in a long time. I expect a spirited auction Saturday."

Cara picked up the dress but didn't bother to put it back on. Despair threatened to overwhelm her.

A new level of her long nightmare had started.

CHAPTER 30

BEN DECIDED CHAIN CLOTHING STORES WOULD BE HIS best bet. They would have a wider selection, better prices, and with any luck, clerks too busy to notice an oddly dressed customer.

He inched along with the bumper-to-bumper traffic on Broadway, the main thoroughfare in Tyler. He sighed with relief when he could finally turn off the busy road and into the parking lot of Kohl's.

Ben killed the engine, got out, and prepared himself for the ordeal ahead. *Now I know what the Bible means by girding your loins.*

Pringle hopped out of the van and joined him. She looked about, excitement dripping from her. She grabbed his hand. "Let's go, Ben Hastings," and tugged him toward the store entrance.

They entered the store and Pringle immediately veered toward the jewelry. "They sparkle, Ben Hastings!" she gushed.

"We're here to find you something to wear, not stuff that sparkles. C'mon."

Ben started off only to discover Pringle headed toward the men's apparel. He groaned. "What're you doing? The women's section is this way."

They walked to the other side of the store and Ben stopped

abruptly. "Oh, my God." Rack after rack of dresses, blouses, pants, and intimate apparel stretched out before him, a sea of clothing. His original plan to get in, buy some clothes, then get out, fizzled like a wet match. He had no idea where to begin.

Ben, pulling Pringle along with him, headed for a clerk folding T-shirts on a display table near them.

"Can you help us?"

A matronly woman with brown hair in a bun, peered down her steel-rimmed glasses at them. Apparently, she'd been in the business a long time, because other than a slight hesitation at the sight of Pringle's odd clothes, she didn't miss a beat.

"Yes, sir. What do you need?"

Ben pointed at Pringle. "She needs some new clothes, and I don't know much about women's clothing."

"Of course." She turned to Pringle. "What's your size, honey?"

Pringle looked at Ben and then back to the clerk. She pointed at herself. "I'm this size."

"Ah, well, neither of us are much into fashion I'm afraid," Ben quickly interjected.

"I can see that," the clerk said.

Ben glanced at her Kohl's nametag with "Martha" stenciled on it. "Look, Martha, can you help us pick some outfits for Pringle? I'd appreciate it."

Martha dropped the T-shirts back onto the table. "No problem. So, we don't know Pringle's size—delightful name by the way—and you want what? Pants, dresses, blouses?"

"All of it. She needs shoes and uh, undergarments as well."

"Just came in from the wilderness, huh?" Martha joked.

"Ha, ha, yeah, something like that."

"Follow me." Martha headed for the dresses.

Ben spent the next twenty-five minutes following Martha as she loaded his arms with a variety of clothing and shoes. He finally had to get a shopping cart to hold all Martha's selections. Her last stop came at the lingerie section.

Martha peered down her glasses at Pringle. "Honey, I have to know your size. You can go into one of the dressing rooms and look at the tags on what you're wearing. Just come back and tell me."

"What's a—"

"She's not wearing any!" Ben blurted. "Can't you just take a guess?"

Martha paused. "You weren't kidding, were you? She *does* need everything." She shrugged. "Come with me, honey." She took a measuring tape from her pocket and led Pringle into one of the dressing rooms. They emerged a few minutes later.

Martha scribbled the sizes on a discarded sales slip. "Okay, so what kind of style and colors do you want? Push-up, lightly padded, or heavily padded bras? As for panties, are we talking thongs, bikini, or regular?"

If he'd been asked for the design and structure of the world's most powerful supercomputer, Ben couldn't have been more clueless. The heat flooding his face and neck felt like he could pass for a lobster.

"To be honest, I don't know."

"Sir, I was asking Pringle."

"Oh." More heat rushed to Ben's face. *Forget lobster and bring on fire engine red.*

Pringle's eyes twinkled. "I want whatever Ben Hastings wants."

"Let's go with regular on the undies and bras," Ben rushed to say before the store clerk could interject another comment.

Martha added several selections to the clothing piled on the cart. "Knock yourself out." She pivoted and left.

Relieved, Ben pushed the fully laden cart to the women's dressing rooms. He collapsed onto a bench. Pringle stood beside him. "What do I do now, Ben Hastings?"

He groaned and stood up. "You need to try everything on starting with the bras and underwear. Pick the ones that fit you the best."

Pringle didn't move.

"What are you waiting for?" Ben snapped

Pringle picked up one of the lingerie items. "How do I put them on, Ben Hastings?"

If Archie had he been there, Ben would have punched him in the nose for suggesting he take Pringle shopping. Angrily, he snatched one of the bras from the pile of clothes. He looked around. No one was looking their way. He reversed the brassiere, attached the hooks, reversed it again, and slipped his arms through the straps. *Who would've thought watching Cara dress would be educational?*

Ben modeled it for Pringle, then tore it off as fast as he could. He handed the brassiere to Pringle, then grabbed a pair of panties. He pointed at the label. "You put on the underwear like the shorts you're wearing, but the label goes in back. Pick a changing room that's empty, and try everything on."

Pringle fingered the bra. "Ooh, pillows. Can I use this one to sleep on?"

Ben frowned. "What?" He peered at the cups. "Oh, it's just padding. They're not pillows."

"Why, Ben Hastings?"

Ben's exasperation reached his limit. "Look, if I answer your question, will you *please* try on the clothes so we can get out of here?"

"Yes, I promise."

"Some women wear padded bras because they think it makes their boobs look bigger and better."

Pringle cocked her head. "What are boobs, Ben Hastings? Are bigger boobs a good thing?"

"Enough!" he cried. "We are not having this discussion in the middle of a department store." He jabbed at the dressing rooms. "Try the stuff on we picked out before we're thrown out of here!"

Pringle skipped into the changing rooms. Ben sagged onto the bench and rubbed his face. *Finally!*

A minute later, Pringle emerged wearing only a bra and

panties. Ben sat up, his breath leaving him in a *whoosh*. Her bare legs led to an impossibly small waist, her breasts mounded into a deep cleavage. *She's gorgeous!*

"Did I put them on right, Ben Hastings? Do my boobs look bigger and better?" she asked with a bright smile.

Ben's brain finally engaged. He leapt to his feet and pushed her back through the entrance to the dressing rooms. "You can't come out here half-dressed!" he hissed. He looked around. Thankfully, no shoppers were in the vicinity.

Pringle's scent distracted him. In the close quarters it was overpowering. *She smells so good. She looks so good.*

He stepped back. *Puppies and kittens, Ben. Puppies and kittens.*

"Uh, just keep them on. They definitely…fit. Put the other clothes on over them."

Thirty minutes later, Ben exited the store pushing a cart piled high with bags. Pringle walked beside him wearing a pair of jeans, sandals, and a simple white blouse. Despite the modest attire, Pringle made it look like something a supermodel would wear.

He loaded the purchases into the van and they both got in. Ben sat back, exhausted. It felt like he'd run a marathon. *If I never set foot in a clothing store again, I'll die a happy man. At least we made it out without being escorted by store security.* Between Pringle's endless questions, and her total lack of modesty, he felt lucky no one had reported them.

He started the VW, but before he could pull out, Pringle reached over and put her hand on his arm.

"Thank you, Ben Hastings."

The look in her eyes and the sound of her voice carried a sincerity that pushed aside his frustration and exhaustion. It made the whole trip worth it.

He put the van in gear and they headed home.

CHAPTER 31

ARCHIE PARKED IN FRONT OF HANK'S SHOP.

He got out of the 'Vette and removed his sunglasses. The late March weather was unusually mild, and he'd removed the hardtop for the drive to Mt. Pleasant. Along the way, he wondered how Ben's shopping foray with Pringle had gone. He resisted calling to find out. Ben could fill him in later. Besides, he had bigger things on his mind.

Like Hank's ancient book on fairies.

He couldn't shake the feeling they'd missed something about Pringle, but despite turning it over in his mind countless times, he couldn't pinpoint what it was. He entered the shop and spied Hank helping a customer. Hank flashed him a smile while he rang up the sale, bagged the item, and handed it to a young woman in jeans and a Hogwarts T-shirt.

"Thanks, Sara. I'm expecting a fresh shipment of the Apple Cinnamon Spice Tea next week."

She thanked Hank and exited the store.

Archie grinned. "Cinnamon Spice Tea? Your sign says 'Antiques and Oddities.' Where does tea fit in?"

Hank stepped from behind the counter. He pointed at a

display of glass containers. They held a variety of bagged and loose teas. "It pays for small shops like mine to diversify to survive."

He shook Archie's hand. "What can I do for you?"

"I thought I'd take you up on your offer to look at the fairy book again."

"Sure. I'll get it for you."

Hank led them to the backroom containing his library. He retrieved the ancient tome and carefully placed it on the table.

"Is there a reason other than curiosity that brings you back so soon?"

Archie hesitated. *What the hell. He already knows about Pringle.* "Yeah, I'm afraid there is. Pringle snuck into the kitchen while Ben was sleeping. She found where he kept the sugar and ate it all. When he woke up the next morning, she'd grown to the size of an adult woman."

Hank shook his head. "That's not good, not good at all. Let me show you why."

He flipped through the pages until he reached another hand-illustrated picture cleverly drawn to give it 3D depth. Archie leaned closer for a better look.

The illustration—divided into a series of pictures—displayed a fairy undergoing a metamorphosis from a tiny pixie to a full-sized adult. Archie drew in a sharp breath. "That's exactly what's happened to Pringle."

"It gets worse. Look at the inscription below," Hank said.

"*Postquam mutata est, reditus esse non potest,*" Archie read out loud. "*Once changed, there can be no return.*"

He glanced at Hank. "No return? What's that mean?"

"I'm afraid it means Pringle may not be able to return to her world."

Archie frowned. "Why can't she just use Ben's clock and go back?"

Hank carefully closed the tome. "Would you agree with me that anomalies are inconsistent with nature?"

"Sure, but what's that got to do with Pringle?"

"She's an anomaly, Archie. The natural order here is not the same as on Almeera."

"Alright, so what's your point?"

"The point is the clock's ticking. There'll come a time when any attempt by Pringle to go back to her world will cause her to sicken and die. Think of it like being poisoned."

"Wait a minute. Ben came back from Almeera without any problems."

"Yes, but from what I understand, his stay lasted only a few days."

Archie drummed his fingers on the table. *The clock's ticking.* "How long before she reaches the point of no return?"

Hank rubbed his jaw. "Ben asked me that already, remember? I can only repeat, days? Weeks? Months? It's hard to say."

"So if Pringle returns to Almeera she'll revert back to being a prawn, and if she stays here, she'll be what? A normal human woman? What about her wings? Do they shrink? Fall off?"

Hank shrugged. "All good questions which I have no answers for. I would assume Pringle would take the characteristics of the world she inhabits, but how deep these changes go I can't say."

Archie narrowed his eyes. "You mean there's something you don't know? You've had all the answers up till now."

"I'm sorry, but there's no way to be sure. If I had to guess, I'd say Pringle's rapid growth would indicate she has days, not weeks or months to safely return to Almeera."

"Damn."

Archie stood up. "Before winning the lottery, I worked with numbers in my previous profession. One of the things I've always liked about numbers is that they are consistent. Two plus two always equals four. But there's something about you, Hank, that doesn't add up. You graduated from UT with a Mechanical Engineering degree, then worked several years for the Grumman Corporation. Now, here you are, owner of a unique shop with a personal library of ancient books any museum would die to have in their collection. And you know things as if you've been there, done that. It doesn't add up. *You* don't add up."

Hank smiled. "I see you've done your homework."

"With internet access and Google, no one's truly anonymous anymore."

Hank took the book from the table, climbed the stepstool, and placed it back in the bookcase. He stepped down and dusted off his hands. He looked up at Archie.

"My personal life is off-limits. As to who I am and what I know, I'm exactly whom you see before you—someone whose curiosity runs wide and deep. I look where no one else looks, follow trails others choose not to follow, and find truth in what many deem as foolish superstition. I don't limit my life based on what others think, so with all due respect, if you feel it doesn't *add up*, that's too damn bad."

Archie grinned. "If I ever start a blog, I'm going to plagiarize the hell out of what you just said."

"Plagiarize away," Hank said with a chuckle. He paused. "So, what now?"

"I'll have to tell Ben." Uneasiness settled in Archie's stomach. "When he and Pringle first came out of that clock and scared the hell out of me, I think Ben would have gladly sent her back. Now…now I don't know."

Hank cocked his head. "What do you mean?"

"I mean in the short time I've known them, some sort of connection developed between them."

"Interesting." Hank tapped his lips. "It's obvious that Pringle has bonded to Ben, but I didn't realize he might feel the same way. Their experiences together have must have strengthened this link."

Hank folded his arms. "One thing I'm certain of. The longer they're together, the harder it will be to separate them."

"Maybe, but I don't think Ben will be as hard to persuade. If he thinks Pringle's life is in danger, he'll convince her to go back to her world."

"Ben's not the problem, Archie. Pringle is."

"C'mon. She has the emotional development of a child."

"Does she? Children grow up, and you told me Pringle is now the size of a young woman. How do you suppose that has affected her emotions? How long before they catch up to her physical development?"

"Hell if I know."

"Exactly. We *don't* know. She's a fairy from another world racing through physical, emotional, and hormonal changes at a phenomenal pace. Her feelings for Ben will rule her thoughts, not logic."

"Sounds like an old girlfriend of mine. She dumped me for someone else."

Hank chuckled. "Old girlfriends aside, think about how a duck hatchling imprints on the first thing it sees—usually the mother duck—and you have a sense of what we're dealing with here."

"So, you're saying it will be impossible to get Pringle to return to Almeera?"

"No, I'm saying *Ben's* the only one who can convince her to return."

CHAPTER 32

BEN ROLLED UP TO THE MANSION, PARKED THE VAN beside the curb, and he and Pringle got out.

He immediately noticed a sheet of paper tied to the gate by a piece of string. It flapped lazily in the breeze. He snatched it up and swore.

"What is it, Ben Hastings?"

"It's the damn HOA agenda. Maude's revised it to add a fine of twenty-five dollars a day if I don't clean up the yard. That's insane! How can you be fined for having weeds? It can't be legal!" He crumpled up the notice and threw it in the gutter. He shook his fist at Maude's house. "You can add littering to the fine, you crazy bitch!" he shouted.

"What's a bitch, Ben Hastings?"

Too angry to reply, he pushed the gate open and stormed up the steps.

"Open up, and unless you want to end up as the ass end of an outhouse, don't say a word!"

The door soundlessly swung open.

Pringle didn't immediately follow. Instead, she studied the large, overgrown lot. A smile spread across her face.

Ben yelled at her, "Pringle, get in the house before Maude decides to ticket you for loitering!"

She bounced up the steps and into the mansion. The door swung shut behind her.

Steamed, Ben mumbled curses under his breath and at first, didn't notice his phone buzzing.

He snatched it from his back pocket and punched a key. "Hello!" he growled.

"Ben? This is Mickey Sledge. You got a minute?"

Ben's mind did an immediate reversal. "M-Mr. Sledge?" he stammered. "S-sure."

"Great. I'll get right to the point. Have you seen or spoken to Cara recently? She didn't show up for work and doesn't answer my calls."

Stunned, Ben tried to refocus his thoughts. *When did we last speak?* "Uh, I called her day before yesterday. We were supposed to meet at Longino's, but she never showed up. Cara's, uh, a little mad at me."

"I see. And why is my daughter mad at you, Ben?" Although he asked the question politely, it carried an edge of hardness, as if Mickey Sledge the trial lawyer, not the father, was asking the question.

"I've been so busy trying to fix up this house I bought, I lost all track of time. Cara was upset I didn't answer her calls and texts."

"You couldn't find a few minutes to call her? Seems a little far-fetched, don't you think, even if you *were* busy?"

Yes it is, but I couldn't tell her I was trapped in a Wizard's Hutch on another world. How's that for far-fetched, Mickey?

"I know, but I wanted to get the house in shape to show her."

"I'm close friends with several realtors, and I know you bought an old mansion. You could spend months working on it and not make a dent." The undisguised suspicion in his voice made Ben wince.

"I wasn't trying to fix up the entire place, just the master bedroom and a few rooms on the first floor." Even though he said it as calmly as possible, Ben knew it sounded like an excuse, something Mickey Sledge wouldn't miss.

Thunder interrupted their conversation. The foyer had darkened, and Ben risked a peek through one of the picture windows flanking the door. Dark clouds scudded across the sky.

"Ben, I'm due in court, but please call me if you hear from Cara." Although phrased politely, there was no mistaking the firmness in his voice.

It wasn't a request but an order.

The call ended. Ben wandered to a nearby chair and collapsed into it. *What happened to Cara?* He could understand her anger with him, but why wouldn't she answer her father's calls? It made no sense.

A louder rumble echoed, followed by the drum of rain on the roof. Distracted by the phone call from Mickey Sledge, Ben didn't realize at first that Pringle wasn't in the room. Normally, he couldn't move without practically tripping over her. He got up and looked for her in the kitchen but found it empty. Thirsty, he opened the refrigerator and took out a bottled water. Unscrewing the cap, Ben stood beside the sink and peered out the window at the blowing rain. *Wow, it's really coming down.*

He took a sip—and immediately spewed it out.

Pringle, naked, twirled and leaped in the sheeting rain. *Prawns like to dance in the rain, Ben Hastings.*

"Oh, no," he breathed.

He dropped the water and sprinted into the main room off the foyer. Old sheets and blankets that had covered the furniture lay piled in a corner. He grabbed one and dashed for the door.

"Open up, open up!" he cried. It swung open, and Ben raced out.

Heart pounding, he tore past Pringle's new clothes lying on the porch, and skidded to a stop. *Where is she?* Lightning flashed and thunder boomed, the storm rising in intensity.

There! Hair plastered to her scalp, Pringle bounded and splashed through the puddles in the overgrown yard.

Ben leaped off the porch and ran after her. Drenched before he'd gone two steps, he caught up with her, but when he tried to stop, his feet skidded out from under him on the rain-slicked ground. He flew into the air and landed flat on his back, the wind driven from his lungs in a rush. When he could finally catch his breath, Pringle stood over him, joy radiating from her dripping face.

"Do you want to dance too, Ben Hastings?"

"You can't run around naked outside," he croaked. "Someone will see you."

Like Maude.

The thought galvanized him. He struggled to his feet and wrapped the wet bedsheet around her. He picked Pringle up, and started for the front door.

Wet, Pringle's heady scent seemed to intensify. It rose from her in aromatic waves of fragrance that made his senses swim. Head nestled against his shoulder, she said, "I danced for you, Ben Hastings. I will always dance for you."

He gazed at Pringle. Even in the driving rain with rivulets of water running down her face, her warm smile and beauty caused him to stop in his tracks. Her emerald eyes held him in a grip he didn't want to break free of.

A harsh voice broke the spell. "Pervert! Sex fiend! What kind of twisted creep has an orgy in his front yard?" Maude stood on her porch, one hand trying to get an umbrella open, while the other hand held a cell phone. She finally got the umbrella open and held up the cell.

"I'm recording all of this you sick—"

The phone slipped from her wet hand. It fell into a puddle with a *plop.* "No!" Maude cried. She dropped to her knees and pawed at the muddy ground for her phone.

Ben, over his momentary distraction, raced for the mansion

carrying Pringle. The door needed no prompting and flew open. Ben placed Pringle on her feet and hurried outside to retrieve her discarded clothing. Once inside, he leaned against the door, trying to slow his breath and the wild staccato of his heart.

He pushed away and pointed at Pringle. "Don't *ever* do that again! Do you want to get us both arrested?"

"I don't understand, Ben Hastings? What is wrong with dancing?"

"Lots of people dance, Pringle, but not *naked*! You have to keep your clothes on."

Ben took a deep breath. He handed Pringle her clothes. "You need to get dressed. Maude probably has a SWAT team already on their way here."

"What's a SWAT—"

"Please! No questions. Just dry off and get dressed."

"Alright, Ben Hastings."

She dropped the damp bedsheet wrapped around her. Nude with water still dripping from her hair, she leaped into the air and flew in dizzying circles around the room, droplets spraying from her wings. Air-dried, she landed beside Ben and picked through her clothing.

"The brazier and punties go on first, right Ben Hastings?"

The breath caught in Ben's throat. The sight of Pringle's nude body stirred such a powerful reaction within him, he couldn't speak, couldn't think clearly.

When he could at last utter a coherent sentence, he said, "It's brassiere and panties. And you can't get dressed in front of me, Pringle. I don't—I can't see you undressed. Don't do it again. Please don't do that again."

"But why, Ben Hastings?" Troubled, Pringle ran her hands up and down her body. "Don't you like me?"

"Of course I like you."

Maybe too much. Far too much.

Chapter 33

Ben opened his laptop on the kitchen table, and checked his course syllabus. He made a few adjustments, then leaned back, satisfied. Everything was ready for his students' return after spring break. A knock came from the front door.

Ben got up and looked through the window. The rain had let up, and Archie stood on the porch twirling a pair of sunglasses in his hand. "Let him in," he called out.

"I live to obey your commands, oh worshipful master," the door replied and swung open.

Archie walked in with a grin on his face. "Door's still a smartass I see."

"Yeah, I'm sure there's a comedy club routine in its future," Ben groused.

Archie frowned. "Sounds like your day hasn't been great. What's got you so pissed?"

"Hmm. Let's see. Where do I begin? The shopping experience from hell with Pringle? A fine for having weeds, courtesy of Maude, who when not filling her role as the neighborhood HOA president, doubles as the wicked bitch of the west? Pringle doing her best stripper routine and dancing butt-naked in the rain? No,

I think the topper has to be the phone call I received from Mickey Sledge, Cara's dad. He hasn't been able to contact her, and he practically accused me of burying her in a dark hole somewhere."

"Man, you *have* had a bad day." Archie looked around. "Speaking of Pringle, where is she?"

Ben pointed upstairs. "Sleeping on my bed." He chewed on his lip. "It's weird because she's doing the usual prawn stuff like buzzing around, doing backflips, and all of a sudden, announces she's sleepy. The next thing I know, she flies up to my bedroom, lies down on the bed, and is asleep in seconds like she's been hit with a tranquilizer dart. She did the same thing at Hank's store, remember?"

Archie rubbed his face. "Yeah, I do, and I think I know why. Look, we need to talk. Still have some beer?"

Ben tried to read Archie's expression, but he hurried past him. A cold tendril of apprehension crawled up Ben's back, and he followed after him.

Archie pointed at the empty bottles on the kitchen table. "Looks like you've already had an early start." He tossed them into the trash.

"You're stalling. What is it you think I need alcohol in order to tell me?"

Archie took two bottles from the fridge, twisted the tops off both, and handed one to Ben. He sat heavily in a chair. "Have a seat, and I'll tell you."

Ben grabbed the beer and joined Archie. "Okay. What's going on?"

"I got another look at the fairy book. This time, Hank showed me an illustration of a fairy undergoing a metamorphosis into a full-sized human. The translated inscription said this change, once complete, means the fairy can't return to her world. It would cause certain death for her to even try."

Ben stared at Archie. "You think that could happen to Pringle?"

Archie toyed with the bottle in his hand. "Nothing's certain, but Hank is convinced. I know it sounds crazy, but the dude knows things no one else does. The fact she grew to full-size like he said she would, means the man must know what he's talking about."

Archie stopped twirling the bottle and put it down with a *thump*. "You probably don't want to hear this, but Hank thinks she may only have days before the change is irreversible. When that happens, there's no going back to Almeera."

Events had moved so fast since Ben walked out of the clock and into Archie's bookstore—with Pringle hiding in his pocket—he'd given only brief consideration to when she would return to her world. At some level, he knew it had to happen someday, but that possibility seemed to push farther into the future every day he spent with her.

Maybe you don't want her to return. Maybe you want her to stay.

"Hank also reiterated that because of Pringle's, uh, *attachment* to you, she won't return unless you convince her to."

Anger gripped Ben. "You mean *make* her go back whether she wants to or not."

Archie spread his hands. "Don't shoot the messenger, dude. Just telling you what Hank said."

Ben scrubbed his face with both hands. "Sorry. It's been a shitty day, and I thought—I thought we would have more time."

Archie cocked his head. He nudged his chin at Ben. "You don't want her to go back, do you? You want her to stay."

"What? Of course I do! She's a prawn from another world, and we have nothing in common. Besides, I *have* a girlfriend, and I need to spend a lot more time with her if we're going to work things out."

Archie dismissed the comment with a wave of his hand. "What's that adage? You can't bullshit a bullshitter? The stuff you're spreading could fertilize an entire pasture. Your *girlfriend* slept with another man and then stood you up the first chance she got, so don't even go there. I've also seen how you and Pringle interact, and you can deny it, but I know this 'bond' Hank mentioned isn't one way. You feel it too."

"You're crazy. You don't know what you're talking about."

"Really? What's Pringle look like now that she's the grown-up version of a fairy?"

Heat crept up Ben's neck. "She looks, you know, like Pringle."

Archie tapped his lips. "Oh, sure, of course she does. You know, I haven't seen Pringle since her growth spurt. How 'bout you wake her up so I can see the perky little prawn."

"Okay, okay," Ben blurted. "She looks good, great, a real stunner. Is that what you want to hear?"

"No, what I want to hear is the truth. How *do* you feel about her?"

Ben started a retort but abruptly shut his mouth. He closed his eyes. Archie was right. He couldn't continue to act as if what he felt for Pringle was transitory, like an irritating rash that would eventually fade away. The fact that Archie wouldn't let it drop, wouldn't let him continue to delude himself, caused his frustration to boil to the surface.

""What's it to you, Archie? Pringle's not *your* problem. I get that seeing a fairy in the flesh is real excitement, something you claim has been missing in your life. I even get that being a millionaire may not be all it's cracked up to be. What I *don't* understand is why Pringle's future or even mine matters to you. You could walk away, right now, go back to your store, book collection, and millionaire life, and no one would blame you, least of all me."

Silence, like a thick blanket, followed Ben's outburst.

Archie took another drink, then looked up at Ben. "You have a lot of friends in college, Ben? How about high school?"

"A few."

"Let me guess. You were on the debate team and probably the secretary of the Student Council. You played sports in Jr. High and found out you weren't good enough to ever play at the varsity level, so instead, you became a team manager. How am I doing so far?"

At Ben's silence, Archie nodded. "That's what I thought. I bet you were a good student, but not good enough to place in the top ten percent, so you had to go to a community college and work your way up to a four-year university."

"What's this got to do with anything?" Ben snapped.

Archie ignored the question. "Me, I was in One Act Play. I can still quote my lines from The Bridge to Terabithia. I entered all the math and computer apps academic competitions in high school, and was a multiple district champion for four years straight. But you know what? My so-called appeal didn't stretch much farther than that. I'm the only black person I know whose lack of rhythm can make a scarecrow look like the second-coming of Michael Jackson. I went through high school and college as good 'ole Archie Jones, everyone's friend but no one's *good* friend."

He leaned closer. "Remember when I told you I became an actuary because I liked numbers? I lied. The real reason is that I decided if I was going to go through life lonely, I might as well get paid for it. And winning the lottery hasn't changed a thing in my life. Not a damn thing."

Archie tipped the beer back and drank the rest of it. He wiped his mouth with the back of his hand. "I thought I recognized you as someone like me, someone who could use a real friend."

He stood up. "Guess I was wrong. Don't worry. I won't bother you anymore."

He turned to leave, but Ben reached out and grabbed his arm before he could take a step. "I'm sorry for being an asshole, Archie. I'm tired, frustrated, but mostly, I'm conflicted…and I could really use a friend to help me."

Archie flashed a smile. "Well, why didn't you say so." He plopped back into his chair. "I'm all ears."

Ben grinned at Archie's reaction. Then the quandary with Pringle returned, and his smile quickly disappeared. "The truth is Pringle saved my life. I would have died on Almeera if not for her. And I'd be lying if I said the prospect of her staying instead of returning to her world doesn't bother me nearly as much as it should."

They sat in silence. Finally, Archie looked at Ben. "Do you love her? Is that what you're saying?"

Ben tiredly rubbed his eyes. "I don't know what I'm saying. So much has happened so quickly, my head hasn't stopped spinning. All I know is I feel something for Pringle that's more than gratitude. And it's not something I've ever felt for anyone else."

Archie studied Ben. "I see. So, here's the big question—what now? Are you going to try to convince Pringle to return to Almeera or not?"

Ben's emotions roiled inside him like a bubbling pot. *Pringle saved my life, and now I can help her save hers. An easy choice, right?*

Then why didn't it feel easy?

Ben didn't consider himself to be particularly brave or noble. Although his moral compass sometimes tended to skew toward selfishness, he felt he tried to do the right thing most of the time. But the situation with Pringle…it left him tied in knots as if his mind and emotions were traveling in opposite directions.

"Ben?" Archie's voice broke his reverie.

"Huh? Oh, sorry," he sputtered. "I-I guess I need to persuade her to return to Almeera."

"You don't sound convinced."

Ben shook his head. "Doesn't matter. She's not from our world, and I won't let her get trapped here."

No matter how I feel.

The patrol car slowed as it passed the silver BMW.

It backed up. Officer Lacy Benson, a twenty year veteran of the Tyler police force, ran the plate. She turned to her partner, officer Rob Forte, driving the patrol car. "We got a hit. There's an APB on the car's owner."

They got out. The sports convertible, unlocked with the top down, allowed them to make a quick inspection of the interior. An expensive French leather purse sat in the backseat. The policewoman put on gloves and fished a wallet out of the purse. She flipped it open and scanned the license.

"Cara Sledge. That's our missing person."

She continued her search and found a cell phone. She tapped the surface, and the picture of Cara Sledge arm-in-arm with a tall young man appeared.

"Call it in," she told her partner. "Tell them we found Cara Sledge's car outside the *Bodies in Motion* fitness center." She studied the picture of the couple on the cell phone.

"And tell Dispatch we may have a person of interest."

CHAPTER 34

BEN SAT AT THE KITCHEN TABLE LONG AFTER ARCHIE left to drive home.

He tried to focus his thoughts on his classes and schedule. However, they kept returning to Pringle. He rationalized that she could make up her own mind and decide whether to stay or not, but his heart wouldn't let him believe such a lie. She lacked the maturity to make such a life-and-death decision, and besides, *he* knew there could be only one course of action.

Return to her world.

Restless, he got up and approached the door. As if sensing his state of mind, it swung open with no comment. He walked out on the porch, and with hands on hips, studied the overgrown yard. The rain hadn't improved the look. Instead of a dry, weed-choked lot, it looked like a *soggy*, weed-choked lot.

"There's no way I can make a dent in this jungle before the HOA meeting," he said to himself bitterly. "Maude's got to be laughing her ass off."

"What's the matter, Ben Hastings?"

Ben spun around. Pringle stood on the porch. "No-nothing," he stammered. "Just trying to figure out how I'm going to get this yard cleaned up before the HOA meeting."

Damn, she looks so good.

She had on the same jeans and blouse she wore out of the store. Despite having slept in them, they remained unwrinkled, her amber-gold hair gleaming in the early evening light.

Pringle's sea-green eyes studied him as if unconvinced. She walked over and threaded her arm through his. "Don't be troubled, Ben Hastings." She gestured at the lot. "It will be taken care of."

"Well, I don't see how." Her closeness, the warmth of her touch distracted him. He slipped an arm around her waist, a reflex act he didn't realize until too late. She snuggled closer. As usual, her scent assaulted his nose. Before he could stop himself, he buried his face in Pringle's thick, honey-brown hair. He inhaled deeply, the aroma of wildflowers, cloves, and rich soil filling his nostrils.

She turned and looked up at him with a gaze that held none of the old Pringle he knew so well. Gone was the happy-go-lucky prawn from Almeera. Instead, she gazed at him with different eyes.

The eyes of a woman.

Ben swallowed. It took every ounce of his self-control to disengage and gently push her away. "We better get inside before Maude sees us and decides to call the police again."

Ben spent time surfing on his laptop, but despite his best efforts to deflect his mind on *anything* but Pringle, his thoughts always returned to her. It didn't help that Pringle made sure to sit in a chair nearby. Instead of her usual effervescent self—an object in constant motion like a firefly on steroids—she just rested in her seat and watched him. The unnerving experience finally proved to be too much.

"What? What is it?" he blurted. "You're looking at me like I'm Humpty Dumpty, as if I'm going to fall and break into pieces."

"I don't know Humpty Dumpty, Ben Hastings. I just like to watch you."

It immediately struck Ben that Pringle didn't ask *who* the nursery rhyme character was—another clue to her state of flux.

Ben closed the laptop and drummed his fingers on the table.

He stood up and fished his keys from his pocket. "I'm hungry. Let's go get some fast food."

"How fast does it run, Ben Hastings?"

Ben couldn't help himself. He chuckled. "You've got a lot to learn, Pringle. I'm talking about a place where you don't have to wait long to get something to eat. C'mon."

Pringle followed him out of the mansion and to the VW. The sun dangled low in the sky as they drove away, and Ben took them to a nearby McDonald's. He pulled into the drive-through and studied the menu. He ordered a Big Mac, fries, and a Coke. After deliberating what to get Pringle, he added a side salad, apple slices, and a strawberry-banana smoothie.

By the time they got back to the mansion, night had fallen. Ben led Pringle back to the kitchen table and distributed their food. Pringle picked up pieces of the salad with her fingers and began to eat. Ben stopped her, and used the plastic fork that came with the salad to spear a piece of lettuce. He held it up and pantomimed putting it in his mouth

"That's how you are supposed to eat."

He put the fork down beside by her salad, and picked up his hamburger.

Pringle stared at the fork. "Why, Ben Hastings?"

"Because people here use utensils to eat with."

"But prawns use their hands."

"You're not on Almeera anymore, Pringle. People use a knife, fork, and spoon."

"But you're using your hands, Ben Hastings, not the 'tensils."

Ben paused in mid-bite.

He put the burger down. "I know it's confusing, but its okay to eat some stuff with your hands."

"Which stuff?"

Ben threw up his hands. "I don't know. A lot of things. And before you ask, I'm not going to go over them all tonight."

Pringle returned to the salad and tried to spear a piece of

tomato with the fork. It dangled precariously on the tip of a tine until she dropped it in her mouth. She pointed the fork at Ben's burger. "What kind of food is that, Ben Hastings?"

Ben glanced at the hamburger. "You mean the patty? It's ground beef, meat from a cow."

"*Eww.*" Pringle turned away in disgust.

Ben kicked himself mentally. He should have known that Pringle, a prawn of the forest, would make food choices that made the most dedicated vegan look amateurish by comparison.

Appetite gone, he threw the rest of the hamburger away. It had been a long day, and he wanted to turn in early. Pringle followed him up to the bedroom and fully-clothed, lay down on the end of his bed. Despite all the time and money spent at Kohl's, it didn't occur to him to buy her a nightgown. He hunted through his closet until he found an old T-shirt. He handed it to Pringle.

"Here. Put this on to sleep in."

Pringle started to put the T-shirt over the clothes she had on. "No," Ben groaned. "You have to take your clothes off, *then* put it on."

She started to undress. "Stop!" Ben held up his hands. "Wait until I'm in the bathroom to get undressed."

He spun around to hurry to the bathroom but stopped and abruptly turned back. "And keep your punties—dammit, I mean panties—on."

He shut the door and leaned heavily against it. *Just get through the rest of the night, Ben. Tomorrow will be soon enough to sort everything out.*

Fifteen minutes later, showered and teeth brushed, he emerged from the bathroom. He breathed a sigh of relief at the sight of Pringle in the T-shirt and sprawled at the end of his bed.

Ben crawled under the sheets. He glanced at Pringle. Head pillowed on her hands, she smiled at him. The sight caused a warm ball of pleasure to bloom in the pit of his stomach.

He turned off the light, rolled onto his stomach, and went to sleep.

Hours later, Pringle stirred and sat up.

She studied Ben. Fast asleep, his chest rose and fell in a regular cadence. Her wings beat the air, and she silently rose into the air. She hovered over his still form, her face inches from his.

She kissed his cheek. "Don't worry, Ben Hastings," she whispered, "I will fix your small forest."

Ben mumbled and turned over.

Pringle darted toward her pouch, reached in, and pulled out two handfuls of dust. She zipped out of the room and down the stairs. The door opened, and she flew out. Once past the porch, she hung motionless in the air.

Rows of hutches—houses, according to Ben Hastings—lined either side of the street in front of her. Some had torches lit, but most were darkened, including the nearby hutch the one called Maude lived in. The distant bark of some creature was the only sound to mar the silence.

Pleased, Pringle shot up into the air. "*Whee!*"

She spiraled in dizzying circles, releasing the dust clutched in her hands. It glittered and sparkled like diamonds as it floated down to cover the mansion and grounds. Pringle clapped in delight as the last of the dust settled. She zipped back and landed on the porch. The door opened.

"Well done—"

The door quieted as Pringle put her finger to her lips.

"*Well done, mistress,*" it whispered. "*Things will certainly be interesting now.*"

Pringle nodded and flew up the stairs. She alighted at the end of the bed, curled up, and went to sleep.

CHAPTER 35

MAUDE SAT AT HER DESK AND STUDIED THE ACTION items on the HOA agenda.

The desk, strategically placed by a large picture window in the living room, gave her a vantage point to see the comings and goings of all her neighbors. As HOA president, she considered it her duty to keep track of the neighborhood activities—and why she was prepared to throw the book at Ben Hastings.

She hit the print key, and a fresh copy of the agenda spat from her printer. She snatched it up and held it to her chest in a lover's embrace. *By the time I'm through with you, Hastings, you'll wish you never bought that dinosaur you call a house.*

The ancient rathole next door was the only black mark to her stellar reign as president. Despite her best efforts to have the place condemned, the old mansion's historical designation stymied her at every turn. When it became clear Hastings wouldn't spend the time and money to fix up the ugly eyesore, she moved on to Plan B, a level she reserved for the lowest of the low—renters. If he wouldn't willingly polish up the place, she'd force him to.

Maude's ruminations were interrupted by an unusual spear of light that flashed through her window. The angle of the light appeared to come from the direction of Hastings' home. She pushed the curtains further aside for a better look.

Her breath caught in her throat.

The agenda dropped from her hand and floated to the floor. She rushed to the front door, jerked it open, and ran out into her front yard. "No," she breathed. "It can't be."

The sight she beheld could pass for a scaled down version of the Biltmore House and grounds. An immaculate lawn spread from the edge of the property to the mansion. Neatly trimmed hedges and flowering shrubs ran alongside the fence, the flagstone path, and along the mansion's raised porch. The flowers, in pastels of red, gold, pink, and yellow, were alive with buzzing bees and gaily-colored butterflies. Redbuds, Dogwoods, Saucer Magnolias, Crepe Myrtles, and other ornamental tress dotted the landscape. The formerly filthy, algae-encrusted birdbath and fountain, gleamed in the morning light, a dainty spray of crystal-line water looping up into the air to splash back into the basin with a pleasant burble.

The ugly, rust-stained wrought-iron fence circling the property, stood rail-straight and glowed under a fresh coat of black paint. Beside the porch, jasmine formed a lattice-like pattern. It threaded its way up a trellis in a profusion of vines that ended in delicate sprigs of white flowers, their delicate scent perfuming the air. Sunlight sparkled off spotless windows, and everything from the corbels to the gothic arches looked brand new. The entire exterior of the mansion looked clean and fresh, as if a team of restoration experts had worked nonstop for months to bring the structure back to its original form.

Anger filled Maude. "What trick is this?" she snapped.

Elbows swinging side-to-side, she stalked up to the gate, shoved it open, and marched up the flagstone path to the porch steps. As she passed the stone lions flanking the steps, their heads turned to look at her. The lion on her left yawned, exposing long, stone fangs.

Maude's hand went to her throat. "Wh-wh-wh—"

"What's the matter? Cat got your tongue?" it asked with a wink. A rumble of laughter rolled from both lions.

A muted scream left Maude. Her hands gripped the railing in a white-knuckled grasp as she backed up the steps.

"Hey, lady. Ease off on the death-grip, okay? You're going to scratch my paint."

Maude spun around. She gasped at the sight of a gargoyle's metal head mounted on the top of the railing. It stared straight at her. Her hands flew to her mouth stifling another scream.

"That's better," the gargoyle said. "Manhandling ain't cool."

Maude continued to retreat up and onto the porch. A pair of white rocking chairs flanked a patio table on her right,. She collapsed into one, her mind doing cartwheels as she tried to process what her eyes and ears had seen and heard.

"I know. Life's a bitch, ain't it?" Her head jerked to the other chair.

A sausage-sized, yellow and black bee reclined in the rocker next to her. Sunglasses perched on its face, a pair of its multiple arms stretched behind its head, it continued, "I mean, all day, every day, its pollinate this, pollinate that. You'd think there'd at least be a holiday for hard-working bees, but no, it's always go, go, go, every stinkin' day."

Maude shot to her feet. She backed away from the bee, her mouth working but no sound came out.

"Madame, do you feel faint? Do you need a cold drink?" the door asked.

Maude drew in a huge lungful of air. "*Aieeeeeeeeeeeee!*" she screamed.

"*Humph!* Serves me right for trying to be polite," the door huffed.

Maude raced down the steps, tripped, and rolled to come face-to-face with one of the stone lions.

"*Grrr,*" it said.

Another scream trumpeted from Maude's lips. She picked herself up, and arms flapping over her head, sprinted down the flagstone steps to the gate. Shoving it open, she fled down the sidewalk shrieking like a diesel train.

A soft kiss on his cheek awakened Ben.

He opened his eyes and sat up. Pringle stood beside his bed beaming.

"Get up, Ben Hastings."

He yawned and stretched. "What time is it?"

"The time is the sun is up."

"Oh...thanks."

He grabbed his phone and checked the time. *Seven in the morning.*

Ben stumbled out of bed, put on an old T-shirt and jogging shorts, then slipped his feet into some flip-flops. With Pringle hovering beside him, he made his way down the steps and into the kitchen. He put a K-cup in the coffeemaker, and while it percolated, poured Fruit Loops into bowls for himself and Pringle. He added milk and showed Pringle a spoon.

"Another 'tensil, Ben Hastings?"

"Yes. It's called a spoon. Eat your cereal with it."

The Keurig beeped, and Ben grabbed his cup. When he turned around, Pringle's bowl was empty and milk dribbled from her chin. The spoon lay beside her, untouched. With a shake of his head, he took a paper towel and dabbed her chin dry.

Pringle tugged on Ben's arm. "Let's go. I want to show you something."

"What? I haven't even had my coffee yet."

She tugged again. "Let's go outside, Ben Hastings," she repeated.

Ben studied Pringle. Excitement dripped from her like rain.

What's up with her? I haven't seen her this amped since we walked out of the clock and into Archie's bookstore.

"Okay," he said with a sigh. "But I'm taking my coffee with me." He pointed at the T-shirt she slept in. "And you can't go outside dressed like that. Put on some of the clothes we—"

Pringle zipped into the air and out of the room before he could finish the sentence. Ben shook his head. "She must *really* have something she wants to show me," he mumbled.

He took a sip of the coffee and ambled to the front door.

"All hail the wonderful, the mighty, the glorious—"

"Yadda, yadda, yadda," Ben grumbled. "It's too early for that shit. Just open up and keep your wooden yap shut."

"Words to live by, Magnificence." The door swung open.

Ben stepped out onto the porch. He sensed an immediate difference, as if the atmosphere around him had undergone a subtle, yet profound change. He sniffed the air. It carried notes of wildflowers, jasmine, and other green, leafy things. The scent carried a familiarity which he struggled to identify. Then it struck him why it seemed so familiar.

The air smelled just like Pringle.

With a buffeting of wind, Pringle zipped out the door and landed beside him. Ben took a step back and studied her. She wore blue jean shorts and a red blouse. He nodded in approval. He half-expected her to be wearing a wildly mismatched set of clothing. However, the only blemish to her ensemble were the mismatched sandals. One was black, the other white.

Pringle swept her arm in an arc. "Do you like it, Ben Hastings?"

Ben casually looked around…and dropped his coffee cup.

The porch, the railing, the steps, the grounds, everything gleamed with a new freshness. Gone were the weeds, the overgrown lot, and in its place, a picture-perfect yard that could grace the cover of *Better Homes & Gardens.*

A huge black and yellow bee buzzed up to him. "Hello,

Guvnor! Top of the mornin' to ya. Well, gotta go. Flowers won't pollinate themselves!" It flew off.

Numb, Ben stumbled down the porch steps. He grabbed the railing to steady himself. The gargoyle head swiveled toward him. "Keep a steady grip, sir. Wouldn't want you to take a fall."

He reached the flagstone path flanked by the stone lions. "Everything's right as rain, chief," the lion on the left said.

"Yeah, except for the crazy lady next door," said the lion on the right. "She lit outta here like her pants were on fire." Laughter burst from the pair.

Ben's brain finally engaged. "Ma-Maude's been here?"

Impatient, Pringle placed her hands on Ben's shoulders and turned him around. "Ben Hastings, *look!*"

At the sight of the mansion, Ben's knees weakened. If not for Pringle's steady grip, they might have buckled. *The entire estate looks brand-spanking new!*

"What—how?" he began. Then it hit him. *She used fairy dust just like she did on the door.*

The sound of a police siren interrupted his thought. He frowned as it drew closer. At the screech of tires turning into the subdivision, Ben turned and a patrol car raced toward them. The police car squealed to a stop at the curb, and two cops jumped out.

Guns drawn.

CHAPTER 36

"KEEP YOUR HANDS UP WHERE I CAN SEE THEM!" BARKED the first officer out of the car.

Ben's hands shot up.

Pringle giggled. "This is fun, Ben Hastings!"

"It's not a game, Pringle! And tell your...*friends* not to move or say a thing!"

With another giggle, Pringle put her finger to her lips, then raised her hands to comply.

As the two officers cautiously approached, Ben recognized the one in the lead. *Maloney* was stenciled on her nametag—the same policewoman who had responded to Maude's call earlier in the week.

Ben cleared his throat. "What's this all about, officer?"

"We received a call about a terrorist act. Are you armed, sir?"

"No, of course not. Look, this is absurd—"

"Hands up!"

Ben clamped his mouth shut and held his hands high. Maloney's partner kept his gun trained on Ben while Maloney patted him down, then she repeated the frisk on Pringle. She holstered her weapon and motioned for her partner to do the same.

Anger boiled within Ben. "Since when is it a terrorist act to have coffee on my own porch?"

A shrill voice cried out before the officer could answer. "Good! Cuff 'em and haul them off to jail!"

Maude hurried down the sidewalk, her bathrobe flapping like a flag in a stiff breeze.

She burst through the gate, stopped beside them, and shook her finger at Ben. "Lock 'em up and throw away the key!"

"Ma'am, are you the one who called in the complaint?" Maloney asked.

"Yes!"

"What terroristic act did these people commit?"

Maude blinked. "What? Are you kidding? Look at this place! Twenty-four hours ago, it could pass as a set piece for a movie shoot in Transylvania. Now look at it!"

Maloney's jaw tightened. "Ma'am, you can't call the police with false or frivolous claims. What you have done is at least a misdemeanor."

"Open your eyes and *look!*" Maude blurted. She rushed over to one of the stone lions. "This statue talked to me." She gestured at the gargoyle head at the top of the railing. "That thing warned me not to grip the handrail too tight. And the bees," she waved at the bees buzzing about the flowers, "one complained about the work it took to pollinate all the blossoms."

Maude pointed an accusing finger at Ben. "Don't be fooled by him. He's not what he appears to be. Nobody could transform this broken-down roach motel overnight. Not anybody normal!" She wheeled on Pringle. "And her! She ran around in the rain without a stitch on, just laughing and acting crazy."

Maloney and her partner shared a look. "I think we've heard enough." She turned to Ben. "Mr. Hastings, we apologize for the misunderstanding."

"That's okay, officer. I know you need to take these things seriously."

Maude stared at Maloney in disbelief. "You mean you're not going to do anything?"

"No, ma'am. I *am* going to do something."

"Good!"

Maloney took a ticket pad from her front pocket, scribbled on it, then handed a copy to Maude. "Sign here."

Maude's hand went to her throat. "You're giving me a citation? For what?"

"Trespassing, ma'am."

"You must be joking. I'm not going to sign anything!"

Maloney removed a copy of the ticket from the pad. "Suit yourself." She handed it to Maude. "The citation includes a toll-free number to call for the date and time to appear in court. Do you have any questions, ma'am?"

Maude stared at the ticket as if it were a poisonous snake. "No," she answered, her voice barely above a whisper.

"Then our business is concluded here." Maloney and her partner moved to either side of Maude. "We'll escort you off the property."

Ben gleefully watched the two officers lead Maude out the gate and onto the sidewalk. They'd taken only a few steps when he called out, "Hey, Maude!"

She stopped. "What?" she snarled.

"See you at the HOA meeting Thursday."

He grinned. If looks could kill, Maude's murderous gaze would have reduced him to a smoking pile of ashes. He spun around, whistling.

So this is what it means to have a song in my heart.

Ben led Pringle back into the mansion, chuckling all the way. He picked her up and swung her around.

"Pringle, you're fabulous. I just wish I'd taken a picture of Maude's face as the police led her away." He pulled Pringle close and hugged her.

A liquid heat tingled within him. It started at his toes and worked its way up to his knees, legs, and the rest of his body. Pringle's warmth, smell, and how her body molded itself to him threatened to drive all rational thoughts from his mind. *She feels so good!*

He kissed her. This time, he held nothing back, and she returned his kiss with equal zeal. "Touch my wings, Ben Hastings," she whispered.

"But you said prawns don't like their wings touched."

"Not to those special to us, Ben Hastings. And you are special to me."

A lump rose in Ben's throat. He gently ran his hands up and down her wings. She shivered and pressed her face against his chest. He lost track of time, didn't know how long they stood together as he stroked her wings, only that he felt more content than at any point in his life.

Then reality wormed its way into his mind.

The contentment slipped away like air from a leaking balloon. *She has to go back to Almeera. I can't let whatever feelings I have for Pringle stop me. It's not fair to her.*

Pringle sensed his discomfort and looked up. "What's wrong, Ben Hastings? Did I do something to displease you? I'll start using 'tensils, I promise."

"No. I don't think you could ever displease me." *Tell her! Tell her she must return to her world or be forever trapped here.*

He swallowed, hard, cold guilt threatening to choke him. "We-we need to talk. But I just don't think I can do it right now."

Pringle studied him. At last, she reached up and ran her fingers across his cheek. "Take your time, Ben Hastings. Whenever you are ready."

Her comment, spoken in a mature, un-fairylike way, gave him yet another clue that Pringle's progression from prawn to woman continued unabated.

She crooked her finger. The door opened, and Ben's dropped coffee cup flew through the air. It floated into his hand.

"Let's finish breakfast, Ben Hastings. This time I'll use a 'poon.'"

Mind swirling, Ben followed her back to the kitchen.

Ben sat on an old, dusty sofa in the mansion's living room.

Pringle's head lay in his lap, fast asleep. Not long after breakfast, she experienced one of her sudden bouts of drowsiness. She curled up with him on the sofa and fell asleep within seconds.

He brushed aside a stray lock of amber hair from her cheek. The delicate tips of her ears protruded like mountain peaks from under her warm rush of hair. He studied her face, a picture of peaceful bliss. Beautiful would be too mundane a term to describe her. Exotic came close but still missed the mark. It was as if a gifted artist had taken several paintings and combined their best elements into a single masterpiece.

Yes, that's it. Pringle is a masterpiece that all others pale in comparison to.

He knew then that he was falling in love with her. Not some sappy, shallow, fleeting love, but a love that ached like a bruise that wouldn't fade. The quandary threatened to tear him apart. He didn't want her to return to Almeera. *It'd be easy. Just do nothing and in a few more days she won't be able to return to her world.*

A totally selfish act, good for him but a death sentence for Pringle.

In preparing for his *Myths & Legends* class, he'd done a fair bit of research on fairies. Although the tales varied wildly, one theme remained constant—fairies are immortal. If Pringle stayed with him, she would lose her immortality, age, and eventually die.

A tear slid down his face. It hung like a glistening dew drop on his chin, then fell onto Pringle's cheek. Her skin rippled like waves on a beach, then flashed a rainbow of colors. It all happened in an instant, and then her flesh returned to a rosy, peach hue.

Pringle's eyes opened. The color of rich grass, they held his in an unwavering gaze. "I will not leave you, Ben Hastings."

Now the tears came in a rush. Ben brushed them aside. "You have to, baby. You have to return to Almeera. If you stay with me, you'll die." Emotion constricted his throat, and he could barely choke the words out.

A sharp knock at the door ripped Ben's attention from Pringle. He slid from beneath her and ordered the door to open. A pair of plainclothes detectives stood outside, a black SUV parked behind them beside the curb.

Ben planted his feet wide, nostrils flaring. "Okay, what's my crazy next-door neighbor told you guys now?"

The first detective, dark hair buzzed short in military-style fashion, flashed his badge and credentials. "Detective Brice Green, sir." He gestured at his partner, "And this is Detective Alvin Torres."

Ben waved his hand. "Yeah, yeah. I repeat, what's Maude Thorne accused me of now?"

"We're not here because of your neighbor, sir."

Ben frowned. "I don't understand. Then why are you here?"

"To question you about the disappearance of Cara Sledge."

CHAPTER 37

"C-CARA?" HE STUTTERED. "SHE'S MISSING?"

"Yes. You weren't aware your girlfriend is missing?"

Ben fumbled to process the news. "No. Of course not."

Green's hard look told Ben volumes. They suspect *me!*

"Maybe I need a lawyer."

"Only the guilty need lawyers, Mr. Hastings. Do you need one?"

Ben held up a shaking hand. "Hold on a second."

He fished out his phone and walked to the end of the porch. He punched a contact number.

"Hello?"

"Archie! A couple of detectives are here. They want to question me about Cara."

"Huh? Why"

"They say she's disappeared."

"Didn't you say her dad acted like you'd done something to her."

"Yes, but that's crazy. I never dreamed he'd contact the police. What am I going to do?"

A long pause followed. Detective Green cleared his throat. "Mr. Hastings?"

"Hold on. Give me a minute."

Archie's voice returned. "I have a lawyer who did a lot of my legal work when I won the lottery. You'd be surprised how much paperwork there is. She's not a criminal defense attorney, but I bet she knows someone who is."

"I need a criminal defense attorney? That's practically admitting I'm guilty!"

"You have a couple of detectives at your doorstep wanting to question you about your girlfriend's alleged disappearance. I'd say that qualifies you as a suspect, whether you like it or not. Let me make a quick call. With a little luck, my lawyer can hook you up with a defense attorney."

Pringle chose that moment to stroll out onto the porch. The detectives' attention riveted on her.

"Excuse me, ma'am," Green said. "Who are you?"

Pringle flashed him a bright smile. "I'm Ben Hastings' girlfriend."

Ben's heart dropped to his stomach. "Make the call. I'll stall them as long as I can." He clicked off and walked back to the detectives.

"I'll gladly answer your questions, but I'll have to talk to my lawyer first. He's, uh, going to call me back."

The detectives shared a smug look. They loosened their ties, and each took a seat in the rocking chairs.

"We'll wait," Green said.

Pringle sensed the tension. She moved to Ben's side. "What's wrong, Ben Hastings?"

Ben led her to the farthest corner of the porch and hooked a thumb at the detectives. "They are," he whispered. "I'll explain everything later. Just don't say a thing, and let me do all the talking."

Eyes wide, she nodded.

The call back—ten minutes later—seemed like it took hours.

Ben snatched the phone from his back pocket like a drowning man would grab for a life preserver.

"Hello!"

"Mr. Hastings?"

"Yes!"

"My name is Elliot Grimes. You were referred to me by a colleague. Am I to understand you need a criminal defense attorney?"

"Yes…but I'm not guilty!" Ben blurted.

"Let's not get ahead of ourselves, Mr. Hastings. First things first, I charge three hundred dollars an hour, including any phone consultation."

Ben gulped. "Th-three hundred dollars an hour?"

Grimes chuckled. "Don't worry, Mr. Hastings. A Mr. Archimedes Jones arranged to pay my fee. Are you agreeable with this arrangement?"

Archie?

"Sure—I mean, yes!"

"Good. Are the police there at your residence?"

"Yes. They're sitting and waiting."

"Have they read you your rights?"

What the hell? Read me my rights? If any doubt remained about how serious Ben's situation was, it evaporated with the lawyer's question.

"No, they haven't."

"Good. Put me on speaker, and let me talk to them."

Ben approached the detectives and held up his phone.

Grimes's voice asked, "With whom do I have the pleasure of speaking?"

Green introduced himself and his partner.

"What's the problem here, Detective Green?"

"We just want to ask Mr. Hastings a few questions."

"I understand. Can you tell me why?"

"We have a missing person whose cell was recovered from

her abandoned car. According to her call record, *your* client spoke to her last."

"Hmm. That's pretty circumstantial, detective. Are you planning on talking to all the others on the missing person's call list?"

"Just following up on all the leads, counselor. However, I find it odd your client is reluctant to answer questions that might help us find his girlfriend. But that's okay. We can come back later if you like—maybe with a search warrant this time."

"A search warrant based on a single phone call? Don't bluff me, detective. Even if you *could* find a judge to issue a search warrant, I'll get it thrown out before the ink has dried on the paper. You'll need to do better than that."

Green, his jaw clenched, growled, "How's this? A witness heard Cara Sledge arguing with your client right before she went missing. Also, our understanding is Ms. Sledge is Mr. Hastings' girlfriend, but when we show up today, *another* young lady introduces herself as his girlfriend."

"Oh, the horrors! A young, single man with more than one girlfriend? Call out the National Guard!"

Ben struggled to keep a grin off his face. Grimes was good—very good.

"I need time to talk to my client, Detective Green, so I'm going to insist you come back later."

Green, his face the color of a sunburned strawberry, gestured to his partner. "We're done here." He whirled on Ben. "Being uncooperative just made you our number one suspect. But don't worry. We'll be back, and *this* time you'll answer *all* our questions!"

They stalked back to the SUV. With a squeal of tires, it roared off.

"They've left," Ben said.

"We've bought some time," Grime's answered, "but I have no doubt the good detective will be back. In the meantime, give me the Cliff Notes version of what's happened. I'll get more detailed information from you later."

Ben's mind squirmed as he considered what he could and definitely *couldn't* tell Elliot Grimes. No one, not even his lawyer, would believe he'd visited an alternate world via an enchanted grandfather clock. He decided to stick with the story he told Cara—he'd been too busy fixing the mansion to call or text her. She became furious with him and then stood him up on their lunch date.

When he finished, Grime's asked for the restaurant's name, when he arrived to meet Cara, when he left, and if he knew the name of the waiter who'd served him. The last thing he asked was for a screenshot of the call log on Ben's phone.

When the call ended, Ben felt drained, as if he'd just run a 5K. He collapsed into one of the rockers on the porch, his mind spinning. *What's happened to Cara?*

Despite her tryst with Bronson Smith and her angry words with him, he couldn't help being worried about her. He took out his phone and visited all the social media sites he knew she frequented. He soon discovered she hadn't posted anything in over two days. A direct hit by a comet ending all life on Earth was more likely than Cara going dark on social media.

A feeling of dread crept up his spine. *Maybe something bad has happened to Cara.* Although he had no proof, he couldn't shake the certainty that she was in trouble.

A lot of trouble.

CHAPTER 38

PRINGLE INTERRUPTED BEN'S MOROSE THOUGHTS.
"Why are you sad, Ben Hastings?"

Ben shook his head. "I'm not sad, Pringle. I'm worried."

"What is 'worry', Ben Hastings?"

How do you explain worry to a woodland fairy who has never been anxious about anything her entire life?

"I'm concerned about Cara. Something might have happened to her."

"Does that mean you still care for her, Ben Hastings?"

The question—out of the blue—summed up Ben's entire dilemma. He'd wrestled with the same uncertainty since his return from Almeera. Was it betrayal he felt over Cara's unfaithfulness with Bronson Smith?

Or relief?

His feelings for Pringle colored everything, even what he *used* to think he felt for Cara. It left him with no clear answer.

"I don't know," he admitted. "Not anymore."

"Do you care for me?"

If her previous question surprised him, this one hit him like a roundhouse punch. He considered being evasive, even lying.

Admitting how he felt would only make her return to Almeera more difficult…for both of them. But they'd come too far, been through too much together for him to take such a cowardly path. She deserved the truth.

He turned and took her hands in his. "Yes. More than I ever thought possible. More than I ever felt for someone else." He squeezed her hands. "And that's why I want you to return to your world before it's too—"

Ben stopped. *Almeera. Pringle's world. That's it!*

Pringle clutched his arm. "Ben Hastings! Your face looks strange."

Ben grabbed his phone instead of answering. He punched a number and tapped his foot while he waited for the call to connect.

"Hey, Ben," Archie answered. "How did—"

"I think I know how to find Cara!" he blurted.

"You do? That's great, but how—"

"Listen! We're coming to your place in Jefferson."

"Uh, okay. When?"

"Just as soon as I run upstairs and get that damn key."

Ben pushed the VW to its limit. The van hummed along at sixty miles per hour, a bit faster going down hills and slower going up.

"Why are we going to Archie Jones's hutch?"

Ben glanced at Pringle. She'd asked the same question a dozen times.

He gave her the same answer. "You'll have to wait till we get there. I need to talk to Archie about what I have in mind."

Pringle crossed her arms with a *humph*. She looked so much like a disgruntled teenager, Ben fought to keep from laughing. The urge quickly faded—*more evidence of her transition to my world and less of hers.*

They pulled up to The Black Swan and got out. Archie waited

for them on the porch. He waved them through the door and followed them inside.

"Okay, what's this great plan of yours?" he asked.

Ben brushed past him and hurried up the steps to the second floor.

"Hey! You going to answer me?"

Ben kept going.

Archie threw up his hands and followed while Pringle launched into the air. They caught up with Ben at the old Otto Albrecht clock. He took the key from his pocket, unlocked the clock's lower panel, and opened it. He peered inside.

A staircase spiraled downward into the gloom.

Ben pumped his fist. "Yes! I can take the stairs back to the wizard's hutch."

Archie stared at Ben as if he'd just grown a third eye. "Huh? After all your warnings about Almeera, how you barely escaped with your life, and now you want to go back? *Have you lost your mind?*"

"You don't understand. It's the only way I can find out what's happened to Cara."

"Look, I don't know where she is, but I know where she's *not*, and that's Almeera."

Ben held up his hands. "I'm not crazy. Just let me explain."

Archie studied Ben for a long moment. Finally, he said, "Alright. Shoot."

"There's a scrying chamber in the wizard's hutch. I used it to, uh, look around. It can even see things in *our* world. I can use it to locate Cara."

Archie shook his head as if trying to clear the cobwebs from a deep sleep. "Whoa, whoa, *whoa!* You're telling me you can find Cara using the Almeeran equivalent of a spy drone?"

"Well…kinda. All I have to do is form an image of Cara in my mind, and it scries until it locates her."

Archie waved his hands. "Okay, stop right there. Start from the beginning and tell me the whole story about this scrying thing."

Ben took a deep breath and related how he and Pringle had stumbled upon the enormous hollow and the scrying chamber located at the top. He described the scrying pool and how he learned to use it. When he finished, Archie gave a slow shake of his head.

"Under normal circumstances, I'd say you need strong medication and serious therapy. But I've seen too many things to doubt you now. Either that, or we're both in a padded room sharing the same delusions. So…what is it you propose to do?"

"Simple. Use the clock to return to the wizard's hutch, find the scrying chamber, and locate Cara."

Archie pursed his lips. "Let's say you find her. What will you—"

"No!"

Pringle grabbed Ben's arm. It felt like a vise had closed over his flesh. "Don't let him go, Archie Jones! Ben Hastings could not even go a short way up the stairs. I flew him up to the chamber because he couldn't get there any other way. He will either get hurt, or fear will keep him from returning."

Ben stared at Pringle. Besides being the longest speech she'd uttered in their time together, she wore an angry, stubborn look as if Archie *didn't* stop him, *she* would.

A moment or two of thick silence passed. At last, Archie said, "You could go with him, Pringle. You could fly him up to the chamber again."

Pringle looked down and released Ben. "I can't, Archie Jones. Once I return, I will not be able to come back. The change…is too far along."

Ben and Archie shared a glance. Ben's heart felt like a lead weight. He turned to Pringle. "That's exactly why you *have* to go back before it's too late." He reached for her, but she skipped away.

"I said I would not leave you, Ben Hastings."

Her wings blurred in motion, and she flew to Archie. She

hovered before him. "Stop him, Archie Jones." Tears dripped from her chin. "I cannot bear harm coming to my Ben Hastings."

Archie cocked his head. "What if I went with him, Pringle? I could look out for Ben, help get him to the scrying chamber and back."

Pringle's eyes widened. "You would do this, Archie Jones?"

"Hold on," Ben cried. "You're not coming with me, Archie. It's too dangerous. I won't let you risk your life when it's my mess."

Archie's eyes flashed. "Pardon me," he said to Pringle and swept past her. He stopped inches from Ben. "First of all, it's my life. I can damn well do whatever I please with it. You got that?"

Ben swallowed. "Uh, yes."

"Second, I consider you a friend, and friends help each other out, right?"

"Right."

"And you'd do the same for me, wouldn't you, Ben?"

"Yes."

"Third, it's *my* clock, and the price for using it is that I come along for the ride. Deal?" He stuck out his hand.

A smile tugged at the corner of Ben's mouth. He shook Archie's hand. "Deal."

Pringle clapped with delight. She flew circles around them in a blur of motion. She alighted by Archie and hugged him.

"Wow. A fairy hug," he said with a huge smile. "Doesn't get better than that."

Archie turned to Ben. He rubbed his hands together. "Looks like we have some planning to do.

"Let's get started."

CHAPTER 39

AN ARRAY OF ITEMS LAY ON THE FLOOR IN FRONT OF THE grandfather clock. Archie scribbled on a pad as Ben went over each item one-by-one.

"Flashlight, batteries, bottled water, rope, grappling hook, gloves, Taser…Wait! Why do we need a Taser?"

"You said there were scary creatures on this world. We need some sort of protection just in case."

"Archie, the hutch is deserted. The only scary thing in the place is a book that growled at me when I opened it."

"What if the wizard returns and finds us trespassing? He could turn us into a frog or something."

Pringle giggled. "You are funny, Archie Jones."

Ben dusted off his hands. "You've been reading too many fairy tales. I don't even know if they have frogs on Almeera. Besides, when I was trapped there, the hutch felt like it'd been empty for a long time."

"Better safe than sorry."

Ben rolled his eyes. "Whatever. Anyway, if the list gets any longer, we'll be so tired carrying all this stuff, we won't be able to get up to the scrying chamber."

Archie snapped his fingers. "You're right." He hurried out

of the room and returned moments later with a handful of energy bars. He tossed some to Ben. "Let's divide everything up." He pushed a backpack to Ben and began to fill his own with the equipment strewn across the floor.

With a shrug, Ben took the backpack and stuffed it with part of their gear, then hefted it onto his shoulders. The weight didn't seem too bad, but he knew how long the distance down the staircase was. What felt light and easy now might feel like heavy boulders later.

Archie slipped his own backpack on. "Okay. Looks like we're ready."

Ben tried one last time. "Archie, are you *sure* you want to do this?"

Archie flipped his wrist. "Of course." He turned to Pringle. "Wish us luck." She hugged him. "*Oof.*" Her firm embrace drove the air from his lungs.

"Be safe, Archie Jones."

She then wrapped her arms around Ben. He held her for a long time, savoring the feel of her warm body and perfumed scent. She lifted her face and kissed him. Her lips tasted of wild honey and clover.

"Come back to me, Ben Hastings. I will wait for you."

Pringle released him and sat cross-legged facing the clock.

Ben forced himself to approach the clock. He placed the key in the lock, and it's runic symbols blazed in reds, blues, and greens before fading.

Click.

The lower panel swung open. Archie entered first, then Ben. Ben took one last look at Pringle. She sat motionless, her eyes focused on him.

He shut the door and they were enveloped in gloom. After a few moments, a pearlescent glow provided enough light to see the descending staircase. The narrow confines of the stairway were such his acrophobia wouldn't be a problem, although it would force them to proceed single file.

With more bravado than he felt, he told Archie, "Follow me."

They began the long descent to the wizard's hutch.

Ben's earlier concern that their *light* packs would become heavier the farther they traveled, proved to be all too true. An hour into their journey, faces dribbling sweat, they were forced to stop and rest. After that, the breaks became more numerous, the traveling times, shorter.

At their next stop to rest, Archie gasped, "How much farther?"

Ben used his sleeve to wipe the perspiration from his face. "Hard to say. You lose perception of time and space going down this rabbit hole."

"Dude, that's the damn truth. I can't tell we've made any progress at all."

A smile cracked Ben's face. "Not so pumped up now, are you?"

Archie extended a middle finger to Ben. "Let's go."

Ben chuckled and started down the stairs.

An hour later, the staircase abruptly ended at a landing. Above it stood the faint outline of a door.

"Thank the sweet Lord!" Archie wheezed.

Ben searched for the lock. *There!*

Located in the middle of the door, the keyhole exuded a faint, otherworldly light. Ben inserted the key and turned it.

The door swung open.

After they stepped through, it closed silently behind them. Ben recognized the familiar sight—the wizard's library. Archie, his mouth open wide enough to drive an eighteen wheeler through, wandered about trying to take it all in.

"This is so cool!" he gushed. He reached for a book in red binding on the shelf.

"No!" Ben shouted too late.

The second Archie's fingers closed on the book, it twisted out of his hand and fell to the floor. With a loud growl, it snapped and nipped at him.

"Hey!" Archie yelped. The book stood on its spine. Pages flapping, it chased him. Backpack bouncing on his shoulders, Archie ran around the library with the red book in hot pursuit. He pawed for the Taser clipped at his belt, pivoted, and fired at the rapidly closing tome.

Bzzzap!

The darts struck the book, electricity coursing through the leads. Smoke rose from the pages. *Yip, yip, yip*. The enchanted book howled and leapt up. Pages flapping like bird wings, it sailed through the air for the bookcase. The darts snapped off as the tome reseated itself on the shelf.

Ben doubled over, helpless with laughter. The ridiculous scene was like something from the Cartoon Network. When he could finally catch his breath, he pointed at Archie. "Don't do that again. Before you touch or pick anything up, ask me first."

Archie hand shook as he rubbed his face. "Believe me, I won't need to be reminded."

After Archie clipped the Taser back onto his belt, Ben led them through a maze of rooms, their progress slowed because Archie wanted to stop and inspect each one. They finally reached a blank wall. Ben stopped.

Archie frowned. "What happened? Did we miss a turn somewhere?"

"Nope. This is the right place."

"But it's a dead-end, a solid wall."

"Is it?" With a smirk, Ben leaned against the wall—and went right through it.

He waited, and moments later, Archie stumbled into the chamber, arms extended as if caught in a thick fog. He stopped and looked around, his mouth open and closing like a goldfish.

"Wow. This is extreme!" he cried.

Ben turned and studied the chamber. It looked the same, an enormous hollow that rose precipitously to the scrying chamber high above. Sconces flickered to life. They spiraled upward magnifying the already dizzying height.

Thump.

Thump.

Thump.

Steps slid out from the wall and curved upward following the contours of the hollow. Ben craned his neck to follow their progress. A cold prickle of fear dimpled his skin. *I forgot how high they go.* His earlier enthusiasm to use the scrying pool quickly faded.

"Look at this place!" Archie cried. His voice echoed about the hollow. "Who needs a video game when you can have the real thing!"

Ben swallowed, his growing dread making it hard to think much less talk. Before he could lose his courage, he approached the stairs. He placed a foot on the first step, then the next. With each step, his anxiety grew. By the time he'd gone only a short distance, a cold sweat drenched his skin. His heart pounded a staccato as if it would burst from his chest.

Then he looked down. Terror filled him and he froze. He couldn't take one more step. *Why did I ever think I could climb these stairs?* The trip back to the wizard's hutch had been a colossal mistake.

I'll never find Cara now.

CHAPTER 40

Paralyzed, Ben couldn't move. He found it hard to even breathe. A hand gripped his shoulder.

"Acrophobia kicking in, huh?" Archie asked.

Ben nodded.

"Well, I wasn't a Boy Scout, but I believe in being prepared." Archie rummaged around in his backpack. "Especially after what Pringle said." He thrust something in Ben's hand. "Here. Put this on."

Ben forced himself to glance at what Archie had given him.

A black mask.

"You want me to masquerade as Batman or Robin? You're not funny."

"It's a sleeping mask, dumbass. Put it on."

"Why? What good will it do?"

"You ever hear the saying 'what you don't know can't hurt you'?"

"Yeah, I guess."

"Good. We're going to try the Archimedes Jones version of 'what you can't *see* can't hurt you'. I repeat, put on the mask."

Ben reluctantly slipped the mask over his eyes. A sense of relief immediately washed over him. His heart stopped pounding, and his chest felt less constricted.

"I feel better. A lot better. But what good is it going to do? I can't see where I'm going."

"*Au contraire*. I'll be your eyes." Archie slipped past Ben and took the lead. "Grab my backpack. I'll go up slowly. The steps are evenly spaced, so just hang on and follow me."

Ben nodded. He took a firm hold of Archie's backpack with his left hand, while his right dangled against the coarse wall of the hollow. "Okay. Let's do this."

After the first few tentative steps, Ben's confidence grew. His suffocating fear didn't return. Within a short time, they established a rhythm, Ben's footsteps up the stair treads matching Archie's. The grueling march upward made for frequent stops, and Ben made sure to keep the mask on during these interludes.

Time became the biggest problem he faced. Traveling blind with caused time to slow, and the trudge upward seemed endless. When his feet at last found a level landing, it caught him by surprise.

"We're here."

Ben removed the mask. After such a long period of total darkness, the muted light of the hollow seemed painfully bright. When his vision cleared, he realized Archie had wisely led them far away from the landing, and they stood beside the entrance to the scrying chamber.

Ben whooped. He grabbed Archie and hugged him. "We did it! You're a genius."

Archie chuckled. "Not bad for an actuary, huh?"

"Are you kidding? Indiana Jones has nothing on you!"

Together, they marched into the scrying chamber. Unchanged from the last time Ben had been there, a circular bowl rose from the middle of the chamber with a wooden chair facing it. Mirror-smooth water filled the basin.

Archie could hardly contain himself. "Is that it?"

"Yep."

"How does it work?"

Ben took a deep breath. "Like this." He sat in the chair and placed his hands in the molds embedded on either side of the basin. He leaned forward, closed his eyes, and concentrated. Bubbles rose, a few at first, then increasing to become a boiling froth. The pool heaved and undulated, then grew still.

Ben opened his eyes. An image formed, a bird's-eye view of the forest canopy. He swooped closer then farther away, the up and down motion like a fast-moving rollercoaster ride.

Archie hooted and cheered. "Awesome, dude! What a rush! When do I get to try?"

Ben removed his hands and sat back. The forest image winked out. "Just testing it, Archie. Remember why we're here. I have to find Cara."

Archie quickly sobered. "Sorry. I guess I got a little carried away."

"I did too the first time I tried to scry, and I ended up face-planting on the floor." Ben cracked his knuckles and rolled his neck from side-to-side to loosen stiff muscles. "I don't know how long this is going to take, but no matter what, you *can't* interrupt me."

Archie raised his hands and took a step back. "Gotcha."

Ben returned his fingers to the hand-molds on the bowl's rim, and leaned forward. He concentrated on Cara and tried to recreate every detail of her face in his mind. A smile tugged at his mouth as he recalled a favorite moment—their last night together. She'd been so excited when he told her he decided to buy a house—"

Light erupted from the pool. Once again, the water frothed and bubbled. When it stilled, an aerial view of a rural panorama appeared. Roads crisscrossed a checkerboard landscape of trees, pastures and rolling hills. A large, multi-storied manor with a string of smaller outbuildings occupied one of the clearings. The scry zeroed in on it, and dived like a peregrine falcon after a fat mouse.

Ben fought to keep his hands firmly in place as the manor rushed to meet them on a collision course. Archie's startled cry echoed behind him, followed by a *thump* as he became disoriented and fell.

The headlong plunge reached the exterior walls of the manor, and passed through the brick and concrete façade as though it were vapor. A dizzying rush down hallways and corridors allowed Ben to catch only blurred images. After another nosedive through the building's concrete foundation, the scry hurtled along a passageway to a room with a single exterior window, entered, and stopped. A young woman dressed in hospital scrubs sat at the edge of a bed, her face buried in her hands Although her features were obscured, Ben recognized her immediately.

Cara.

"It's her!" he cried.

Archie managed to regain his feet and move closer. "Is she in a hotel room? It looks pretty cramped."

Ben moved his fingers, and Cara's face zoomed closer. Tears trickled from between her fingers.

"Something's wrong. She's crying."

Archie peered over Ben's shoulder. "Can you zoom in on the door and window?"

Ben made slight adjustments with his fingers. The front of the room moved closer.

Archie pointed. "Look, there's a deadbolt above the door jamb but no way to unlock it from the inside. And the window is tinted. I bet it's one-way glass. Cara can't see out, but anyone outside can see in. Let's check the back of the room."

Ben shifted the scene to a stainless-steel sink and toilet at the rear of the room.

Archie turned to Ben, his face grim. "She's locked in, Ben. I think she's a prisoner."

Apprehension crept up Ben's spine. "No. You're wrong. There must be some other explanation."

"Maybe, but I don't think so. Can you go back out to the passageway? We need to see what else is going on."

Ben nodded and moved the scry out of the room. A long corridor ran in both directions. Spaced at intervals, rooms like Cara's lined the passageway.

"Go to each window so we can look in."

Ben moved the scry and positioned it before the window in the room next to Cara's. A trio of young girls dressed in the same blue scrubs, sat listless beside each other. He moved to the next chamber. A pair of young men occupied the room. Like the girls, they wore a look of hopelessness.

Archie's face twisted. "Human traffickers!" he spat.

Ben risked a look over his shoulder. "Are you sure?"

"A hundred percent. Those people, including Cara, are going to be sold like cattle."

"But, Cara—"

"They must have kidnapped her. I don't know how, but you can be damn sure she didn't go willingly."

Anger blossomed inside Ben. He leapt up and the image in the scrying pool winked out. "We have to do something!"

"We will. I just don't know what yet. We need proof to contact the police. Can you imagine what will happen if we tell them you *scried* to find Cara and those other poor victims? They'll laugh us out of the building."

Archie paced the room. "Whatever we do, we need to be careful. Life is cheap to these motherless bastards, and they play for keeps. If we make one wrong move, tip them off in any way, they'll kill Cara and the others to get rid of the evidence. A few dead are nothing but a product loss on their ledger, a minor inconvenience."

Ben fumed. "I don't know what we'll do either, but we have an advantage they don't."

Archie snorted. "What?"

"A forest prawn with a pouch full of fairy dust."

CHAPTER 41

BEN BOLTED OUT OF THE SCRYING CHAMBER.
"Hurry! We gotta get back. There's no telling when the smugglers will sell Cara and move her."

"Come back! You haven't thought this out," Archie protested.

"What's there to think about? Every second we waste puts Cara's life in greater danger."

"So your great plan is to rush out of here, get Pringle, and launch an assault against the traffickers? You're going to get yourself killed and maybe Pringle too."

Ben stopped. Fists clenched, he said, "We can't just stand here and do nothing."

"We *are* going to do something."

"Like what?"

"Like finding out *where* they're holding Cara. We need a location, an address."

"How are we going to get that?"

Archie pointed to the scrying pool. "The same way you found her."

Ben felt heat rush to his face. *Of course.*

He moved to the scrying chair. "Thanks, Archie. At least one of us kept his head."

"Don't worry about it. If someone kidnapped my girlfriend, I doubt I could think straight either."

Ben reactivated the scrying pool. A few minutes later, they were soaring above the traffickers' mansion. Archie moved beside the pool and got out his phone.

"What are you doing?" Ben asked. "Your phone won't work on Almeera."

"I know, but the camera function works just fine. Zoom down to the mansion so I can take close-up photos."

Ben manipulated his fingers, and the estate moved closer.

Archie snapped pictures, then said, "Now backtrack down the drive all the way to where it turns off the road." Ben complied, and Archie took pictures of the county road sign. Five minutes later, they had a pictorial record of every road sign leading to the mansion.

"Okay, I have what we need to find this place," Archie said. "Go back so I can get exterior shots of the mansion." Ben nodded and angled the scry for frontal, aerial, side, and back views of the manor.

"Now for the hard part. We need pictures and film of every part of the interior and the goons in it. Start at the front door and work back from room to room until we have the complete layout. The last thing is the underground complex where Cara and the other victims are. If worse comes to worse, we can at least forward the images to the authorities."

Ben directed the scry to the tall and thick front door. It looked like it could take a round from a grenade launcher and remain standing. Once inside, they discovered the manor was filled with gleaming marble floors, original works of art, and other luxurious furnishings. A handful of suspiciously fit "servants" moved about the mansion, muscles bulging from under their uniforms. Ben tracked their movements, and it soon became obvious their only duty seemed to be patrolling the mansion and grounds at regular intervals.

Guards.

A search of the rest of the mansion revealed little else of interest. Ben moved to the underground complex. A network of corridors branched off like spokes on a wheel. Guards even larger than the ones in the manor, stood watch at each intersection. More locked rooms lined each of the passageways. Ben briefly inspected each one and found most were occupied with other abducted victims. A smoldering anger grew inside him at the sight of each scared and wretched face.

"What filthy excuse for a human could do this to other people?"

Archie released a derisive snort. "Read your history. Buying and selling slaves dates back to before the Babylonian Empire. What we're witnessing is the twenty-first century version, and for the same shitty reasons. There's big money to be made selling the poor and innocent to the rich and powerful."

"We can't leave these people here, Archie. We can't!"

Archie placed a hand on Ben's shoulder. "I know," he said softly. "Maybe if we can figure out a way to free Cara, we can help the others too."

Ben fought the urge to pound his fists against the rigid edge of the basin. He took a deep breath, then redirected the scry. Soon he returned to the aerial view above the estate. Far below, a car turned off the county road onto the drive leading to the mansion.

Ben tilted his head. "Hmm. What've we got here?" He zipped down and into the car. A hulking chauffeur drove, while an equally large man rode on the passenger side. A woman in a conservative grey pantsuit sat in the backseat. Midnight black hair curled around her shoulders while ice-blue eyes studied her phone. Beside her sat a man with such wide shoulders that there was barely room for the both of them.

Archie leaned closer. "I wish we could hear what they're saying."

"Me too. I—"

A rapid stream of conversation filled the chamber.

Startled, Ben almost jerked his hands away from the basin.

"Way to go!" Archie cried.

Ben mentally kicked himself. *I forgot the scry has audio.*

"Uh, yeah. Great!"

They listened, but the car's occupants spoke in a language neither understood.

Archie rubbed his chin. "I can't be sure, but I think they may be speaking in Russian." He tapped his phone to record the conversation. "Follow them, and let's see what happens."

A full-size Mercedes sedan drove up to a six-car garage adjacent to the manor. A bay door opened, and the sedan pulled in and stopped. The chauffeur got out and opened the door for the woman. She unfolded a pair of long legs and pointed at a touchscreen mounted on the wall.

"I want to check on our products for Saturday's auction," she said in heavily accented English.

"*Da.*" The brute in the backseat walked up to the touchscreen.

"Quick! Zoom in on that control panel!" Archie cried.

Ben manipulated his fingers, and the touchscreen's image filled the scrying pool. Archie filmed while the man's beefy fingers punched a sequence of numbers. It beeped, and a rumble filled the air. The section of floor the Mercedes rested on began to descend. It came to a stop on a lower level. Ben recognized the area immediately.

The place where Cara and the other kidnapped victims were being held.

"So that's how they transport and transfer the people they snatch," Ben murmured. "The garage has a false floor. No one would ever suspect there's an underground compound beneath it."

"Yeah," Archie growled. "The excavation and construction costs, not to mention paying off contractors to keep their mouths shut, had to be enormous. It shows just how lucrative the market for human trafficking is." He angrily shoved his phone into his back pocket.

Ben removed his hands, and the scrying pool returned to mirror-still water. The concentration needed to operate the scry had required his total focus….and it came with a cost. Sweat poured off his face, and fatigue settled on his shoulders like a leaden blanket. He fished one of Archie's energy bars from his pack, ate it in two bites, then drained a bottled water.

"You look like you spent an hour too long in the sauna," Archie commented.

"Yeah, I know," Ben admitted.

"Well, if it makes you feel any better, we've got everything we need to find the smuggler's place and come up with a plan." Archie practically danced around the chamber. "Who needs a GoPro when we have a scrying pool?"

Even drained, Ben couldn't help but smile at Archie's enthusiasm. He quickly sobered at what lay ahead—another hair-raising trip down the stairs of the giant hollow, then an exhausting trek up yet another set of stairs to the clock in Archie's bookstore. *Why couldn't the wizard have devised a levitation spell instead of stairs?*

Archie sensed Ben's trepidation. "The scrying took a lot out of you. We can hang out here for a while if you like."

Ben waved him off. "No. The woman mentioned an auction Saturday. Once they sell Cara, they'll smuggle her out of the country. That means we've got to move fast. Just give me another one of those energy bars and let's go."

Archie tossed him a protein bar. After eating it and washing it down with more water, Ben felt somewhat refreshed. With a groan, he stood and dug the sleeping mask out of his backpack.

Archie took the lead, and Ben took a firm hold of Archie's pack.

"Okay. Let's get back."

CHAPTER 42

To Ben's relief, their trip down the narrow, winding stairs was much faster and less excruciating. The return to Archie's clock was not.

The steep staircase challenged their tired legs. Their progress, rather than steady, came in fits and starts. Frequent stops were the norm, and both soon wheezed like fourth-stage emphysema patients.

"How much farther?" Archie panted during a pause.

"Don't know," Ben gasped. "It doesn't matter anyway because each round of steps feels like a mile."

"If we ever get back, I'll never set foot on another set of stairs. In fact, I plan to install an elevator. I might even remove the second-story stairs and replace them with a slide."

Ben grinned at Archie's comment. "It won't help your book sales, but you'll be a big hit with the neighborhood kids."

They both chuckled, and the laughter eased their fatigue. After a moment more to rest, they resumed the trek upward.

Stop, rest, continue. Ben's feet moved by reflex, his mind dulled to the point no conscious thought was required. When at last they finally reached the clock's landing, neither Ben nor Archie realized it at first. Bent over and winded, Ben finally found the energy to straighten. A faint light etched the rectangular door of the clock.

He pointed a shaky finger. "Look. We made it!"

"Thank you, Lord," Archie gasped. "Thank you, thank you, thank you!"

Ben pushed the panel open. Pringle sat where they'd left her, the same place on the floor. She jumped to her feet and hurtled toward him.

Ben caught her and staggered backward from the impact. Pringle, her wings buzzing furiously, carried him upward. Together in midair, they spun like a top. "I missed you, Ben Hastings!"

He laughed. "I missed you too, but I'm getting dizzy."

They drifted back to the floor.

Pringle, her face pressed against Ben's chest, tightened her arms around him. The feel of her body against his produced a distraction that made it hard to think clearly. Reluctantly, Ben unwound from her embrace and held her at arm's length.

"We need your help."

"I will always help you, Ben Hastings."

"It's not for me. It's for Cara."

Pringle stiffened. "The girlfriend?"

"Yes. She's been abducted, and her kidnappers plan to sell her."

"I don't understand, Ben Hastings."

Ben searched for the right words. "Do you remember the Taluk?"

She nodded.

"And the little ones and others captured by the Taluk?"

"The fingerlings? Yes, I remember, Ben Hastings."

"Good. Remember what happened to them, how the Taluk mistreated them?"

Pringle's face darkened. "They were tied together and beaten."

"My world's version of the Taluk has captured Cara. And they will do the same to her."

A look crossed Pringle's face, one he'd never seen before.

Rage.

"Then we must help the girlfriend Cara, Ben Hastings."

A range of emotions roiled through Ben. Relief that Pringle was eager to help, guilt that her involvement would likely put her own life in danger, and a second dose of guilt over his conflicted feelings. Since Pringle had rocketed into his life with a whirr of fairy wings, his connection to Cara had steadily weakened. Instead, *Pringle* occupied his thoughts. She moved him in ways he never thought possible.

He shook his head to clear it. *This isn't the time to soul-search.* "Pringle?"

"Yes, Ben Hastings?"

"How much dust do you have left in your pouch?"

Archie's office became a war room of sorts. Ben and Archie bounced ideas off each other while Pringle sat in a corner, plucking grapes from a cluster and munching on them. Her head swiveled back and forth as they fired one salvo after another at each other.

"We need a distraction," Ben said, "something that will draw away the guards so we can rescue Cara and free the others."

"Look, we've been over this a hundred times. Short of detonating a bomb, we don't have the means to create a diversion big enough to draw away *all* the guards."

"It beats your idea to try and sneak past them," Ben retorted.

"I can, Ben Hastings."

Ben and Archie stopped arguing and looked up. Ben vigorously shook his head. "No! Too dangerous. That's why I want you to use the fairy dust to create the distraction *Archie* says won't work. Then we'll sneak in to free Cara and the others."

"Archie Jones is right."

Ben threw up his hands. "Why?"

"Because they will still be able to see you, Ben Hastings." In a blink she appeared to vanish. "But they won't see me," her disembodied voice continued. Pringle reappeared and popped another grape into her mouth.

"What—what just happened?" Archie asked.

"Camouflage," Ben answered. "Pringle can mimic any background." He paused and studied Pringle. "What other mischief can you conjure up?"

"Toot fruit. Forest prawns like to play tricks."

"What is toot fruit?"

Pringle giggled and stuck out her tongue. "*Phwaaat!*"

"Does that sound like what I think it does?" Archie asked.

Ben rolled his eyes. "Yeah. A fart. And I still don't see how that helps. The traffickers can pass gas and shoot at the same time."

"*Tee hee*, it is great fun, Ben Hastings. The Taluk will not be able to control themselves."

Ben cocked his head. "How would you get this to all the guards?"

Pringle held up her hand and pretended to sprinkle fairy dust. "I will scatter the dust in the air. Once they breathe it in, *phwaaat!*" This triggered another round of giggling.

Ben glanced at Archie. "It might work. If all the guards have *intestinal* issues, they'll be incapacitated, and we can free all the prisoners and escape."

"No."

Ben glanced up at Pringle. She wore a determined look.

"You and Archie Jones will not free the fingerlings and the girlfriend Cara. I will."

"But—"

"The Taluk leader almost captured you, Ben Hastings...and he would have killed you. These Taluk will do the same to you and Archie Jones."

"But—"

"You cannot do this. Only I can."

Ben started to protest, but Archie firmly clutched his shoulder. "She's right, Ben. We both know that."

Ben glared at Archie. "I'm not going to let her risk her life!"

Pringle put down the grapes. Her wings whirred, and she landed to face Ben. "It is not your choice to make, Ben Hastings." She planted a finger on his chest. "It is mine."

"If anything happened to you," Ben gently closed his hand on her finger, "I just don't think I could live with it."

With a buffeting of wings, Pringle rose to eye level with Ben. She sighed, the sound like the passage of a soft breeze. "Do not worry, Ben Hastings. I will not be seen or caught."

"How can you be so sure?" Ben persisted.

Pringle's eyes twinkled. "Because I'm a prawn…and prawns are good at games."

CHAPTER 43

BEN AND ARCHIE SPENT THE NEXT FORTY-EIGHT HOURS preparing for what Archie dubbed *Operation Flatulence*. Although the title provided some needed light-hearted humor, Ben had no illusions about what lay ahead—a dangerous and potentially fatal rescue attempt. The fact that Pringle would lead the charge only raised his level of anxiety. She would be directly in the smugglers' crosshairs.

If there had been any way to convince the authorities that the country estate was a human trafficking center, Ben would have gladly pulled the plug on their Hail Mary rescue. But the first question the police would ask is how they came by their video and picture evidence.

Sure officer. See, there's this whole other world that can be accessed by a pair of grandfather clocks me and my buddy own. One leads directly to a wizard's hutch with an honest-to-God scrying pool. We used it to spy on the traffickers and found out where their victims are held. What's that? Have I been drinking? Am I a drug user?

And from there, it would go rapidly downhill. They couldn't help Cara and the others if they were detained in a drunk tank or a psych ward. Worse, it might even tip off the smugglers if they had any contacts among the authorities.

Now the day had arrived to launch Operation Flatulence.

Ben glanced at his watch. *5:30 am. Archie should be here anytime.*

Crunch, crunch, crunch. He looked up and smiled at the sight. Pringle sat cross-legged on the kitchen table eating a bowl of Lucky Charms. Although he had convinced her to use a spoon, it was still a work in progress, and a tiny drop of milk trickled from her chin.

He took a sip of coffee and watched the trail of milk grow. Unable to help himself, he grabbed a paper towel and dabbed her chin.

"You really are something, you know that?"

Pringle paused her chewing. "I'm not a something, Ben Hastings." She pointed at herself. "I'm a prawn."

He chuckled. "You certainly are."

And I'm not only letting you head straight into danger, I'm taking you there.

Pringle paused and studied Ben. She set her bowl down, then flitted into the air. She landed beside him and took his face in her hands. "You have *that* look again, Ben Hastings."

Ben wanted to turn away, but Pringle's forest-green eyes held his like a magnet. He licked his lips. "You know why. I'm worried you're going to get hurt."

"I told you, prawns are—"

"Good at tricks! Yes, I know." He clutched her hands. "But unless you have a trick that can outrun a bullet, this whole shitty mess might get you killed."

He shoved away from the table and stood. "When Archie gets here, I'm going to tell him we just need to go to the police and show them what we've got. Even if they think we're crazy, the pictures and video might at least get them to investigate."

"But you said that would cause the Taluk to kill the girlfriend Cara and the fingerlings."

"*I know what I said!*"

Pringle recoiled at Ben's harsh retort. She sprang into the air and circled the room, wings whistling.

Ben immediately regretted his outburst. He ran his hand through his hair. "I'm sorry. There are no good choices here. You're risking your life while my contribution is to sit on my ass in a van a safe distance away."

Pringle halted abruptly in front of Ben and drifted to the floor. Arms crossed, she marched to within inches of his face. "I have learned to trust you, Ben Hastings. When will you learn to trust me?"

Pringle's angry expression looked alien and out of place. His hands moved to her waist, and he could feel the tension hum in her like a high-voltage line.

"I—" she paused as if searching for a word. "I *worry* too. About you. That is why *I* must be the one to free the girlfriend Cara and the fingerlings."

If Ben had any previous doubts about Pringle's feelings for him, they evaporated with her comment. *She's falling in love with me…and God help me, I'm in love with her too.*

"Besides, my friends have agreed to help me."

Ben blinked. "Huh? What friends?"

The tautness left Pringle in a rush. She giggled, flew to the kitchen door, and opened it. Ben's mouth fell open as a parade of bees flew in, followed by one of the stone lions.

"Heard we got us a situation, Guvnor," the lead bee growled.

Ben recognized him immediately. Large, with yellow and black stripes, he was the bee that had greeted him on the porch. He hefted a piece of metal pipe in one of his multiple sets of arms.

"Nothin' a good head-knocking won't solve, Guvnor." His fellow bees, similarly armed with clubs, buzzed in agreement. "And since the Queen kicked us drones out of the hive, all we do is hang out pollinatin' and drinkin' nectar. We're gettin' rusty and need a good fight!"

The stone lion stood on its hind legs and shadow-boxed. "A

good right cross to the jaw will knock some sense into the bug-gers…er, no offense."

"None taken," the head bee said. "Where's your brother?"

"Someone's got to stand guard, and Larry's the odd-lion out. We played *rock, paper, scissors* to see who had to stay, but we both kept picking rock. So we arm-wrestled, and I won."

The head bee buzzed up to Ben. "What's the plan, Guvnor?"

Ben tried and failed to form a coherent reply. "Uh, I don't, you see…" His voice trailed off.

"Beggin' your pardon, Guvnor, but it sounds like it needs some work."

"What's going on here?"

Archie stood in the open doorway, his eyes the size of din-ner plates.

Ben finally found his voice. "Pringle's brought in some, uh, *reinforcements.*"

Archie grinned. "Way to go, Pringle!" He turned to the bees. "The plan is to kick some serious ass, rescue the hostages, and re-turn home as heroes."

The bees cheered, and the lion roared. The head bee buzzed up to Archie. "Lead on, Guvnor."

Archie winked at Ben and high-fived the bee. "Let's load my stuff into the van and go. We need to get in position while it's still dark." They filed out with the lion bringing up the rear. Only Pringle and Ben remained.

Pringle crooked a finger. "Let's go kick some serious ass, Ben Hastings."

Hand-in-hand, they headed for the van.

It took twenty minutes to reach the place Archie selected as the control center for their rescue attempt. On an isolated section of rural road half a mile from the trafficker's estate, they stopped at a place off the road's shoulder. At one time it had been a gravel stockpile, and the crescent-shaped piece of ground remained bare of vegetation. Partly obscured by trees, it was a perfect location.

Archie got out and removed a frisbee-sized drone from the van. "Special-ordered this baby and had it overnighted."

Ben studied the drone. "It's not very big."

"Doesn't need to be. In fact, the lighter, the better. Added weight reduces the flight time. The main thing is the optics and battery life. Its camera can zoom close enough to read the print in a book, and the battery is rated for 40 minutes—more than enough for what we need."

Archie powered up the drone and ran a system check on his iPad. "Okay, everything looks to be in the green."

Ben pointed at the iPad. "You can use that to fly the drone?"

"Yep. All I need is Wi-Fi, and I can split the screen for both the controls and the live feed from the drone's camera."

He paused and glanced at Ben. "You ready? It's now or never."

Ben clenched and unclenched his fists. Pringle's voice echoed in his mind. *When will you learn to trust me?*

"Yeah. Let's do it."

Archie's fingers danced across the touchscreen. The drone rose into the sky. "Pringle, you're up!" he called out.

"Whee!" With a blur of wings, she emerged from the van and streaked after the drone, the stone lion tucked under one arm. *Bzzzz.* The bees trailed after her. Soon, they disappeared into the murky, early morning sky.

Ben and Archie returned to the van. Archie kept the drone on course until the estate appeared below. He waggled the drone to signal Pringle. She peeled off and dived, the bees close behind like fighter jets in a bombing formation.

Archie increased the camera magnification until the front of the manor filled the screen. Ben twisted his hands.

All we can do now is watch and wait.

CHAPTER 44

PRINGLE LANDED BESIDE THE STOUT FRONT DOOR. The bees took position above her and out of sight. When she set the stone lion down, he sidled off to the side and crouched.

She knocked. When no one answered, she knocked again. At last, the door opened. A large guard filled the space, the seams of his servant's uniform straining to contain his bulk. He squinted suspiciously at Pringle.

"What you want?" he asked with a heavy accent. "We don't need no girl scout cookies."

Pringle beamed. "I'm not a girl scout. I'm a prawn."

"I don't care. Leave!" The guard took a threatening step.

The lion sprang forward and stomped on the guard's foot. He cried out and doubled over in pain.

Now at eye level with the faux servant, the lion grinned, exposing stone fangs. "Nighty, night." His closed paw crashed against the guard's chin.

The trafficker dropped as if boneless, out cold.

"Okay, lads. One down and hopefully more to go," the head bee cried. "Stuff 'em in the nearest bin."

The bees picked up the limp guard and tossed him into one

of the large entry closets. Another guard rushed into the large foyer area, gun drawn.

"High bridge!" the head bee shouted. The bees formed a gauntlet.

Bap, bap, bap, bap, bap. The sound, like tires traveling over rumble strips, rang out as each bee took turns clubbing the second guard. He face-planted, unconscious, onto the floor.

"Low bridge!" The bee leader cried when another guard rushed in. The bees buzzed lower and bludgeoned the sentry's legs. The guard pitched forward, slid a short distance, and came face-to-face with the lion.

Crack, crack. The lion knocked out the guard with a right-left combination. Both unconscious "servants" joined their fellow team members in the closet.

The head bee saluted Pringle. "We got this. Time to rescue the lasses and laddies."

Whoosh! Pringle streaked away, sparkles trailing behind her like the tail of a comet. She zoomed down the hallway and through the door leading to the garage. She stopped and hovered in mid-air. A box truck sat in one of the parking spaces.

Zip. Pringle flew to the touchscreen mounted on the wall. She pulled a paper from her pouch with a picture Archie had downloaded. It displayed the number sequence to activate the hidden freight elevator. *Blip, blip, blip, blip, blip.* Pringle punched the numbers in rapid succession.

A soft whine followed, and the platform holding the truck lowered. Pringle rode the box truck down until, with a *thump*, it came to a halt twenty-five feet below the garage. She darted off the platform and studied the twin corridors that branched from the elevator. A pair of guards, alerted by the noise of the elevator's arrival, hurried up to the truck. Both wore suits shielding shoulder holsters, and both were muscular giants. The only noticeable difference between them was hair color. One had black hair, the other blond.

"We expecting a delivery?" the black-haired guard asked.

"Nyet."

"Then what—"

Pringle zipped up to the guard. Startled, he stumbled back and reached for his gun. "Who are you?" he demanded.

"I'm Pringle, and you are a bad Taluk." She flung dust into his face, then with a blur of speed, did the same with the other guard.

The sentries brandished their guns, searching for a target.

"Where is she?"

"Don't know. I—*braaat!*"

"I told you not to eat the borscht. It always gives you—*brrraaaatttt!*"

One explosive fart after another followed, like a string of fire-crackers going off.

Pringle giggled and zipped down one corridor, then another. Every guard she encountered received a faceful of toot fruit dust. Soon the entire underground complex sounded like a NASCAR race, with rumbles, roars, and backfires echoing off the walls.

With the Russian guards incapacitated, Pringle flew to one of the locked rooms. She effortlessly wrenched open the door. A pair of young girls turned frightened faces toward her, and cringed as she approached.

"You are free. Go to the truck and hide in the back."

The girls clung to each other. At last, one stood and crept to the door. The riotous noise caused her to pause. "What is happening?"

Pringle smiled. "The bad Taluk will not stop you. Hurry."

The girl motioned to her sister. She stopped beside Pringle. "Are you an angel?"

Pringle giggled. "No, I'm a prawn."

Hand-in-hand, the girls ran out and down the corridor.

Pringle repeated the process for each room. Those victims too frightened to move, she picked up and flew them to the box truck.

At the last room, when Pringle forced the door open, a young woman sat on the bed, her knees pulled up to her chest. She cast a look of dread at Pringle. "Is it time for the auction?" A sob left her.

Pringle recognized her immediately. "You are the girlfriend Cara."

Cara wiped her eyes. "Yes, but I haven't been sold yet." Another sob rocked her. "So I don't know who I'll belong to."

"I'm Pringle, and you need to do the truck."

Cara looked up. "D-do the truck? I don't understand."

Pringle pantomimed turning a steering wheel with her hands.

"You mean drive?"

"Yes!" Pringle cried.

In a blink, she whizzed to Cara, picked her up, and carried her out of the room. They careened down the corridor, Cara's screams competing with the explosive, nonstop farts. Pringle dropped her beside the box truck.

Cara leaned against the door, gasping for air. "What's happening? What's happening? What am I supposed to do now?"

Pringle led Cara to the back of the truck. Dozens of frightened faces looked back at them. "Drive," she said.

"You want me to drive *them* away from here?"

"Yes. Archie Jones said you would know where to go."

Cara took a deep breath. "I guess that would be the nearest police station."

Pringle reached into her pouch and pulled out a small rectangular object. "Archie Jones said to give you the burning phone."

"Burning phone? Do you mean *burner* phone?"

"*You're not going anywhere!*"

The black-haired guard staggered toward them, his gun pointed menacingly. *Brat, brat, brat, brat.* A farting sonata accompanied each step. *Brat, brat, brat, BRAT!* Red-faced and sweating, the guard could barely keep a grip on his gun.

"Now, turn around, and—"

A groan escaped from his lips. *BRAAAAAAATTTT!* The shriek of gas sounded like a mortar shell had been dropped into the Russian's pants. The explosive release lifted him up and launched him into the air. He landed on the concrete with a *thud*, rolled over, and lay motionless.

Pringle clapped. "Time to go, girlfriend Cara!"

Cara stared at the guard's still form. "I'm dreaming. I must've been drugged because none of this is real. It's not possible!"

"Dreams are good, but you must leave, girlfriend Cara."

Pringle whizzed to the touchpad on the wall and tapped the same sequence of numbers. With a soft rumble, the platform and truck rose. The section of floor came to a stop inside the massive garage.

Cara shook her head, and rubbed her eyes. When she opened them, a moan escaped her lips. "No. Everything's still here. I'm going cra—"

Pringle snatched her up and flew to the driver's side. She opened the door and shoved Cara into the seat. "The toot fruit will soon wear off. You must leave *now*."

Cara released a shrill laugh and started the engine. "Why not? In just a few minutes, I'll be in Never Never Land. And look! The bay door's still down. No problem. I'll just drive straight through it."

She gunned the engine, and the truck leaped forward.

Pringle reached into her pouch and flung dust on the bay door seconds before the truck crashed into it. The door shook and rolled up, the truck passing through with inches to spare. It roared down the drive.

Pringle zipped out of the garage. She brought her fingers to her lips and whistled. The mansion's front door banged open. The bees poured out followed by the stone lion. He leaped up, and Pringle caught him in her arms.

"Great fun, mistress!" the head bee cried. "We gave them what for, didn't we lads?" The bees buzzed loudly in agreement.

"Was the mission a success?" the lion asked.

Pringle laughed. "Yes. The fingerlings and the girlfriend Cara have been freed from the Taluk."

A rousing roar and exuberant buzzing followed her announcement.

"What now?" the boss bee asked.

"We return to Ben Hastings and Archie Jones. Then," she paused. A word drifted into her mind, one both unfamiliar and comforting at the same time. "Then we go *home*."

CHAPTER 45

Ben cheered at the drone's footage of the truck racing away.

"We did it! They escaped!" he shouted. The VW rocked as he celebrated.

Archie, busy flying the drone, said, "They're not in the clear yet." He dug a new cell phone out of his pocket and punched a preloaded number. It rang and rang.

"C'mon, c'mon," he mumbled. "Pick up, Cara."

"Hello?"

"Cara! Don't hang up!"

"Who-who are you?"

"A friend, and right now, that's all you need to know. Listen to me carefully. Turn right onto the road the private drive leads into. You probably haven't a clue where you are, but you're not far from Tyler. I'm going to lead you there. When you get close enough to get your bearings, call 911 and do whatever the police tell you. And Cara?"

"Yes?"

"It's not just you. The truck's carrying twenty other kidnap victims, and they're depending on you. Keep your shit together and get yourself and them to safety."

Silence followed.

Finally, with a shaky voice, Cara said, "Okay."

"Great! You've got this. Just follow my directions and drive."

Archie had the drone follow the truck for another five minutes. He relayed directions to Cara until she said, "I know this road. I know where I am! Thank you...whoever you are."

"Awesome. Just one last thing."

"Yes?"

"The police will have a lot of questions, including how you managed to escape. You don't want the sons of bitches who did this to get away with it, do you?"

"No!"

"Then don't tell them *exactly* how you got away. Makeup something like you managed to pick the lock on your door, steal a key from a guard, anything but what actually happened. Otherwise, when they catch and prosecute the subhuman shitballs that abducted you, your testimony will sound like something out of a Grimm's fairy tale. No one will believe you and any competent defense lawyer will have the case thrown out."

A long pause followed. "You want me to lie?"

"No, I want you to omit some of the facts. You *did* escape, you *did* find the truck, and you *did* drive it and the other kidnap victims to safety. What happened in-between is subject to interpretation, end of story."

"You sound like my father."

Archie chuckled. "See? If it's good enough for Mickey Sledge, it'll work for you. Gotta go. Goodbye and good luck, Cara." Archie clicked off.

"I wish I could have talked to her," Ben said.

"We already went over that. How would you explain any of what's happened? It's best for you, me, and Cara if she thinks some mysterious benefactor intervened to help her and the others."

Ben shook his head. "I know. But still—"

Pringle zipped up to the van. Ben opened the door, and she

flew in with the bees close behind. "Did the girlfriend Cara escape the Taluk?"

"Yeah. She got away."

Pringle clapped and danced, the bees buzzed.

Archie landed the drone, secured it, then climbed into the passenger seat. Ben got behind the wheel, and turned to Pringle. "You did good. You and your friends saved Cara and all those kids."

He pointed at Archie. "Actuary my ass. The way you helped plan this rescue would make any senior FBI and CIA agents look like green rookies."

Archie grinned. "I'll be sure to use you as a reference when I apply to the FBI Academy."

Ben high-fived Archie, and they shared a laugh.

He started the van and put it in gear. "We're done here. Let's go home." As they started down the highway, Archie wiped off the burner phone to remove his prints, and tossed it out the window.

Mounted high in a pine tree beside the road, a faint red light blinked on from a digital camera…and started recording.

A persistent shake woke Petrova. Sleeping late was a rare exception to her iron routine, a luxury she guarded closely.

She sat up. "This had better be good," she growled.

Ivanov stood next to her bed. A thin sheen of sweat beaded his forehead.

"What the hell is wrong?" she asked.

"All of our product has escaped. We have to get out of here before the authorities arrive."

Any vestige of sleep left her instantly. She knew better than to doubt Ivanov, a stone-cold killer who dealt only in stone-cold facts. Not bothering with modesty, she stripped off her nightgown and quickly dressed. They hurried out of the bedroom.

"Have everyone evacuate."

"Already started."

"Good! Now tell me what happened."

Ivanov handed her a tablet. "It's better you see it for yourself."

While they hurried to the garage, Petrova scrolled through the video footage. Little in the world could still shock or surprise her, but the security montage managed to do both. Her men staggered about farting like a muffler-less Russian Lada, while their product fled in the very truck that had transported them here. But what floored her, what caused an icy chill to creep up her spine, was the blurred images of their liberator. Even viewed frame-by-frame, the rescuer moved so fast that the images remained fuzzy. Petrova could make out just enough to determine the person was female and that she possessed…wings.

Ivanov opened the door to the Mercedes sedan and Petrova got in. He slid in beside her, tapped the driver on the shoulder, and they pulled out of the garage. "Who is she? *What* is she?" Petrova demanded as they drove off.

Ivanov shrugged. "Don't know, and I don't know how anyone can move that fast. But I think I know how to find out."

He took the tablet from her and scrolled through the footage. "Here." He handed the tablet back.

Petrova studied the video. An old Volkswagen van stood parked beside a rural road. The VW pulled away, and someone on the passenger side threw out an object. She turned a questioning look to Ivanov.

"We have motion-activated cameras hidden in strategic locations on every road leading to our *dacha*." He zoomed in on the object being tossed away. "That's a burner phone. The time stamp on this footage matches the escape of our product."

Petrova swore. "Did the video capture images of anyone in the van?"

Ivanov shook his head. "*Nyet.* But I got something just as good." He manipulated the controls on the tablet, and handed it back to her.

A smile slowly spread across Petrova's face. The screen displayed the VW's license plate.

They reached the end of the private drive and pulled over. Petrova and Ivanov got out. Several cars filled with security personnel followed, and the brawny bodyguard waved them on. With the windows down, the *brat, brat, brat* of guards still suffering from farting spasms filled the air.

Petrova reached for her cell. She punched a sequence of numbers. "*Self-destruct in three minutes,*" a feminine voice intoned. A countdown ticked off on her phone's screen.

She sighed. The construction of her *dacha* had taken almost two years. When completed, she'd had the perfect facility to hold and traffic her human cargo. Now, it was about to be turned into a smoking crater of rubble. Not that she had any choice. She couldn't leave any evidence for the authorities.

Petrova shrugged. Regrets were for fools. Her *dacha's* destruction was the cost of doing business. She'd make a hundred times what it cost in the next year.

Revenge, however, was different.

She turned to Ivanov. "Hosseini brought us the girl. Find him." Cold rage built within her.

"Then trace the plate and get me a name and address."

CHAPTER 46

BEN WOKE TO THE PERSISTENT TRILL OF HIS CELL. Groggy from the epic celebration that lasted well into the night, where he, Archie, and the bees had managed to put away a case of beer…or maybe it was two or three. His muddled mind couldn't remember. He *did* remember the drones' capacity for alcohol far surpassed their size—a discovery he and Archie realized too late when they tried to match them drink for drink. While his Bluetooth speaker had blared Queen's, *Another One Bites the Dust*, over and over, the bees and Larry the stone lion had joined in the boisterous sing-along. Even the normally dour door hummed along.

With the throb of his hangover pulsing at his temples, Ben tried to gather his thoughts. *Where is my damn phone?* He followed the sound, dug under the covers, and found the cell lying close to his feet.

"Hello?" he rasped.

"It's all over the news!" Archie cried. "Cara's being called a heroine. A picture of her with the other escapees is plastered all over social media. She's the lead story in every newsroom across the country!"

Munch, munch. Ben glanced up. His bleary eyes spied Pringle hovering above the bed, eating an apple. Unlike his own still-wobbly brain, she looked fresh and vibrant.

In a blink, she zipped down to him. "Hi, Ben Hastings." The suddenness of her approach overwhelmed his tenuous senses.

He fell off the bed, his cell skittering away.

"Ow!" The pain of landing on his butt helped clear his head, and he crawled after his phone.

"What happened?" Archie asked.

"Just a typical good morning from Pringle—sudden and in your face."

Archie chuckled. "The little pixie does have her ways, doesn't she?"

"Not so little anymore," Ben grumbled.

Archie's cheery voice sputtered. "No, I guess not."

Ben rubbed his eyes. The exhilaration of rescuing Cara was quickly replaced by another reality—one he couldn't ignore any longer.

"You need to call Cara." Archie reminded him. "I'm sure her phone is blowing up, but you still need to try. If you can't get her, text her then call her father. Remember, you've got to act surprised and relieved. That would be the normal reaction as her boyfriend."

"Yeah, yeah, I get it."

"Once you've done that, we'll," Archie paused, "we'll move on to Plan B."

Plan B. Their code name for Pringle.

And the scheme to send her home.

Maude, hunched over her computer, scanned Tyler's municipal building code. Long on legalese, sections, and subtitles, but short on plain language, she'd searched the code fruitlessly for hours.

"There must be something here I can use against Hastings," she muttered. "Something to get his entire property condemned."

A knock at the door disturbed her search. She pulled the curtain aside and peeked out. A large man in white coveralls stood on her porch. A white panel van stenciled with "Termites R Us" was parked in her drive.

She frowned, went to the door, and cracked it open. "Can I help you?"

The big man smiled. "Hi, I'm Ivan from Termites R Us," he said with a heavy accent. "We're canvassing the neighborhood to see if any residents would like a free termite inspection."

"No thank you. I had an inspection last year."

She tried to shut the door, but found it blocked by the man's foot.

"I insist."

Indignant, Maude opened her mouth—then quickly snapped it shut at the sight of the gun pointed at her.

"Don't say a word. Open the damn door ," Ivan growled.

Maude stepped back. "Take whatever you want. I don't have much money, but you can have all my jewelry," she said, her voice choked with fear.

"Shut up!"

Ivan closed the door and looked around. "Is anyone else in the house?"

"No."

"What about your husband?"

"I'm divorced."

Ivan took out his phone and punched a number. "I'm in."

He put the cell away and shoved her into a chair. He quickly bound her hands and feet, then squatted beside her, the nose of the gun resting against her cheek. "Remember, keep your mouth shut."

Maude nodded, her heart threatening to erupt from her chest. Ivan patted her head. "Good."

He hurried away, and Maude heard the garage door open, followed by the rumble of an engine. Moments later, Ivan came back with two others—a swarthy, smaller man, and a woman with midnight black hair. The fear on the second man's face matched Maude's.

The woman pulled up a chair next to Maude. She sat and studied her with glacial blue eyes.

"Now…tell us everything you know about your neighbor."

Petrova stood at the window looking at the gothic mansion next door.

"She doesn't know much," Ivanov said. "And some of the stuff she said is crazy."

Petrova pointed at the vintage VW van parked at the curb. "We know enough. The burner phone was tossed from *that* vehicle, and it's owned by the neighbor next door."

She turned to Ivanov. "And *crazy* is in the eye of the beholder. Would you say *crazy* describes what we saw on the security footage? Because if you do, I'm inclined to believe her."

Ivanov shook his head. "Maybe we should cut our losses. Something doesn't feel right."

Petrova snorted. "Scared of ghosts and goblins? Maybe I need another enforcer."

"*Nyet!* I fear nothing made of flesh and blood. But this, this—"

"Isn't real? Doesn't bleed?" Petrova finished for him. "We'll find out soon enough." She returned to the window and resumed her study of the mansion.

"Because tonight we're going to pay the neighbor a visit."

Archie parked his 'Vette behind Ben's van.

He glanced at his watch. *Eight pm.* He wanted to put this off until the next day, but Ben insisted they couldn't wait. He worried that each passing second could be Pringle's last as an immortal.

So…the time had come to send Pringle back to Almeera. If all went well with their Plan B strategy—and with Pringle, who knew how *that* would go—their ruse would be for Ben and Pringle to follow him back to the Black Swan and continue the celebration. Once there, they would use his clock to send Pringle back to the wizard's hutch and her world. Of course, it would've been simpler for Ben to take her to Jefferson himself, but he'd begged Archie to come to Tyler so they could leave together. Although he didn't explain why, Archie thought he knew.

Ben didn't trust himself. He needed Archie to make sure Pringle went back.

Archie shook his head. The emotional tug-of-war within Ben had to be titanic. He loved Pringle, but that same love couldn't allow her to stay—not if it meant sacrificing Pringle's immortality. *If you love somebody, let them go.* Archie always thought the saying to be so much clichéd bullshit, but now…now it held a ring of truth.

Archie sighed and got out of the 'Vette. Preoccupied with his thoughts, he didn't realize someone had come up behind him.

Until a gun jabbed into his back.

CHAPTER 47

"SHUT UP AND DON'T TURN AROUND," IVANOV HISSED. Archie froze.

Two other figures approached. In the gathering dusk, Archie couldn't make out their features until they reached him—a statuesque woman and a shorter man. The woman stepped closer. Even in the failing light, her eyes carried a flint-hard look. She hooked a thumb at the mansion.

"Who lives here?"

When Archie was slow to answer, the gun barrel dug against his spine.

"M-my friend, Ben."

"Take us to meet him." The woman's steely tone left no doubt she expected immediate compliance.

Archie swallowed. "Okay."

They frog-marched him through the gate to the veranda steps. The stone lions turned their heads and growled.

Petrova didn't miss a beat. "Unless you want to eat a bullet, you'll tell your…whatever they are, to back off."

A shaky laugh escaped Archie. "Hey guys, please don't do anything."

The lions crouched on all fours, tails swishing. But they made no move to intercept Archie's captors.

As they went up the steps to the mansion, the gargoyle's head on the railing turned. "Want me to sound the alarm?"

"No!" Archie cried. The gun stabbed his back again.

"Keep your voice down!" Ivanov hissed.

"A djinn. It's a djinn!" Hosseini wailed. "Mistress, we must leave—"

Petrova whirled and grabbed Hosseini's silk shirt with both hands. "You started all this with the girl you brought me. *I'm* the one you need to fear, *so shut up and do what you're told!*"

Whimpering, he nodded. She released Hosseini.

Petrova grabbed Archie's arm and led him to the door. "Open it!"

Archie grasped the door handle, but it wouldn't budge. He tried again. "It won't move. It must be locked."

Petrova gestured to Ivanov. He tried the handle. It didn't move. "*Da.* He's telling the truth."

She pushed Archie. "Knock."

He rapped on the door, but no sound resulted. He tried again, harder this time, but with no better luck. Ivanov shoved Archie aside. His meaty fist pounded the door.

The wood didn't even creak.

The bodyguard looked at Petrova. "I don't know. Maybe there's a sound deadening layer under the wood.

A face materialized on the door's wooden surface. "There's no sound because you haven't been invited in. Really, the lack of intelligence on this world continues to stagger me."

Hosseini fell to his knees. "Another djinn! Mistress, I beg you. Before we are all lost, we must leave!"

"Hmm. Add superstitious too. What a backward lot."

Petrova moved to the door. "Let us in…now!"

"Oh, let me see. So many replies to choose from. Which one? I have it!

"No."

She motioned to Ivanov. He spun a silencer onto his gun. *Pfft, pfft.* He fired two bullets into the door.

"I'm hit! I'm hit! Oh, what a cruel world. Just as my wood had reached the right amount of seasoning. I'm coming home, Ma, coming home to that great big lumberyard in the sky. I-I—"

The door's voice faded away.

Ivanov tried the handle again. He frowned. "It's still locked."

Ptooey, ptooey, plink, plink, two bullets were spat out by the door. "Of course I am. I'm made of wood, you moronic idiot. Is there anything that passes for education on this world?"

Ivanov stepped toward the door, his body shaking with barely controlled rage. "No one talks to me like that!"

"Then it's a good thing I'm not a *no one*, otherwise I'd be so scared my hinges would rattle."

"Enough!" Petrova hissed. She scanned the neighborhood behind them. Although night had fallen, she knew they were still exposed. The longer they stayed out in the open, the greater the chance someone might notice and call the police.

"Get his phone," she ordered. Ivanov patted Archie down and pulled his cell from his pocket. He gave it to her.

Petrova handed the phone to Archie. "Call your friend and tell him to let you in." She leaned closer. "And if we're not in the house in the next thirty seconds…" She put her finger against his head, and pantomimed pulling a trigger.

Archie made the call.

Ben had spent most of the day reading online news reports about Cara's daring escape. Dubbed a heroine by social media and the authorities, Cara finally made a public statement at the law offices of her father, Mickey Sledge. He tapped his iPad and watched the video clip yet again. Mickey stood beside his daughter and spent as much time answering shouted questions as Cara did.

The trill of his phone interrupted the video clip. "Hello?"

"Ben, I'm here. The door won't let me in."

"That damn door," Ben grumbled. "Okay, hold on."

He stalked into the foyer and to the door. "Open up!"

"I wouldn't advise that, magnificent sir."

"Let Archie in!"

"Wise are your words. As you wish."

The door swung open.

A huge man shoved Archie in, a gun jammed against his head. A smaller, whimpering man followed. Last, a statuesque woman entered. She appraised him like a cobra preparing to strike.

"Ben. We finally meet. I'm Zelkova Petrova, and my large associate is Ivanov. We have a lot to talk about." She pointed a small, silver handgun at him. "And you're going to tell me everything."

"The bad Taluk!" Pringle cried.

Petrova reacted instantly. She grabbed Ben, and jammed her gun against his ribs. "Show yourself!"

Pringle appeared beside her. "I'm here." She vanished and reappeared beside Archie and the Russian enforcer. "Here I am." She disappeared again.

"Whee!" Pringle appeared above them rocketing in circles.

"*Aieee!*" Hosseini cried. "More djinns! They'll steal our souls!"

Ben grunted as Petrova ground the gun against his chest. "Is your friend faster than a bullet?" she hissed in his ear. "Tell her to stop, or you'll be my first test subject."

Ben licked lips suddenly gone dry. "Pringle, stop. Otherwise the Taluk will hurt me and Archie."

In a blink, Pringle hovered beside them, her face a mixture of anger and fear. "Do not hurt my Ben Hastings or Archie Jones."

"That will depend on their answers." Petrova waved the revolver at a nearby Victorian-era sofa. "Let's get comfortable."

Ivanov shoved Ben and Archie to the couch. Guns trained

on them, Petrova barked, "Sit! And you!" she snapped at Pringle. "Join them. Remember, try anything and I'll shoot them both."

Pringle zipped beside Ben and sat, hands in her lap.

"Good!" She pointed the revolver at Pringle. "Tell me who and what *she* is."

"A djinn, a djinn!" Hosseini babbled. "She's a demon from the depths of hell!"

With a quick step, Petrova moved to the Iranian and back-handed him. His head snapped back. "Say another word and you're a dead man!" she snarled.

Snot mixed with tears rolled down the Iranian's face. "Yes, Mistress." He scuttled a safe distance away.

When she turned back to Ben, his heart almost stopped. The promise of violence in her eyes carried an unspoken message. *Far worse things are in store for us if I don't answer her questions.*

Petrova pointed the gun at Ben.

"Talk!"

CHAPTER 48

"**P**RINGLE IS A PRAWN," BEN SAID.

"What's a prawn?" Petrova asked.

"Prawns are like fairies. They live in the forests of Almeera."

Petrova paused, digesting the information. "What she did to my men, the way she moves and disappears—how is that possible?"

"Pringle's a magical creature. It gives her extraordinary abilities."

Petrova's look hardened. "Do you think me a fool? There's no such thing as magic."

She gestured to Ivanov. "Kill his friend."

Ivanov raised his gun.

"No, wait! I can prove it!" Ben cried.

Petrova gave a slight nod. "One chance. Prove it." Ivanov lowered the weapon.

Ben indicated the grandfather clock at the base of the grand staircase. "The entrance to Almeera is inside the clock." He took the key from his pocket. "I can show you."

A cruel smile spread across Petrova's face. "Okay, I'll play along. But if I'm not completely convinced, your friend is dead." She motioned with her gun. "Proceed."

Ben got up, and Petrova pressed her gun against the base of his skull. He moved to the clock. His hands shook as he inserted the key and turned it. The runes glowed and the lower panel swung open.

He glanced over his shoulder. "We have to go in."

Petrova pushed him aside and peered inside the clock. "What do you mean? It's too small. We can't fit—"

The words died on her lips. "What—what's this? There's enough room for several people."

"It's the way to Almeera. If we go inside, you'll see the staircase."

Petrova nodded and followed Ben into the clock. He pointed at the stairway. It spiraled downward and disappeared. "The stairs lead to Pringle's world."

Petrova's look of astonishment deepened at the sight of the staircase. "Back outside!" she ordered. She circled the clock, examining every side. "Impossible. The interior dimensions are larger than the outside. How do you explain that?" she demanded.

"Magic," Ben answered. "That's what I've been trying to tell you."

Petrova shook her head. "A new world," she mused. Her astonishment was replaced with another look—calculation. "And a new world means new possibilities."

She turned to Ben. "You're going to take us to this world."

Fear coursed through Ben. "Wait! You don't understand. I barely escaped with my life. It's too dangerous."

The cold muzzle of Petrova's gun traced a path across his cheek. "More dangerous than me?" she cooed in his ear. "Want to bet?"

"N-no."

"Good!" She gestured to Ivanov. "Tie up his friend and gag him. It looks like we're going on a trip." She pointed at Hosseini. "*All* of us."

"Mistress, please," he pleaded. "You don't need me. I can stay behind and watch the prisoner."

"And when I return find you've escaped down some rathole? You must think I'm a fool. I should just kill you now."

"No!" Hosseini cried. "A thousand pardons, Mistress. I'll gladly go with you."

Petrova smirked. "Of course you will."

"Finished," Ivanov growled. Archie lay bound and gagged on the sofa. The Russian enforcer nudged his chin at Pringle. "What about her?"

"She's going with us. Still have the silencer on your gun?"

The enforcer nodded.

"Good. Time for a demonstration." Petrova grabbed an embroidered pillow off the sofa. "Pringle, here's an example of *my* magic." She tossed the pillow high in the air. "Shoot it!" she ordered Ivanov.

Pfft, pfft. The silenced gun put two rounds through the pillow. An eruption of feathers showered the air.

"Now imagine the pillow is Ben. If you try anything, I'll shoot him. I'll kill him right in front of you. Do we understand each other?"

Pringle crossed her arms. "You are a bad Taluk."

"Don't know or care what a bad Taluk is. I *do* care that we understand each other." Petrova trained her gun on Ben. "So, what's it going to be?"

"I understand bad Taluk. Do not hurt Ben Hastings."

A thin smile creased Petrova's face. "Great. Everybody inside the clock."

Ben's mind raced. "Can I say something to Pringle first?"

Petrova eyed Ben suspiciously. "Why?"

"Prawns don't have long memories. They tend to forget stuff. I just want to remind her how we made the trip back from Almeera. It'll save us time and trouble later."

"You're lying. What's so unusual about a staircase?"

"Remember, they're magical stairs. They can get tricky the farther we travel. Pringle will make it easier for us."

Petrova studied Ben. "Okay. Go ahead. I think you know what will happen if you're bullshitting me."

Ben released a pent-up breath. "Thank you."

He had no illusions about their fate. Once the Russian mobster felt they'd outlived their usefulness, she'd kill them all. They had one and *only* one advantage.

Only Ben had traveled through *this* clock.

His plan, wild, risky, and full of holes, depended entirely on Pringle.

I trust you, Ben Hastings. When will you learn to trust me too?

"Remember the stairs?"

"Yes, Ben Hastings."

"Be ready to help us out when they get quirky."

A pause followed. *Say yes, just say yes*, Ben silently pleaded. She smiled at him. "Yes, Ben."

Ben, not Ben Hastings. Pringle *never* called him by his first name. *She understands!* For the first time a glimmer of hope rose in his chest.

Petrova shoved him forward. "Lead the way."

Ben reentered the clock. The staircase, like the one in Archie's clock, forced them to proceed one-by-one. Petrova followed Ben, behind her Hosseini and Pringle, with Ivanov at the rear. They moved steadily downward in silence, the only sound the scuffling of feet. The vivid memory of what happened the last time he took these stairs, scrolled through his mind. He hoped and prayed it would happen again. If not, they were all as good as dead.

They continued their descent. *I can't be certain, but it seems like we're past where—*

The stairs wobbled, stilled, and wobbled again. The narrow walls around the staircase began to melt like butter in a hot saucepan.

Then the stairs disappeared completely.

Petrova's startled cry joined Hosseini's panicked screams, and Ivanov's roar. All of them slid downward faster and faster, until everything blurred. Suddenly, a pair of hands jerked Ben up and into the air.

"Let's go home, Ben Hastings."

With a whir of wings, they shot upward.

CHAPTER 49

PETROVA LANDED HARD, THE WIND KNOCKED OUT OF her.

Thud, thud.

Ivanov and Hosseini landed on top of her.

Petrova pushed them off and staggered to her feet. Once she could catch her breath, she looked around. Dry, dusty grass and soil stretched for miles under a blazing sun. She shaded her eyes and turned in a circle. She stopped at the sight of an odd grouping of humps on the horizon.

Ivanov stood and dusted himself off. "Where are we?" he asked.

"My guess is Almeera, the world Hastings mentioned."

Hosseini lurched to his feet. "I think I broke my ribs," he moaned.

Ignoring the Iranian, Ivanov asked, "Where is Hastings? I don't see him anywhere."

Petrova took a moment to answer. "I don't know. He might have tricked us somehow." That galled her to admit, even more than losing her *dacha*. A glint in the grass caught her attention. Her gun. She picked it up and pointed at the collection of lumps in the distance.

"Those may be buildings of some sort. Maybe we can get some answers there." They started off.

"Wait!" Hosseini pleaded. He clutched his ribs with both hands. "I-I don't think I can keep up."

Petrova turned, raised her gun, and fired. A bloom of red erupted in the middle of Hosseini's head. He stood for a moment, a puzzled look on his face...then toppled over.

"Good shot," Ivanov commented. "Nicely centered."

"Didn't want to waste a bullet on the greasy bastard, but I couldn't listen to one more word."

After twenty minutes, they reached their destination. "Tents? They all look abandoned," Petrova said.

Pavilions of assorted sizes formed a large circle on the dry ground. Covered in a thick layer of dust, the tents were in various stages of collapse. Debris lay everywhere, and Petrova picked up a broken haft with a sharp metal tip. "This looks like a spear."

"Over here," Ivanov called.

Petrova walked to where he stood beside skeletal remains. The bones, picked clean by scavengers and bleached by the sun, gleamed in the harsh sunlight.

Ivanov poked the bones with his shoe. "What kind of creature has a skeleton like this?"

"Nothing human," Petrova replied.

Her sharp ears caught a low rumble. She turned, and in the distance, plumes of dust rose in the air. The source of the dust drew nearer, and Petrova could begin to make out more detail. She sucked in a breath at the sight of riders and their mounts.

Thick hind legs supported the mounts, and wide, leathery wings spread from their shoulders. Small, short arms protruded from their chests, and their muzzled mouths were lined with sharp, carnivorous teeth. They looked like smaller versions of a Tyrannosaurus Rex.

The riders were as alien as their mounts. A beaklike snout protruded from their heads with a ridge of bone that ended above slitted nostrils. At the sight of Petrova and Ivanov, they stopped and formed a skirmish line.

"How many?" Petrova asked.

"A hundred or more," Ivanov estimated.

A commotion disturbed the line, and the riders parted. A larger rider emerged. What distinguished him from the other creatures was a purple wattle of flesh that crowned his head.

Like a rooster comb.

He smiled at the sight of Petrova and Ivanov, exposing sharp teeth. He raised a spear-like weapon over his head and released a piercing cry.

The riders charged.

Held snugly in Pringle's grasp, wind whistled past Ben's ears as they sped upward.

Seconds later they emerged from the clock. "We're home, Ben Hastings," Pringle announced.

She deposited him beside the couch and Archie's bound form. Gagged, all he could manage was a muffled cry. Ben quickly untied him and removed the gag.

"Wh-what happened?" Archie gasped.

"Pringle saved the day—again," Ben replied. He then explained what happened, how Pringle caught him before he fell back into Almeera.

"So, the Russians are trapped there?"

"Unless they can find another clock, they're never coming back."

Archie released a relieved sigh. "Good." He glanced at Ben. "What now?"

Ben took his time answering. Heart heavy in his chest, he said, "We go to your place…and implement Plan B."

Ben and Pringle rode in Archie's car back to The Black Swan in Jefferson. For the most part, they made the trip in silence, even though Pringle repeatedly asked Ben what was wrong. All he could bring himself to say was, "Wait until we get there."

When they arrived and got out, the silence continued. Even Archie's normally effervescent personality seemed to be muted.

Once in the bookstore, Archie turned on the lights. Without a word, Ben made his way up the stairs to the second floor with Archie and Pringle close behind. Ben stopped at Archie's clock. He took out the key and inserted it in the lock. A glow of magic emanated, and the panel swung open.

Ben turned to face Pringle. "We had this elaborate plan to trick you into the clock. Then I'd tell you to go back to Almeera, that you didn't have a choice, and I'd lock the clock. But I can't do it. I can't lie to you, and won't try to make you. Instead, I'm going to *ask* you to go back to your world, Pringle."

Pringle flitted into the air, arms crossed. "No. I will not leave you, Ben Hastings."

"Don't you see? Every second, minute, and hour you spend in *my* world makes it more difficult to return to *your* world. The time will come when you *can't* go back, and you'll be trapped here."

Pringle thrust her chin out. "No, Ben Hastings."

Ben reached out with his hand. After a moment, Pringle took it. He gently pulled her out of the air and wrapped his arms around her until they were face-to-face. "I love you, Pringle. I've tried to fool myself into thinking it must be something else, but I can't do it any longer. You brought color into my life, took my average, ordinary days, and made them bright and vibrant. And even though we've been through some scary stuff together, I'd do it all again just so I could be with you."

Ben gripped Pringle's shoulders. "But I can't watch you die. I couldn't live with myself. If I've learned anything since we've been together, it's that love is selfless. And that's why I have to let you go, why you have to let *me* go."

A tear slid down Pringle's cheek. She reached up and touched it. "I hurt inside, Ben Hastings. I don't know why, but it hurts."

"I know. I hurt too."

Ben felt himself unraveling. He forced himself to hold his emotions in check. He led Pringle to the grandfather clock, and they stepped inside. He kissed her and inhaled Pringle's scent one last time. He released her and stepped back.

"Goodbye."

Pringle touched her lips, her green eyes meeting his. Then, with a whir of wings, she lifted into the air. She streaked down the stairs.

And was gone.

Chapter 50

Three Months Later

BEN SAT AT LONGINO'S, WAITING FOR CARA.

He glanced at his phone. *Late as usual.* An untouched bottle of red wine rested in an ice-filled bucket on the table. Since her escape from Petrova's clutches, she'd become quite the celebrity and in great demand as a speaker and for media interviews. Consequently, her already tenuous concept of timeliness had been stretched to the breaking point.

Their on-again relationship rested on similarly shaky ground. Ben couldn't decide if it was his own apparent lack of enthusiasm or Cara's. Since Pringle's return to her world, he didn't see Cara through the same lens. Her clothes, car, jewelry, all her trappings of wealth no longer intimated or impressed him. Even her beauty seemed artificial and narcissistic. *So why do I keep trying to revive the spark?*

Because of Pringle.

Time had not closed the gaping hole left in his heart by her absence. If anything, it had grown wider. Like a drowning victim, he tried to snatch at anything to ease the pain and keep his life afloat. He taught extra classes at the university, took up jogging, started the research needed to publish an academic paper on modern myths, and of course, picked up where he left off with Cara.

None of it worked.

When he awoke in the morning, his first thought was of Pringle. When he went to bed at night, his last thoughts were of Pringle. Any free time in between became a constant battle to focus on his daily tasks, not *her*.

A breathless Cara interrupted his morose meanderings. She rushed in, threw herself into the chair, and checked her phone.

"Sorry to be late, but this whole day's been crazy! Three different producers want to make a movie about what happened to me. Even though Daddy's doing the negotiations, I keep getting phone calls from them. I mean, I can't even get a free moment to catch my breath." She paused. "So, how are you?"

Ben shrugged. "Okay, I guess."

Cara studied him. "No, something's wrong. I may be busy, but I'm not *that* busy. What is it?"

Ben shook his head. "I don't think it's going to work."

"What? What's not going to work?"

"Us."

If he had chosen that moment to grow a third eye, Ben didn't think Cara could have been more surprised. She blinked and sat back.

"You...you want to break up with me?"

He nodded.

"I know I've been busy, but I can—"

"It's not you, Cara, it's me. I-I don't know how to explain it other than to say I'm not in a place to have a relationship with you or anybody else."

Ben got up and tossed a few bills on the table. He leaned down and kissed her on the cheek.

"I'm proud of you. You saved those people as well as yourself. Someday, you'll find someone who will love and appreciate you the way you deserve to be loved and appreciated. I'm just not the one."

He walked out without a second glance.

When Ben got home, the lions didn't greet him, and the door opened and shut normally. The mansion's magic had slowly faded, more evidence of Pringle's absence. Even the "For Sale" sign planted in Maude's front yard failed to lift his spirits.

He sighed, opened the door, and headed straight for the kitchen. He grabbed a beer from the refrigerator, and went up the stairs to his room to change. Ben opened the closet, kicked off his shoes, then paused at the sight of his clothes. A single garment hung separated from the rest.

The shirt Pringle had slept in.

He set the beer aside, and with great reverence, took it off the hanger. He sat on the bed and lifted the fabric to his face. Ben inhaled, Pringle's rich scent filling his senses. Like the mansion's magic, her lingering fragrance had begun to fade.

"I miss you," he whispered.

"I have missed you too, Ben."

He dropped the shirt and jumped to his feet.

Pringle stood at the door.

She wore a short, denim skirt, a white blouse tucked into the waist, and white leather sandals. Earrings dangled from her ears, their pointed tips covered by hair that flowed well past her shoulders. She clutched a purse in one hand, gold bangles encircling her wrists. If he didn't know better, she could pass for an ordinary—albeit pretty—woman.

"What? How—" Ben sputtered.

"I never left, Ben. I never intended to."

"But I locked the clock. I saw you leave!"

"You saw me disappear, not leave," she corrected him. "I hid inside the clock."

She strolled up to him. "And you of all people should know a lock is no match for a prawn, magical or otherwise." She laughed. "You should have seen Archie's face when I flew out of the clock."

Ben thought his eyes would pop out of their sockets. "You mean Archie's known the entire time?"

"Of course. He helped me with my Becoming."

"*Becoming?*"

"You know. My transition to your world."

"But why?" Ben cried. "You know the cost."

Pringle put her arms around Ben. "Did it ever occur to you the price was one I was willing to pay?"

Ben shook his head. "But—"

She put her finger on his lips. "No more buts."

Pringle pushed him onto the bed and straddled him. "I love you, Ben Hastings. And I would rather live a mortal life in love with you," she leaned down and kissed him, "than an immortal life without you. I would make the same choice a thousand times."

Every wall Ben erected around his feelings for Pringle crumbled to dust in an instant.

To hell with my ethical concerns. Why should I be the strong one?

He pulled her to him, joy filling every pore of his body. Pringle's wings extended to their full length.

"And now you get to stroke my wings *every* night."

CHAPTER 51

ARCHIE WATCHED A LINE OF GUESTS OFFER BEN AND Pringle their congratulations.

"Quite a wedding, eh?" he said to Hank.

Hank nodded. He gestured at the grand pavilion and the mansion's grounds. "What a beautiful place for a wedding."

Flowers of every color lined a red-carpeted path to a podium. Even the steps up to the platform were blanketed in flowers. Rows of chairs, laced with vines and flowers, faced the pavilion. Immaculate green grass, trees, and shrubs dotted the grounds.

"Let's get a refill," Archie said. They carried their glasses to a nearby table that held a magnificent three-tiered cake. Next to it, pink champagne bubbled from a multi-tiered silver fountain. A 3D printed image of the wedding couple crowned the cake. Wings sprouted from the bride.

"Nice touch," Hank commented.

Archie grinned. "I thought so. I've always wanted a 3D printer, and the wedding gave me the perfect opportunity to try it out." He raised his glass. "To the happy couple."

"Here, here," Hank replied. Their glasses clinked.

"So, am I to understand Pringle stayed with you a few months before she approached Ben?" he asked.

Archie nodded.

"May I ask why?"

"The best I can describe it is that she didn't want Ben to view her as a *prawn* anymore, but as a *woman*. That meant uh, well, you know, becoming womanly."

Hank chuckled at Archie's discomfort. "I'm not sure what that entails, but I'll take your word for it."

Archie stared wistfully at the couple. "I'm happy for them. Ben's a great guy, and Pringle...well she's Pringle. Never a dull moment."

Hank studied Archie. "Maybe one day you'll have your own escapade, your own story to tell."

Archie laughed. "I don't think lightning strikes the same place twice, but I guess anything's possible."

"If you truly believe that, you're already halfway to adventure." Hank tapped his nose. "I know a little about these things."

Cheers interrupted them. Ben and Pringle hurried through a shower of rice to Ben's van.

Archie gestured to Hank. "C'mon!" They ran to join in on the rice cascade.

Just married in white letters covered the windows of the VW. Gaily-colored streamers and cans trailed from the bumper. Ben opened the door for Pringle, then ran to get in the driver's side.

The VW beeped as they pulled away, the streamers fluttering and cans rattling. When they reached the end of the block, the van stopped. Pringle's arm stretched out the window and tossed something into the air. Glittering dust in reds, blues, greens, and yellows, glinted in the sunlight, then burst into butterflies. They fluttered after the van.

Until both disappeared from sight.

ABOUT THE AUTHOR

Multi-Award winning Author Michael Scott Clifton lives in Mount Pleasant, Texas with his wife, Melanie. An avid gardener, rapacious reader, and movie junkie, his books contain facets of all the genres he enjoys—action, adventure, magic, fantasy, and romance. His fantasy novels, *The Janus Witch*, and the *Conquest of the Veil* series, (*The Open Portal, Escape From Wheel, A Witch's Brew, and Cavern of the Veil Queen*) all received 5-Stars from the prestigious Readers Favorite Book Reviews. *The Open Portal* has been honored with a Feathered Quill Book Finalist Award. In addition, his YA novel *Edison Jones and The Anti-Grav Elevator* received a Feathered Quill Book Award Bronze Medal. Two of his short stories have earned Gold Medals, with *Edges of Gray* winning the Texas Authors Contest, and *The End Game*, winning the Northeast Texas Writer's Organization Contest. Professional credits include published articles in the *Texas Study of Secondary Education Magazine*. Visit Michael's official website at: www.michaelscottclifton.com or google him at @authormsclifton.